THE KILLING KIND

ALSO BY CHRIS HOLM

THE COLLECTOR SERIES

The Big Reap
The Wrong Goodbye
Dead Harvest

THE KILLING KIND

CHRIS HOLM

MULHOLLAND
BOOKS

Little, Brown and Company
New York Boston London

Mulholland Books
Hachette Book Group
1290 Avenue of the Americas, New York, NY 10104
littlebrown.com

First Edition: September 2015

Mulholland Books is an imprint of Little, Brown and Company, a division of Hachette Book Group, Inc. The Mulholland Books name and logo are trademarks of Hachette Book Group, Inc.

The publisher is not responsible for websites (or their content) that are not owned by the publisher.

The Hachette Speakers Bureau provides a wide range of authors for speaking events. To find out more, go to hachettespeakersbureau.com or call (866) 376-6591.

ISBN 978-0-316-25953-8
Library of Congress Control Number: 2014960165

10 9 8 7 6 5 4 3 2 1

RRD-C

Printed in the United States of America

For Katrina—again, or for the first time

Nor is there any law more just, than that he who has plotted death shall perish by his own plot.

—OVID

We can't all be saints.

—JOHN DILLINGER

THE KILLING KIND

1.

THE STREETS OF downtown Miami shimmered in the evening heat, the summer air rich with spice and song. Neon and rum and the warm ocean breeze conspired to make the city thrum with lurid anticipation. It was, after all, a Friday night in one of the most vibrant cities in the world. Still, no one who walked that night beneath the broad modern portico of the Morales Incorporated Building suspected they'd briefly occupied the spot where a man was about to die.

Edgar Morales pushed through the revolving doors of the gleaming steel-and-glass building that bore his name and stepped onto the sunbaked concrete. After a day spent in climate-controlled comfort, the hot breath of the city set him sweating. He checked his watch. It was precisely six thirteen p.m. Most days, Edgar's car would come around to pick him up at precisely six fifteen—but today was not most days. Today Edgar's car would not be coming, for it had been disabled. Fixing it would delay his driver long enough to leave Morales exposed so that the man the Corporation—as the Cuban Mafia calls itself—sent to kill him could complete his task.

He wasn't exposed *enough* for Michael Hendricks's taste.

Hendricks watched Morales through the telescopic sight of his M40A3 sniper rifle from his perch some four blocks down the street. His vision was distorted slightly by the tinted window through which he peered, and by the stolen Escalade's vibration as its AC labored to cool its spacious interior. Hendricks had found the vehicle in a long-term parking lot at Miami International a few hours back. Gleaming black with chromed-out rims, an enormous cabin, and tinted windows all around, it made the perfect downtown Miami sniper blind. He would have preferred to set up in one of the many towers that faced Morales Incorporated—shots from above were less likely to encounter an obstruction prior to finding their target, and both witnesses and routes of egress could be more easily planned for and controlled—but that damned overhang shielded the entryway from view at such an angle. So instead, he made do, slipping a valet a hundred bucks for the privilege of parking in the far corner of a boutique hotel's parking lot, which had decent sight lines to the building's entrance. Time was, a hundred bucks could have gotten you a *room* in this town—but not anymore, and certainly not at *this* address.

He'd been sitting there for an hour watching traffic roll by, the AC blasting in a vain attempt to keep the heat and humidity at bay. The air was so heavy and still, the strips of fabric he'd tied to the street signs to serve as wind indicators hadn't moved since he'd first parked. The lack of wind was to Hendricks's advantage. Wind was second only to gravity in its ability to alter a bullet's trajectory, and since its force was not constant, it was far harder to account for. But he'd need to take the humidity into account. Air this water-laden was sure to slow his bullet down—enough, at this distance, to lower his point of impact by three full inches. Three inches could be the difference between a kill shot and a graze.

This muggy weather was disgusting, Hendricks thought, much like the cup of café con leche that sat un-drunk in the cup holder beside him—thick, cloying, and sticky. And the palette of the city grated on him—everything was canary and coral and aquamarine. Hendricks missed the dark greens and cold blues of northern New England, where even the hottest summer sun failed to warm the deepest hollows of the forest, and the water ran cold all year long. Miami was beautiful, sure, but that beauty was as garish and artificial as the siliconed women who walked its streets.

Everything about the place felt insincere.

Best to get the job over with and get out of here.

Through his scope, Hendricks watched Morales look left and right, surveying the busy street as if for his missing ride, and then descend the wide concrete steps toward the curb. Men in business suits jostled for position beside bronzed women in skimpy beach gear, waiting for the crosswalk light to change.

"We're a go," Hendricks said. He turned the key in the ignition, cutting the engine but leaving the battery en-gaged. The world around him went silent, and the car's vibration stilled. "Tell me you're in the system."

"I'm in," came the reply through his Bluetooth, "but understand, the security is first-rate. It cycles through its diagnostics at five-second intervals. If any unauthorized command is detected, an alarm is triggered. And if that happens, the cops'll be at your position in minutes."

"You saying you can't do it?"

"I'm saying once you give the go-ahead, you'll have three seconds, no more."

"Guess I'd better make those seconds count," Hendricks said. "On my mark."

Morales reached the curb. Hendricks pivoted his rifle first left, then right, taking in the scene through his scope. He gave a nod of satisfaction at what he saw and lowered the passenger-side front window, sighting his target through the opening, his weapon's bipod steadied against the leather sill.

"Mark."

At once, the lights for blocks around changed so that the intersections were red leading to this stretch of road, and green leading away. As traffic cleared in front of the Morales building, the light at the crosswalk changed as well, and the crowd around Morales stepped out into the street.

"Three," said the voice in his ear.

Hendricks drew a measured breath and held it. His body processed the complex math behind the shot by instinct, making fine adjustments to account for the heat, air pressure, and distance from sea level. His heart beat slow and steady in his chest.

"Two."

His body motionless, Hendricks squeezed the trigger—three pounds' pressure, no more, no less.

"One."

A crack like thunder echoed down the street.

When Morales heard the shot, he hit the deck. Hendricks had to hand it to the guy, he had good instincts—he reacted a full second before anyone else in sight. But ultimately, his gesture of self-preservation was futile; by the time you hear the gunshot, the bullet's come and gone.

Lucky for Morales, he wasn't Hendricks's target.

Hendricks's target was Javier Cruz—the hitman the Corporation had sent to kill Morales. A button man for the Corporation since their early days running *bolita* rackets out of Little Havana, Cruz'd killed more men than he could count.

Not that anyone would know to look at him. Those he passed on his stroll down Brickell toward Morales Incorporated were like as not to smile at the kindly old Cuban man in his crisp white guayabera shirt, raw linen pants, and straw fedora. They had no idea his steel gray mustache hid beneath it the grisly scar of a lip split by a policeman's baton, or that the policeman in question hadn't lived to see the sun rise the following morning. They didn't realize the limp in his gait wasn't age or sciatica, but the result of two lead slugs fired off by the wife of a local politician who'd made it his business to disrupt the Corporation's. She woke to find him in her bedroom while her husband was out of town, and if she hadn't been so beautiful—or so very, very naked—perhaps Cruz wouldn't have allowed her time to reach the gun in the nightstand. She buried two bullets in his leg, and he buried her in half a dozen spots the state over, leaving only a bedroom full of blood and a ring finger for her husband to find on his return, resting atop a photo of their four daughters. That man never spoke a word about the Corporation again.

Those Cruz passed didn't know they were in the presence of a monster. But unfortunately for Cruz, Hendricks knew.

And unfortunately for Cruz, Hendricks never missed.

When Hendricks pulled the trigger, Cruz's head exploded. For a moment, what was left of him stood there, inches from Morales, a steel blade gleaming in his hand—his bloodied fedora fluttering to the ground behind him. Then his body slumped to the sidewalk like a dropped marionette.

As the gunshot's echoes died, the night was filled with the sounds of panic. The shriek of voices and tires both. The bleat of car horns. The wail of a distant siren fast approaching. Everyone within earshot had been trained by one awful news report after another to await that second shot, or third, or fifth. Trained to wonder if they'd prove another victim in the killer's tally.

Hendricks, on the other hand, calmly withdrew the rifle and raised the blackened window. He knew it would take them several minutes to determine where the shot had come from—more than enough time for him to make his escape.

"You get out of the system clean?" he quietly asked.

"Who do you think you're talking to?" the voice in his ear replied. "They'll never even know I was there."

"Good," said Hendricks. "Signing off."

"Safe travels."

At the curb outside his office building, Edgar Morales scrabbled to his feet, ashen and trembling. Though he tried, he couldn't tear his gaze from his would-be killer's corpse. If he'd had any inkling it would come to this when he'd begun buying up cheap tenements in Miami's dodgy

Goulds neighborhood with an eye toward gentrifying the area—and cleaning up a stronghold of the Corporation's narcotics sales in the process—his altruistic streak would have taken a backseat to his healthy sense of self-preservation. But he hadn't known, any more than he'd known until this very moment that he had no stomach for killing, even in self-defense.

His phone rang in his pocket. Morales flinched as if slapped, and then answered.

"H-hello?" he said.

"Are you all right?" Hendricks asked.

Morales hesitated. As a point in fact, he was pretty fucking far from all right. But instead, he told Hendricks, "Yes. I trust my payment was received?"

"If it wasn't," Hendricks said, "you wouldn't be around to ask me that."

Morales laughed—brittle, barking. "That's not exactly a comforting thought."

"Well, just think: now you've got your whole life to come to grips with it. Pleasure doing business with you."

And then the line went dead.

2.

IT WAS A COOL August night on the southern shore of Lake
Geneva, and Jean-Luc Vian's château was alive with
candlelight—a glimmering jewel nestled in the crushed
velvet of the French countryside, its rich greens fading to
black as the soft light gave way to darkness. The grounds
were bedecked for a grand party, and the flagstone drive—
which led from the rural one-lane road, past the massive
iron gates and guest quarters, and up to the main house—
was lined with luxury automobiles. BMWs and Mercedes,
mostly, interspersed with a few Jaguars, a Bentley, and even
one god-awful yellow Lamborghini, the last driven by that
boorish football player Caravagas that Vian's wife had insisted he invite.

No doubt that deceitful cow had by now lured the
man to one of their many bedrooms, Vian thought, where
their exploits would join those of her prior dalliances

as the talk of every dinner party from Paris to Haute-Savoie.

If it weren't for the fact that she was daughter to the foreign minister, his pride would have insisted he leave her long ago. Theirs was a marriage of political and social expediency, not love—a fact that was too well known amid the corridors of power for Vian's taste.

Then again, Vian thought, for all her faults, at least *she* was enjoying the party. He, on the other hand, apparently had work to attend to, having been summoned by text to dial in to an emergency conference call—though what could be so pressing at this late an hour, his employer didn't say.

Vian punched his security code into the keypad on his office door, waited for the electronic whir as the lock disengaged, then stepped inside. As he shut the door behind him, the lock engaged once more, and the sounds of the string quartet and drunken laughter dropped away, deadened by his office's soundproofing.

It wasn't until he raised the lights that he realized he was not alone.

"Who are you?" Vian asked the man in French. "How did you—"

"—get in here?" his uninvited guest ventured, his own French excellent but accented. "Mr. Vian, there's no need for a man of your breeding and intellect to be so trite—or so dreadfully sincere. You don't *really* expect me to answer your first question, do you? And as to your second, I suspect if you ruminate upon it for a moment, you could save me the tedium of explaining."

So Vian ruminated upon it. It made no sense. How could this man have breached the gate and slipped past all his guards? Vian was sure he hadn't been *invited*, for his employer—who, in addition to supplying his personal security detail, ran background checks on all attendees of Vian's parties—had sent along the dossiers they'd compiled for everybody on the invite list just yesterday, and this man was not among them.

Perhaps he'd bluffed his way through, then. Certainly, the stranger was dressed for the role of partygoer, in his slim black suit, crisp dove-gray shirt, and matching tie. He was seated in Vian's own leather desk chair, his black oxfords propped atop the desk. Black kid gloves graced his slender hands.

But bluffing alone could not have gained him access to this room—only Vian had the access code. Well, Vian, and his employer, who had installed the door locks, the encrypted phone and Internet connections, and the sound-proofing as well.

And then, at once, Vian understood. The late-night summons. The lack of dossier on this man. The breach of Vian's inner sanctum.

It seemed the terms of his employment had been reevaluated.

The stranger noted with some satisfaction the change in Vian's expression from puzzlement to despair. "Sit down," he said, withdrawing his feet from the desk and plucking a silenced firearm off the blotter as he rose.

Vian did as the man instructed, dropping heavily into one of the high-backed chairs that faced the desk from this side.

"Good," the man said, a smile dancing across his face. "Now: tell me why I'm here." That face was neither young nor old—oddly wise, yet unlined, as though he'd never in his life encountered a troubling thought. His hair was sandy blond, perhaps interspersed with white, perhaps not. Vian was struck by the fact that—despite the dramatic circumstances of their meeting—if he passed this man on the street a month from now, he probably would not recognize him.

But Vian knew he would not be passing anybody on the street a month from now. Vian knew his life would end tonight.

"You are here to kill me," Vian replied.

The stranger laughed. "Well, *yes*, but do you know why?"

"Does it matter?"

"It does to the man who hired me, which means it does to me. You see, I've been asked to send a message. Your death is merely to be the punctuation mark at the end of said message."

"All right then, what's the message?"

"I've been instructed to tell you your work in the Sudan was unacceptable. I'm told that will mean something to you. It does, does it not?"

It did. Vian's employer was, on paper, a security contractor, one with fingers in a great many pies at France's Ministry of Defense, including the manufacture and distribution of weapons and ordnance, the contracting of private military personnel, and consulting for strategic planning. Off book, his firm was responsible for three quarters of all weapons sales on the continent of Africa, including those to all sides of the Darfur conflict. Vian, for a time, was in charge of such sales, but he found that even his own prized moral flexibility had its limits. He'd begun funneling communiqués to the UN in secret—communiqués which implicated his employer in breaking the UN African Union arms embargo. Though nothing was made of these revelations publicly—due to his firm's ties to not only French defense but to many other NATO nations as well—his actions led to his company losing seven billion dollars' worth of contracts.

He'd thought he covered his tracks such that his involvement would never be discovered.

Vian could only nod, certain it was far too late for him to deny it. At least, he thought, I will not die denying the only decent thing I've ever done.

"Good. I've been further instructed to glean from you, if possible, whatever I can about who *else* may have been involved in your unacceptable performance."

"Why on earth should I cooperate with you?" Vian spat. "You've already told me you plan to kill me, and my wife is too public a figure for you to harm, which means you've no longer any leverage."

"That's not *entirely* accurate," the stranger said, and then he shot Vian in the knee.

Vian shrieked. Every muscle in his body tensed at once. He jerked out of his chair, spilling onto the floor. The pain in his knee was white-hot, exquisite. It spread up through his groin and settled like lead in his stomach. Waves of dizziness and nausea shook his body, and unconsciousness encroached, spotty black at the edges of his vision. And all the while, beyond the soundproofed walls of his office, the party continued unabated—his guests oblivious to his suffering.

Somewhere, a thousand miles away it seemed, a mobile phone chirped. The stranger looked startled for a moment, and then reached into his suit coat, removing from his inside pocket a cheap, pre-paid burner phone.

"Yes?" the stranger snapped, impatience hiding puzzlement.

"This Engelmann?" The voice was coarse, uneducated—American, to his ear.

"Where did you get this number?"

"My organization has worked with you before," he said.

"You're with the Council?" Engelmann asked. They were the only Americans for whom he'd ever worked. The Council was a group of representatives from each of the major crime families operating in the United States—Italian, Russian, Cuban, Salvadoran, Ukrainian, you name it. Though their organizations were often rivals, Council members convened on occasion to handle issues on which their respective organizations' interests aligned. American organized crime was often too parochial to tap someone such as Engelmann; each family had their own little fiefdom, their own way of doing things—their own hitmen should any hitting be required. Only rarely when they came together did they deign to hire outside themselves—and even then, Engelmann suspected, it was simply so they needn't decide which family got the job, the risk, the blame should the hit fail, or the glory should it succeed.

But on the rare occasion they did hire out, they paid very, *very* well.

"That's right," said the American. "We've got a job for you." He paused a moment then, noting for the first time Vian's anguished wailing in the background. "I, uh, catch you at a bad time?"

"Not at all," said Engelmann. "In fact, you've just rescued me from the most *dreadful* party." Then he held the phone to his chest, covering the mouthpiece, and said to Vian, "I'm sorry—I have to take this."

The silenced firearm jumped three times in Engelmann's hand—each report no more than the popping of a champagne cork—and Vian's cries ceased. Such a waste, thought Engelmann; given time, Vian would have told him anything he asked. But in reality, the loss was minor—Vian was hardly the worthiest of subjects for Engelmann's more esoteric ministrations, and the bonus he'd been promised for any information obtained would doubtless pale before the sum the Council would likely offer.

"Now," Engelmann said into the phone, "where were we?"

3.

A SINGLE DROP OF RAIN smacked against the windshield of Evelyn Walker's Jetta as she turned off the narrow country road and onto her rutted dirt drive. Seconds later, the sky opened, unleashing sheets of heavy rain. Evie sighed and turned her wipers on as fast as they would go, but still her visibility was reduced to nothing. She slowed to a crawl and felt her tires sinking in, the ruts they traveled now twin rivers of churning, muddy water. Rain pounded on the car's roof as loud as hail.

It was sunny when I left Warrenton, she thought with a sigh. Still, she shouldn't have been surprised. During summer in Virginia, the weather had a habit of turning on a dime.

The Jetta fishtailed as Evie rounded the bend that brought her rambling, buttercream farmhouse into view, her groceries jostling in the backseat. The trees that crowded the length of the driveway gave way to rolling lawn. Evie pulled in next to Stuart's pickup and waited a moment, car idling, for the rain to abate before deciding it wasn't likely to slow anytime soon. So she thumbed the ignition and the car shuddered off, heat and humidity encroaching immediately once the air conditioner stopped.

Getting out of the car was harder than it had been a few months ago, before she'd started to show. Took three tries and one decidedly un-ladylike groan. As soon as she stepped out, one wedge-heeled sandal sank into a mud puddle. Muck, cool and slimy between her toes, yanked the sandal from her foot as she took a step toward higher ground.

By the time she got the rear door open, her shirt clung heavily to her swollen belly, and her hair was plastered to her face. She hauled the groceries out of the backseat—standing cockeyed with one sandal on and one bare foot—and glanced toward the deck, where the French doors stood open. There was still no sign of Stuart. Strange. Ever since he'd seen that blue plus sign four months ago, Evie hadn't so much as opened a pickle jar or carried a load of laundry—at least, when Stu was home to stop her. To be honest, his constant hovering drove her nuts, even though she knew that it was well intentioned. She was surprised he hadn't rushed out to lend a hand the second she'd pulled in. She thought the sight of her carrying two overflowing bags of groceries would be enough to bring him running, hollering at her to put them down.

Figures, she thought. The one time I actually need some help.

"Honey?" she shouted toward the open doors, the light on within.

Stuart didn't answer.

"Hon?" she called again, hobbling up the stairs to the deck—the bags sodden in her arms, her gait loping and awkward now that her left leg was down a couple inches from her right. She reached the open doors and peered inside through the screen. The house was ablaze with light—just like Stuart, she thought; you'd swear he thinks those switches only work in one direction—but Stuart was nowhere to be seen.

Evie eyed the screen-door latch and heaved a sigh of consternation. Then she contorted herself into an awkward crouch-turn—an upside-down comma—so that if she squeezed the bag with her forearm and twisted her wrist just so, she could maybe kinda sorta get a grip on it and... crap. The bag in her left hand tore, spilling groceries everywhere. A tomato rolled across the deck. Egg white oozed from the upturned egg carton.

Where the hell was Stuart, anyway?

Evie stuffed the groceries back into the torn bag and yanked open the screen door. She put the bags down atop the kitchen island and turned to close the door behind her—trailing muddy footprints across the tiles—only then realizing she could have simply set the bags down on the patio table and then opened the door with ease.

Damn pregnancy brain.

A click of nails on hardwood, and Abigail trotted into the kitchen with as much brio as a six-year-old bulldog can muster.

"Abby, where's Stu?" Evie asked. Abigail glanced back the way she came for just a moment before stretching upward into Evie's head-scratch, her stubby tail wagging with glee. Then she shuffled off toward her empty food bowl, giving Evie sad eyes the whole way.

"Why didn't Daddy feed you?" Evie asked, her delicate features set in a frown. But if Abby knew, she wasn't spilling. Evie fetched Abby's kibble from under the sink and shook some into the bowl. Abby crunched away with abandon.

"Stu?" Evie called. A clap of thunder shook the house, and the lights flickered all around her. She headed for the living room—the room from which Abigail had emerged.

As she neared the doorway, she spotted something that set her mind reeling.

Stuart's feet, unmoving—clad in plain white gym socks, the red stripe at the toe of each pointed ceilingward.

Evie's mouth went dry, and her heart leapt.

"Stuart?" she shrieked, her shrill tone piercing the silence of the farmhouse and echoing back at her like a mockingbird's reply. She hit the doorway at a sprint, and then stopped short.

Stuart was lying on his back amid a sea of dowel rods and hardware beneath a half-assembled crib. When he heard her call, he jerked upright into a seated position—his forehead smacking against the wooden frame and causing the rickety structure to collapse atop him.

"Son of a—" he cried, and then caught himself. He'd been doing that a lot lately—as if the overgrown bean sprout in Evie's uterus were absorbing every swear word within earshot, and would emerge five months from now cursing a blue streak.

"You asshole," she said, ignoring his reproachful look. "You scared the shit out of me! Not answering when I called, leaving Abby unfed, and then…"

Stuart yanked the iPod earbuds from his ears and climbed stiffly to his feet. "Evie, I'm sorry—I didn't hear you come in! I was trying to surprise you by getting the crib together before—" and here he noticed the rain through the French doors. He knitted his brow. "Before you got home. But these directions are ridiculous, and I guess I just lost track of time. I swear, I didn't mean to scare you—do you forgive me?"

"Of course," Evie replied. She was now crying and found it hard to catch her breath. She had no idea why.

"Hey," Stu said, taking her in his arms. He knew her well enough to know she'd blame this on her mood swings. And he knew her well enough to know that wasn't true. "It's okay. I've got you. And I'm not going anywhere."

Stuart held her close and waited for her panic to abate. Then he kissed away her tears and led her to the bedroom— both of them trying hard not to think about the fiancé she'd lost years back to a roadside bomb somewhere north of Kandahar.

The farmhouse burned bright against the dimming sky as day evened into night. Eventually, Stu and Evie came back downstairs and cooked dinner both tired, both happy, both content. They sat awhile and watched TV with Abigail at their feet until their eyelids grew heavy. Then Evie shuffled off to bed. Stuart and Abigail followed shortly after, only delaying long enough to wander the house's perimeter—Stuart shutting windows and checking locks.

And from the darkness of the forest, Hendricks watched unnoticed—as he'd been doing for hours, and as he'd done so many nights before. He watched until the only light that showed in any of the windows was the flicker of the TV in the master suite. He watched until even that went dark. He watched until the sky began to lighten to the east. Then he hiked back to his rental car and headed north, toward home.

4.

Union Station in Utica, New York, is a structure oddly out of time and place.

The city itself is a decaying industrial town nestled in the Mohawk River Valley, five hours and a world away from the bustle of Manhattan. Its streets are run-down and ill-traveled, and many of its storefronts sit empty. The factories that once provided jobs for its residents are now boarded or bricked up; the few windows left exposed are gapped by decades' worth of vandals' stones.

Yet Utica's train station—which, these days, services more buses than trains—is an imposing marvel of Italianate architecture a full city block in size, with a vaulted ceiling, elaborate cornices, and an interior rife with gleaming marble. Massive columns jut upward toward skylights through which the gray light of the perpetually overcast Upstate New York sky streams through. Long, low wooden benches shiny from lacquer look out of scale for so large a space and lend the interior an oddly ecclesiastical air. In addition to a proper shoe-shine stand, the building also boasts a barbershop and restaurant, the latter an authentic lunch counter of the type that once appeared on street corners in every town in America.

The terminal was built in a fit of optimism, when rail was king, by the same architects who'd designed Manhattan's Grand Central—but Utica's fortunes were even then on the wane, having peaked decades before during the heyday of the nearby Erie Canal. Now the station seemed not so much preserved as forgotten, like an apparition doomed to walk the same halls again and again.

For the past fifty years, Utica hasn't been known for much of anything—unless you count the violent struggle between four crime families that stretched the length of the seventies and eighties for control of the city.

Gazing dully out the window of his chauffeured Lincoln as it conveyed him from the private airstrip to his destination, Alexander Engelmann couldn't for the life of him guess why organizations as powerful as the Genovese and Colombo crime families, as well as Outfits out of Buffalo and Scranton, would bother spilling blood over such a place. It seemed any money this town once possessed had been wrung out long ago. But he had to admit, their train station was really something. Perhaps it was pride that motivated their bloodshed.

Engelmann's calfskin Ferragamos clacked against the marble floor of the terminal. Despite the summer heat, he wore a charcoal sport coat of worsted wool, a pair of pressed chinos, and a crisp white shirt, open at the throat. He carried neither bag nor weapon—his only luggage, a small carry-on, was in the Council's hired jet, and he never traveled armed, preferring to procure any weapons in-country as needed and discard them after use. The terminal was empty but for Engelmann, two students with dreadlocks and dreadful clothes waiting for a bus, and a hulking mass of steroid-enhanced Mafia muscle shrink-wrapped into a black suit that bulged suspiciously at armpit, back, and ankle. Why this gorilla needed three firearms was beyond Engelmann, as was how anyone with that much muscle would even have the flexibility to reach an ankle holster.

Not that his assessment mattered—it was habit, nothing more. This occasion did not call for violence. Which was a pity, really; stiff and irritable as Engelmann was from his hasty trip halfway around the world, he could have used a pick-me-up.

As he approached the gorilla, the gorilla jerked his head to indicate the barbershop beyond. Engelmann strode past him without breaking stride, pushing through the glass doors and stepping into 1953.

Dime-sized hexagonal tiles, once white but now the color of old teeth, covered the floor, the grout between long since gone to black. Above waist-high marble wainscoting stretched walls that aimed for sunny yellow, but missed. Rounded mirrors hung above small vanities piled high with products Engelmann would have guessed ceased production decades ago. At each station was a pedestal sink and a barber chair of black vinyl, white trim, and ornate, tarnished bronze.

In one chair was a man, beside whom stood an aged barber. Whether the man was tall or short, fat or slim, Engelmann couldn't tell, because he was mostly hidden beneath a black cutting cape—and his face was wrapped in steaming white towels in preparation for a shave, so that only his nose and thick black hair showed. His head was tilted back, his nose pointing skyward. His hair was slicked down such that even at the angle of his head, gravity held no sway over it.

At the sound of Engelmann's footfalls, the man in the chair raised one finger—his hands until then both curled around the edges of the armrests—and the barber, a slight man with gray hair, gray eyes, and a lined, gray face, disappeared without a word.

"I kinda figured you'd be taller," said the man, his gruff, coarse tone confirming him as the one who'd called Engelmann two nights ago.

The man's statement was a joke—with a hot towel draped over his eyes, he could no more see Engelmann than could Engelmann see him. But Engelmann did not laugh.

"Someday," said Engelmann, "you'll have to tell me how you obtained the number of a burner phone I'd not used until that very night."

"No, I don't think I will. Sit down."

Engelmann did not sit down.

The man shrugged. It was a token act of defiance, nothing more. Engelmann had come when called. He may be one of the most gifted contract killers in the world, but in this room, at this moment, Engelmann was more house cat than lion.

"We have a job for you," the man said from within his wet folds. "A pest in need of exterminating."

"And what, pray tell, is this pest's name?"

"I wish to hell I knew," said the man, "but if I did, I wouldn't have had to call *you*."

"Ah. I see. I trust, then, that you've no idea where I might find him, or even what he looks like."

The man bristled. "Not specifically, no."

"Then perhaps we should begin with what he's done to so offend."

The man gestured vaguely toward the oak vanity behind him. "Check the left-hand drawer."

Engelmann did. Inside was a manila envelope with a string-and-button enclosure, fat with documents. Engelmann unwound the string and lifted the flap. Not documents, he discovered—or at least not mostly.

Mostly, they were pictures.

Some were glossy black-and-white eight-by-tens. Some were color copies of police reports, blown up so large the images had pixelated, and the typeset words around them were five times their normal size. On the back of each was a location and a date, scrawled in a tight, controlled script. The dates stretched back as far as three years. The most recent was just two days ago—the day Engelmann received the phone call summoning him here.

Each photo was of a murder scene.

No. Not just a murder scene. A hit. Cold. Calculating. Professional.

Engelmann thumbed through them, transfixed. Some of them, like San Francisco in October of 2010, or Wichita this January past, were precision long-range kills—needle-threading sniper shots from what had to be twelve hundred meters away. Some of them, like Green Bay or Montreal, were close and messy—the former a stabbing that took place past security in an airport, and the latter a garrote at the opera during a Place des Arts performance of Gounod's *Faust*. Of the close kills, it was the former that impressed Engelmann the most. Smuggling a weapon past security, while not impossible, poses some degree of difficulty—but to then commit murder and vanish undetected is quite a feat indeed. Which clearly this man had done, for if his visage had been captured by security cameras, the Council would have doubtless obtained the footage. They had, after all, tracked Engelmann without difficulty.

"You believe this all to be the work of one man?" Engelmann asked.

"I do."

"Magnificent," he muttered.

"You sound surprised."

"Most in my profession have a preferred method, something tried and true from which they never deviate. Whoever did these is proficient in a variety of techniques. Few in the world can claim such skill. Even fewer can make good on such claims."

"You can," said the man, steel creeping into his voice. Despite himself, Engelmann drew a worried breath, wondering for a moment if this had all been some elaborate setup to lure him here. But then, from beneath his towels, the man laughed. "Relax, Al—I didn't ask you here so I could whack you. We've had an eye on you since this guy's Reno job a few months back; we know you weren't anywhere near Miami two nights ago when he last hit. He popped a guy from ground level across four blocks of busy city street, if you can believe it. Turned the poor bastard into a fucking smear."

"These targets," Engelmann asked. "They were La Cosa Nostra?"

"Some," allowed the man in the chair. "Some were Salvadorans. Some Russian. One was Southie Irish. Truth is, there's not an Outfit in the country ain't been touched. Which is a good fucking thing as far as I'm concerned, 'cause if any of the families had been spared, everybody who got hit would be gunning hard for them, figuring it for some kind of power play. Shit, it's just a matter of time before one family points the finger at another anyway, just 'cause they don't like the look of 'em. This situation is a—whaddaya call it—a powder keg."

"Hence the involvement of the Council."

"Yeah," the man said drolly. "*Hence.* Tensions among the families are running high. This don't get resolved soon, there's gonna be a war. Which is why we're willing to offer you a million flat to find this guy and seal the deal. That, and whatever resources are at the Council's disposal."

One million dollars.

One million dollars, plus the combined resources of every crime family in America.

Engelmann could scarcely contain his excitement. But he managed. One does not attain a reputation such as his without mastering one's emotions.

Engelmann smiled, showing teeth. "Euros," he said.

" 'Scuse me?"

"One million *euros.*"

The man in the chair was silent for a moment, and then he nodded his assent, his towels bobbing.

"Excellent," said Engelmann. "Consider me in your employ. I'll send you the number of my Cayman account, and you can wire the money at your convenience."

"No need," said the man. "We've got the number."

Engelmann, unnerved, swallowed hard, and then changed the subject. "His victims," Engelmann asked, "have they any commonality? Apart from their employers' extra-legal status, that is."

"Yeah. They're all hitmen. And every one of 'em was on a job when they got whacked."

For a moment, Engelmann thought he'd misheard, then realized he hadn't. That one man had perpetrated such a variety of kills was impressive. That his victims were themselves all hired killers made the accomplishment all the greater.

"You are telling me you've a hitman killing hitmen, and now you're hiring a hitman to hit him back?"

"I'm telling you I've got a problem, and you've got one million reasons to fix it."

Engelmann smiled again, for he in fact had more than that. For the first time in a decade, he had a job that posed a significant challenge and a quarry worthy of pursuit. For the first time in a decade, he had reason to fear for his own safety—reason to question whether he was equal to the task. Of course, this man would not have the combined resources of every crime family in America at his beck and call—but then, it seemed his wits had served him well thus far in the face of such resources.

This man, thought Engelmann, was not to be trifled with.

This man, whoever he was, would be an honor to square off against.

This man, he would have killed for free.

5.

S PECIAL AGENT Charlotte Thompson flinched as her cell phone chimed. She knew before she glanced at it the text was from her sister; she'd texted fifteen times today already. Jess was Charlie's baby sister—just three years out of college. A waitress who fancied herself an artist and insisted her meds quieted her muse.

Usually, when Jess was in a manic phase, it fell to Charlie to talk her off the ceiling. But today, she had neither the patience nor the time. She'd spent the past seven hours crammed into the back of a surveillance van with three other FBI agents and a tangled heap of audiovisual equipment. Seven hours of listening to the tinny patter of Albanian played through headphones, and the Bureau's translator—a slight, olive-skinned man by the name of Bashkim—converting it into flat, dispassionate English beside her. Seven hours with no AC and no fan, the van amplifying the August heat until the cabin reeked of sweat and the agents' clothes were plastered to their skin. Between the dehydration and the constant discordant input of two languages at once—not to mention her new partner Garfield's inane chatter before she finally told him to shut up—Thompson's head was pounding. The last thing she needed was a dose of Jess at her most tightly wound.

Thompson silenced her phone with a sigh and stuffed it into the glove box. Thirty seconds later, she heard it vibrate—rasping against the van's registration like a rattlesnake's warning.

"Lovers' quarrel?" Garfield quipped, his eyes glinting with mischief. He'd been making pointed comments like that all day long. She wondered what he'd heard—how much he knew. But she didn't want to get into it with him, especially in a van full of potential witnesses. Besides, they had a job to do. Bad guys to catch. That's what her dad, now a captain with the Hartford PD, told her as a kid every time he left for work. It had never failed to make her smile back then—and much to her father's consternation, it turned out to be the only thing she'd ever wanted to do when she grew up.

The surveillance van was parked on one of the narrow side streets off Allegheny Avenue, in the Port Richmond neighborhood of North Philly. It was a working-class neighborhood—Polish, mostly, though the Albanian population had been on the rise of late, as had that of the Latvians, Ukrainians, and Lithuanians—and, in contrast to the swanky, condo-studded neighborhoods that'd been popping up all over Philadelphia, the only concessions to luxury in sight were the ass-ends of several window-mounted air conditioners, dripping onto the concrete below.

The sign in the storefront window declared Little Louie's closed, but there'd been two men inside all day. Armed men, if the outlines of their tracksuits were any indication. Mostly, they just sat and drank, the better part of six hours spent shooting the shit about soccer, vodka, and assorted sexual conquests both real and imagined.

It wasn't until Petrela showed up that their conversation turned to the missing girls.

Luftar Petrela was perhaps the single unlikeliest proprietor of an Italian restaurant who'd ever lived. Ghost-pale and wire-thin, he looked as though he'd never felt the kiss of the Mediterranean sun on his cheeks or experienced the warm comfort of a bowl of spaghetti Bolognese. His hair and eyebrows were thick and dark, but in a manner that suggested Slavic, not Italian. And of course, there was the fact he'd never actually learned to cook—he'd been too busy hurting people at the behest of his uncle, Tomor Petrela, local capo of the Albanian Mafia.

None of which mattered much to the clientele of Little Louie's, who to a one worked for Petrela, and mostly showed up so his list of people who needed hurting didn't include them.

A burst of rapid-fire Albanian, followed by Bashkim's uninflected translation.

Petrela: "Have they eaten?"

Purple Tracksuit: "They claimed they were not hungry."

Petrela: "They must eat. They will not fetch a decent price if they're malnourished."

Lime-Green Tracksuit: "The blonde was acting up again. Gouged at Enver's arm when he opened the door."

Petrela: "We'll raise her dose. Soon she'll decide she likes the junk more than she likes fighting back. And there are some who'll pay a premium for such feistiness."

Bashkim looked to Thompson, as if to ask if this was enough. Thompson removed her headphones—her hands trembling slightly from anger and adrenaline. The moment was three months in the making. Three months spent canvassing homeless shelters, arresting pimps and street thugs, and chasing wire transfers—all to connect a dead runaway from Duluth to the men who used her until there was nothing left to use.

Thompson gave the order.

In moments, the sidewalk was alive with agents, armed for battle and wearing body armor head to toe: FBI SWAT. They moved into position with silent precision. The three men inside had no inkling and no chance.

When the battering ram connected with the door, Petrela and his men scattered. Purple Tracksuit broke left, diving behind the faux-mahogany bar as if three-quarter-inch medium-density fiberboard was going to protect him from a fully automatic Heckler & Koch. If he hadn't fired on the agents as they fanned out through the dining room, he wouldn't have needed protecting. But he had, and was quickly silenced.

Lime-Green Tracksuit had better instincts, if not more smarts. He took off for the back door at a sprint. Why the idiot thought a team of highly trained federal agents would neglect to cover the alleyway behind their intended target, Thompson had no idea. Maybe she'd ask the guy someday, since he was apprehended without a shot.

Petrela, though, was another matter. He didn't stick around to shoot it out. He didn't flee. True to his reputation, when the SWAT unit made its move, he beelined for the girls, determined that if he was going down, he'd take as many of them with him as he could.

"Ma'am," the call came over the radio, "Petrela's retreated into the basement! The door's reinforced steel; it'll take a sec to cut through!"

Thompson swore. "He armed?"

"Affirmative!"

But by the time the answer came, Thompson didn't need it. The distant *pop-pop-pop* from somewhere below street level was answer enough.

Thompson dashed from the van, the other agents close behind. She leapt onto the street, the stiffness in her limbs momentarily forgotten, and wheeled around, frantic to find some way to reach the girls while there were still some of them left. Her eyes lighted upon the sidewalk basement door.

The door comprised two dented, rust-streaked panels of checkered steel, set into the sidewalk a few feet from the front entrance—intended to allow direct basement access for deliveries. There were no handles or other outside access points, but thanks to frost heaves and foot traffic, the seam between the panels was far from flush.

"Hey!" Thompson shouted to one of the tactical agents nearby. "You carrying a Hallagan?"

The man removed the tool from his belt and tossed it to Thompson. Hooked at one end like a fireplace poker, with a flat, forked end like that of a pry-bar, a Hallagan is a favored tool of SWAT and firefighters both. Thompson jammed the hooked end into the space between the panel doors and yanked. Rusted hinges shrieked, and one panel moved, but not enough to get a man through. Two SWAT agents joined her, wrapping gloved hands around the exposed edge, but the damn thing wouldn't budge.

And that's when the new guy had a bright idea.

Hank Garfield had only been with the Organized Crime Section a couple weeks—he'd transferred over from the MS-13 Task Force, where he'd been working undercover. He'd spent the past two years trying to infiltrate the brutal Mara Salvatrucha street gang, followed by six months rehabbing from a shoulder through-and-through after someone loyal to the gang spotted him meeting with his handler at a sidewalk café two hours north of the gang's turf. It was a wrong-place, wrong-time bit of bad luck that illustrated just how far Mara's reach extended, and it nearly cost him his life. Garfield's handler wasn't so lucky—he wound up in the ground. Word was that the two of them were close.

It probably would have been better had Garfield asked—or, failing that, warned her at least. But he hadn't; he just yanked a flash-bang grenade off one of the SWAT guy's belts and lobbed it through the narrow aperture of the jammed sidewalk door. Thompson barely had a chance to shield her ears and turn away before the thing went off, loud as a firework and bright as the goddamn sun. Even though she'd closed her eyes, a ghostly green afterglow danced in Thompson's field of vision for a good five minutes afterward.

"Garfield, the fuck was *that?*"

Garfield grinned. "It stopped him shooting, didn't it?"

Thompson strained to listen over the ringing in her ears. I'll be damned, she thought. The crazy bastard's right.

Moments later, SWAT breached the inside basement door to find Petrela lying unconscious in the middle of the concrete floor, both ears bleeding, his eardrums blown.

Turned out the shots they'd heard hadn't been directed at the teenaged girls held captive there, but at the padlock fixed through the walk-in freezer's latch. In his haste to get downstairs, Petrela'd forgotten to grab the key; it hung on a hook just outside the basement door. Once SWAT popped the lock, they found the freezer wasn't so much a freezer as a holding pen—sweltering and smelling of human waste— full of very frightened and very *loud* teenaged girls. They were destined for the sex trade, or white slavery. But with time, Thompson hoped, they'd be all right. The human mind and body were more resilient than they were given credit for.

What a sight it must have been for them, these goggled, helmeted, armed men streaming into the walk-in after weeks of cramped captivity and ushering them upstairs, where ambulances waited to take them to St. Joseph's for treatment.

It was no wonder they wouldn't stop screaming.

Thompson stood in Little Louie's squalid kitchen, massaging the bridge of her nose with thumb and forefinger to soothe her aching head as one by one the girls came up the stairs. Garfield was inspecting the pots bubbling away on the massive cooktop, seemingly oblivious to the filth and the girls' racket.

He removed a lid, dipped a spoon into a stockpot, and fished out a meatball covered in red sauce. Though it was piping hot, he stuffed the whole thing into his mouth, sauce dribbling down his chin.

"The hell you think you're doing?" snapped Thompson.

Garfield chewed and made a face. "Hey, gimme a break—ain't like a meatball's *evidence*. Besides, I'm starving; we've been in that van all goddamn day, and I ain't had so much as a bite to eat since dinner last night. Which—no disrespect to Petrela here, 'cause he seems like a real good guy and all—is the only reason I could even choke that fucking thing down. No wonder the poor bastard turned to a life of crime—his meatballs taste like ass."

"Bold play back there with the flash-bang," was all she could think to say.

Garfield shrugged. "It worked."

"This time," Thompson amended. As far as she was concerned, Garfield was dangerous, stupid, and too cocky for his own good. His swagger no doubt served him well going up against street thugs, but it could prove a liability chasing down the more established crime families their unit covered. Those families didn't survive on guts and brutality alone—they were businesses, and they ran like multinational corporations. They had deep pockets and long reaches, patience and subtlety. Going up against them required patience and subtlety, too. "But what if the girls hadn't been locked up?"

Garfield nodded toward the storefront windows, through which Thompson could see Petrela—strapped unconscious to a gurney and flanked by armed agents—being loaded into one of the waiting ambulances. The girls were loaded into the others in twos and threes. "Guess then they would've been easier to carry out."

"Hey, boss?" It was Littlefield, the equipment tech from the van. In his hand was Thompson's phone. "This thing's been going nuts for twenty minutes straight."

"It's just my sister," she said. "She's been texting me all day."

Littlefield shook his head. "Nope. These were calls—from HQ, it looked like."

"You were snooping around my phone?" Thompson asked, a bit too sharply.

"I glanced at it, is all," he said defensively. "Figured it might be important."

He handed her the phone. Five calls, all from Thompson's supervisor, Assistant Director Kathryn O'Brien. Five calls, and not one voice mail.

Thompson called her back. Told her the op went fine.

"I'm glad," O'Brien replied, "but I'm not calling about the op. There was a shooting two nights ago in Miami. I want you and Garfield to go down and check it out."

"Yeah, I saw it on the wire. Some old guy gunned down in broad daylight. But why me? If it's federal, I'm sure the Miami office can handle it. Shootings in Miami are a dime a dozen."

"This wasn't some random shooting, Charlie. It was a hit."

Thompson felt a tingle of excitement—the kind of rush that meant a case was on the verge of breaking. "And the vic?"

"A Corporation enforcer by the name of Javier Cruz."

"You're kidding."

"I'm not."

"Any witnesses?" Thompson asked.

"You tell me, Special Agent—that's kind of your job."

"We'll be on the next flight down."

"I thought you might be," O'Brien said.

Thompson was smiling when she ended the call.

"What was that about?" Garfield asked around a mouthful of God knows what.

"We're headed to Miami," Thompson replied. "It would seem my ghost has struck again."

6.

THE BELL THAT hung above the entrance of the Bait Shop clanged as the door swung open and a gust of chilly salt air blew in from the streetlit night, rattling bottles and settling atop the scuffed copper bar. Just a couple miles inland, it was a stultifying summer night in Maine—windows thrown open, fans on high—but the city of Portland was blanketed in fog, the bank extending the length of Casco Bay.

The fog had put a damper on the night's business. Like any of the bars in Portland's Old Port—a historic district of renovated fish piers and nineteenth-century architecture—the Bait Shop was usually hopping all summer long, Sundays included. It wasn't as swanky as the tapas place around the corner, or as much a mainstay of the bar-crawl scene as the Irish pub just down the street. And unlike half the places in town, it didn't have a deck, ocean-view or otherwise. But it did have Lester Meyers behind the bar, and the man was known to have a heavy hand with the drinks—which made the place a hit with locals if not tourists.

Tonight, though, the place was so dead that Lester closed up around ten thirty, ushering a couple shitfaced lobstermen out into the night, where they were forced to make their way home with exaggerated care over the old paving stones. Then he'd killed the neon in the window, and locked the doors—which is why it was odd to hear that bell clang.

Lester, who'd been behind the bar breaking down his garnish station, craned his neck to see over the bar and past the chairs that sat upturned atop the tables. But try as he might, he couldn't see the door from where his wheelchair sat. The bitch of being four feet tall, he thought. After twenty-eight years, four months, and thirteen days of being a solid six-two, his brain had never quite adjusted to the change.

"Sorry, pal," he called, "we're closed."

Lester sat and listened for a moment, but if there was anyone there, he couldn't say—and after six years with Special Forces running black ops throughout the mountains of Afghanistan, his ears were as attuned to subtle cues as anybody's could be.

He gripped his wheels and rolled himself backward just a hair to see if he could get a better look. As he did, he could have sworn he heard a rustle of fabric.

He stopped.

It stopped.

He rolled another couple inches, and there it was again.

"Look, this ain't funny," Lester said. He put on some speed—whipping a quarter-spin as he passed the end of the bar and drawing the Beretta M9 Velcroed to the underside of his chair, so that when he came to a halt, he was facing the door head-on, his gun sight trained on…nothing.

He sat like that a moment, lungs and limbs searing from the sudden exertion, but then a sound behind him made him start.

The sound of a beer bottle being opened.

Lester spun, his gun hand swinging toward the noise, and coming to a stop aimed precisely at the bridge of Michael Hendricks's nose.

"Hiya, Les."

Lester let his hand drop. "Jesus, Mike—you scared the hell outta me! I coulda shot your fucking face off. Which—I don't mind telling you—mighta been an improvement. You look like shit. You get out okay? Was worried I stayed in the system too long after all and got you nabbed."

"Nope," said Hendricks. "Job went fine. Your trick with the lights worked like a charm."

The fact was, though Lester's hack worked perfectly, Hendricks wished they hadn't had to go that route. He preferred his kills to be a little less of a tightrope act than the Cruz job had been. If he'd had his druthers, Cruz would have been in the ground long before he ever got within striking distance of Morales. But then, he hadn't had much time to prepare; Morales had taken his sweet time scraping together Hendricks's fee.

Michael Hendricks had a unique business model. He didn't accept contract kills. Didn't work for any criminal organization. And he never killed civilians. He only hit hitters. He wasn't the kind of guy you called if you wanted to pop somebody who'd pissed you off or done you wrong. In fact, he wasn't a guy you called at all—*he* called *you*. And when he did, you'd be advised to take the call, because it meant someone, somewhere, wanted you dead.

Morales's hesitation was understandable. It was clear he thought at first that Hendricks was trying to shake him down—and even for a billionaire, two hundred thousand dollars isn't exactly chicken feed. But the price the Corporation had placed on Morales's head was $20K, and Hendricks's rate to make a hitter disappear was ten times the hitter's payout. Always up-front. Nonnegotiable.

The smart ones paid. The ones that didn't weren't around too long to regret it. And until the text came through from Hendricks's bank in the Seychelles six hours before Cruz was to make his move, Hendricks had no idea which Morales would prove to be.

Guess he'd done his homework. There were plenty of rumors of Hendricks's existence for those who knew where to look—not to mention examples of his handiwork. And now Edgar Morales would live to piss off the Corporation another day. Most hired guns wouldn't touch a job that got a predecessor popped, for fear they'd wind up meeting the same fate. Killing was a whole lot harder once you took away the element of surprise—and the scrutiny a failed attempt attracted from law enforcement made finishing the job damn near impossible.

Still, Morales ought to consider beefing up his personal security for a while. Or maybe flee the country in one of those fancy charter planes his company owned until things back home cooled off. Hendricks's services were one-time offers; in his business, it didn't pay to offer lifetime guarantees.

"Cruz wasn't any trouble?" Lester asked. "I hear tell he was supposed to be one nasty motherfucker."

Hendricks shrugged. "Emphasis on *was*."

"Then why the holdup getting back? And what're you doing *here*? Not that I ain't happy to see you—but I figured you'd be eager to get home."

"Needed to recharge my batteries," said Hendricks, too dismissively. "Decided I'd take my time. Drive up the coast. See the sights."

"Yeah, you *look* recharged," said Lester, his words dripping sarcasm. "This drive of yours didn't happen to take you through Virginia, did it? Past Evie's place, maybe?"

Of course it did. And of course Lester knew it. In all the world, the only person left who really knew Hendricks was this man—now that Evie thought him dead.

"She looked good," Hendricks said—his expression pained.

"It's Evie, dude—of *course* she looked good."

"How far along is she?"

Damn it, thought Lester—so *that's* why Mike came straight here, instead of going home. He decided to play dumb. "Come again?"

"Don't pull that shit on me, Les. You really expect me to believe you didn't know? You and Evie are Facebook friends. She and *Stuart*," he spat, as though the man's name was an epithet, "invited you to their fucking wedding."

"Ain't like I went," he said, giving the chair a twirl. "Not much for dancing these days."

"How far along, Les?"

Lester sighed and looked at his lap. "Gotta be five months now, almost. She's due in January. And shit like this is exactly why I won't let you see her feed."

Hendricks set his beer down on the bar. Hard. Foam rose and ran over, like the bile rising in his throat. He kept the latter down by force of will and mopped up the former with a bar rag.

"Look, I'm sorry, man, but what did you expect? Poor woman thinks you're dead. She went outta her head mourning you—we all did. The day you walked through that door," he said, nodding back toward the front of the bar, "it was like the clouds had parted; you got no idea the weight of guilt you lifted offa me when you came back. I know you've got your reasons for not seeing her, and as much as I think you made the wrong damn choice, I understand it ain't my place. But you can't leave a girl a widow at twenty-six and not expect her to move on."

"I didn't," Hendricks said.

"You didn't *what?*"

"Leave her a widow." It was true. They never married.

Lester snorted in dismissal. "Why, because you didn't have a fucking piece of paper? You think that mattered to her? You made a promise, and so did she. The rest is nothing more than, you know, fodder for the bureaucrats."

Lester was right. Of course he was. But it didn't mean that Hendricks had to like it.

Hendricks and Evie met their sophomore year at Albemarle High, which was nestled in the foothills of the Blue Ridge Mountains outside Charlottesville, Virginia. Evie's parents were Southern upper-crust types; her father taught law at the university, and her mother didn't work, insisting a woman's place was in the home. Home was a sprawling redbrick mansion Evie's three-greats granddad built before the War of Northern Aggression, as her family still called it, and her mother's idea of playing housewife was bossing around the team of servants it took to tend it. Hendricks—

then a skinny kid in ill-fitting thrift store clothes—had never seen such opulence. Evie's parents were genteel enough in their disdain for him to hide it behind a veneer of Southern charm—supposing, perhaps, the whole affair would blow over soon enough.

By the time Hendricks's relationship with Evie reached the six-month mark, her parents weren't speaking to him.

And when, after graduation, Evie agreed to marry him, they weren't speaking to her, either.

Evie and Hendricks ran off together—just hopped into his old pickup truck and headed north. They moved into her father's family's summer cabin in New Hampshire, unused for decades on account of Evie's mother's disdain for the wilderness. That summer, Evie worked weekends slinging soft serve, and Hendricks—who aimed to enlist as soon as his eighteenth birthday came around—picked up the odd construction gig. They had barely ten dollars between them and not a care in the world, lounging and laughing and making love in their shabby forest home.

They talked of using his meager soldier's salary to get Evie a degree. They talked of making it official and starting a family once his tour of duty was through. They talked of nothing at all for what seemed like days, lost in lust and love.

Looking back, it was hard for Hendricks to imagine how it could have all gone wrong. How he could have gone from love-struck, duty-bound kid eager to fight for God and country to cold-blooded killer-for-hire.

Truth be told, the progression was simple enough. But simple wasn't the same as easy.

* * *

There was a dream that plagued Hendricks every time he closed his eyes. No matter how hard he tried to change the outcome, it always played out the same way.

In the dream, Hendricks is a fresh-faced patriot straight out of basic training—a soldier so green, he barely knows which end of his rifle is which. He brims with pride as he's given his first assignment downrange: guard duty for a dignitary and his family. The dignitary is a kindly older gentleman, beaming as he introduces Hendricks to his wife and children and thanks him for his protection, his dedicated service.

The men arrive at nightfall. Silent. Lethal. Clad in black, cowards operating in darkness. He watches, helpless, as they kill his brothers-in-arms; the dignitary he's sworn to protect; the dignitary's family.

He's helpless because his throat's been slit, a vulgar smile, warm blood pooling on the floor beneath him.

And as his life slips away—just before he returns gasping to the waking world—he can sense the fresh ghosts of the cooling dead all around.

Hendricks is that soldier every night—honorable and dying—but in life, he never was.

He was the black-clad man who killed him.

In boot camp, Hendricks was identified as having certain qualities. Qualities the military finds valuable in a covert operative. To this day, he wasn't sure what put them onto him. He supposed it could have been his instinctive understanding of military tactics, his knack for firearms and bladed weapons, or his talent with shaped charges. But it seemed likelier to him their barrage of psychological examinations revealed some dark aspect of his psyche, like the shadow of a tumor on an X-ray, that told them he was the killing kind.

Whatever it was, they weren't wrong. Hendricks took to the training like a dog to the hunt, and why wouldn't he? Special Forces was his chance to make a difference. To tip the balance. To make the world safe for democracy.

But his idealism didn't last long.

The job itself proved just the antidote.

His was a false-flag unit, operating under orders of the US government, but without the safety net of military backup or diplomatic support. They specialized in missions the details of which the Pentagon didn't want to see the light of day.

Most of those missions were political assassinations.

Even now, Hendricks was forced to admit he and his team had done some good. Many of the threats they neutralized were legitimate. But some weren't. Some were murders, pure and simple.

Hendricks honestly couldn't say whether that dignitary needed killing or not. He *could* say they didn't need to kill his wife and kids. Or his entire security detail, who weren't any more a threat to an elite team of commandos than the wife and kids had been.

But they did. They killed them all.

Hendricks wasn't sure why—given all he'd seen and done—the young soldier was the one who haunted him. He'd kicked the door in to find Hendricks standing over the dignitary, knife in hand, and Hendricks got to the kid before he could unsling his rifle from his shoulder. Cut him ear-to-ear, clean through his windpipe, and listened to his strangled cries as he died. Poor kid looked so *surprised*, Hendricks recalled, as if he couldn't square exactly how it had come to this. For that matter, Hendricks couldn't square it, either—but something told him that would've been cold comfort to the boy as he lay dying.

Maybe Hendricks felt some kinship with him. Maybe he'd just had his fill of taking orders from those who refused to get their hands dirty. Hell, maybe it was the phase of the fucking moon.

Whatever it was, after he killed the kid, Hendricks withdrew into himself. He stopped writing Evie. Stopped calling. He didn't figure he was worthy of her love on account of what he'd done.

He wanted to die. To disappear. And when a roadside bomb outside Kandahar destroyed his unit, Hendricks got his wish.

They were returning back to base after a mission. Recon in the hills just north of town. Seventy-two hours without rest and a sort of delirious exhaustion set in. Lester was running point—walking ahead of the team's two Humvees to scout the unmarked dirt track on which they were traveling. Hendricks was tasked with bringing up the rear, slowly surveilling their perimeter.

As the Humvees rolled past a stand of brown scrub brush, Hendricks spotted something. A rustling in the bushes. Protocol dictated he radio ahead to halt the team and investigate, but he didn't. It was probably nothing, he thought. Turned out, he was right—as he crouched to peer into the underbrush, he found it was just a common hare, fleeing as they approached.

Then the high-desert stillness was ripped apart in a fury of light and sound, of flaming metal and flying rock. An improvised explosive device, Hendricks later learned. In the scant moments before consciousness failed him, he thought it was the wrath of hell.

Turned out Lester had been asleep on his feet. Maybe if he hadn't been, he would have seen the warning signs. Then again, maybe not. It was the dead of night, after all, and Afghani rebels had been waging war against various occupiers for over thirty years—they'd learned a thing or two about disguising booby traps along the way. Odds are, not a man alive could have spotted that device in time.

Not that knowing that helped Lester sleep at night.

By some standards, Les was lucky: he only lost his legs. The men in both Humvees lost their lives. It was the first of the two that set off the device—two bricks of C-4 packed all around with shards of rock—but when the bomb blew, it threw the first vehicle backward onto the second, collapsing both vehicles on themselves and leaving nothing to bury back home. Hendricks was thrown some thirty yards from the roadway and knocked unconscious. He stayed that way for days, buried beneath a layer of ash-gray dirt.

Lester crawled for two miles trailing blood from the stumps of his ruined legs before collapsing, determined to find help for his brothers-in-arms, and was picked up on the verge of death by a routine patrol. By the time Hendricks came to—fevered, concussed, and nearly dead of starvation and exposure—all evidence of the ruined caravan was gone and all mention of their missions scrubbed from the record.

And why wouldn't they have been? Officially, they had never existed. They were disavowed in death as they would have been in any other failure. And those few who knew the truth—about his unit and their demise—thought Hendricks to be among the dead.

It took Hendricks a month to walk out of Afghanistan. At first, he was near feral, operating on instinct. His memories were ragged, his injuries severe—so he holed up, living off the land as he recuperated. He didn't know whom he could trust, so he hid from insurgents and American patrols. Once his fever broke and the swelling in his brain abated, his memories returned—and with them, the crushing guilt of all the innocents he'd killed. He supposed he could have come in from the cold, but why? As far as the military was concerned, Hendricks was dead—which meant Evie thought him dead as well. It was for the best, he told himself. He never could have faced her knowing what he'd become—a monster, a ghost. And so he hiked southeast, toward Pakistan, where the border was rendered porous by treacherous terrain and tribal control.

Once in Pakistan, he set about gathering new papers, crafting a new identity—building a new, if hobbled and incomplete, life. He thought even this damnable half-existence was better than he deserved.

This gig hitting hitters started out as retribution, of sorts. Hendricks figured once you agree to kill an innocent, you deserve whatever's coming to you. That ridding the world of people who murder for a living was some kind of public service.

The irony of his chosen vocation wasn't lost on him.

Or maybe his motivations were simpler than that. Maybe he killed because he was good at it. Maybe he killed because he didn't know how to do anything else.

It's also possible that he kept at it because he figured one day somebody was going to turn the tables on him and put him in the ground.

God knows he deserved it.

7.

A BEAD OF SWEAT trickled down Charlie Thompson's side as she paced the sidewalk in front of Miami Police Headquarters, her cell phone to her ear. Garfield was inside, enjoying the relative comfort of the building's air-conditioned lobby. They'd arrived over an hour ago and had been waiting for their department contact to collect them ever since. In that time, Jess had called twice. It seemed yesterday's manic episode led to boy problems with a tequila chaser, and somehow it was up to Charlie to set Jess's world right again. She wasn't wild about the idea of Garfield overhearing her family drama, so she took the calls outside.

The building she paced beside was a squat, imposing concrete structure accented with tile the color of rust and red desert sand. It sat to the east of the city center, just blocks from Biscayne Bay, two miles and change from where Cruz met his fate. Low concrete barriers lined the building on all sides, disguised halfheartedly as retaining walls or planters for exhaust-choked palm trees. But they were architectural flourishes in a building devoid of architectural flourishes, and they weren't fooling anyone. They were battlements, intended to protect the building and the people within from a street-level assault, or from a vehicle on a collision course. In a town full of drug smugglers and gunrunners, terrorists and gangbangers, an attack on police headquarters wasn't entirely out of the question.

"Look," Thompson said into the phone, "I'm not saying he shouldn't have mentioned they were back together, Jess. All I said was snooping through his phone probably wasn't the best idea."

Jess gave Thompson an earful in reply while she wilted in the morning's rising heat. Her brow beaded with sweat. She dabbed at it with her sleeve as she paced.

"Well, if you can't trust him," Thompson said, "maybe you shouldn't be sleeping with him."

An old woman with a hooked nose and oversized sunglasses eyed Thompson with disdain as she walked by, her hair rinse silver tipping toward blue. The way she cocked her head, she looked to Thompson like a cartoon owl.

"No, you shouldn't text her back and tell her off." A pause while Jess, riled up, responded. "Because he's the one who fucked up—not her. Damn it, Jess, I don't care how pretty he is—you deserve better. Yes, you *do*."

It took a while, but eventually she talked Jess down. By the time she reentered the lobby, her patience was wearing thin. Garfield, for his part, looked unruffled: his suit was clean and crisp; his tie too flashy but well knotted; his collar buttoned and pressed. But then, that might've been because Garfield spent the hours after the Petrela collar catching some Zs, taking a shower, and changing his clothes, while Thompson had been perched atop her hotel room's bed with her notebook computer on her lap, cranking through the necessary post-bust paperwork and poring over the file on the Cruz hit—which meant she hadn't slept or showered in forty hours. Even as the night wore on, she'd been unable to stop her brain from cycling; she couldn't force herself to sleep. Not when they were so close.

"Spill it," Garfield had said, flipping through the file on his lap as Thompson piloted their rented Focus from the airport to police headquarters. "What's this 'ghost' thing all about?"

Thompson smiled at the question as she weaved through Route 112's dense morning traffic, though it was less a smile of amusement than vindication. The term had started as a joke. She'd been on this case since long before her fellow agents thought there was a case at all, and in the early days, they'd ribbed her mercilessly for it. Much as she loved her job, the FBI was still a good ol' boys' club at heart; the instincts of female agents were called into question far more often than those of their male counterparts. But she hadn't cared what they thought—she'd known in her gut she was right. That there was a new player in the game. Someone talented. Dangerous. And one hundred percent off the Bureau's radar.

Every time Thompson had added another kill to her whiteboard, another report to her file, her colleagues would tease her, saying, "Thompson's ghost has struck again." And whenever a case on her list was proven to be the work

of some low-level thug—in the early days of her investigation, she'd yet to discern the pattern and had cast too wide
a net—she'd never heard the end of it.

But then a pattern *did* emerge, and the killings escalated
to the point that the Bureau brass could no longer ignore
them. By the time the deputy director appointed Thompson, the resident expert, to head up the investigation, her
colleagues had stopped laughing.

Garfield gripped the dash and inhaled sharply through
clenched teeth as Thompson threaded their rental between
a minivan and a delivery truck. Somewhere behind them, a
horn blared.

"It's not a *what*," Thompson replied, "it's a *who*. Some
new hitter on the scene. Relatively new, at least. Bagged
thirty-five kills we know of in the past two years alone,
though I suspect his CV stretches farther back than that."

"And you think this Cruz was number thirty-six?"

Thompson didn't think Cruz was thirty-six—she knew
it. "Has all the hallmarks."

"What hallmarks?" Garfield asked. "He shot a guy.
Seems to me anyone can pull a trigger."

"You kidding me? I wouldn't call popping a guy from
four blocks away just *pulling a trigger*," said Thompson.
"But anyway, that wasn't what I meant—he rarely kills the
same way twice."

Irritation flickered across Garfield's face. "Okay then,
what're the hallmarks?"

"For one, his hits are flashy. Asphyxiation in the middle
of a crowded convention center. An airport knifing. A precision shot on a busy city street. Hell, he once used a shaped
charge to blow a theater chair—and the guy inside it—to
pieces without injuring the patrons on either side. And for

two, despite the fact that they're so flashy, no one's ever managed to get eyes on him."

"Not even traffic cams? Surveillance footage?"

Thompson shook her head. "Disabled or obscured."

"Then I'm guessing he ain't the sort to leave prints, either."

"You're guessing right. But I haven't told you the best part yet."

"And that is?"

"My ghost only hits other hitters."

At eleven a.m., after nearly two hours' wait, their contact finally arrived. A stocky, hirsute man in a cheap gray suit bounded across the atrium with a vigor that belied his heft. Both his suit and bald pate gleamed beneath the lobby's fluorescent lights.

"Agent Thompson? Agent Garfield? I'm Detective De Silva."

He extended a hairy-knuckled hand to each of them in turn.

Thompson shook it.

Garfield didn't. "*Special* agent," he corrected. Thompson winced. The Bureau doesn't have a rank of agent—all investigators are titled special agent—but it was a common enough mistake, and one only a supercilious prick would bother to correct. Particularly when the person that supercilious prick was correcting was someone whose cooperation was far from guaranteed.

"Detective," Thompson said, as De Silva let the hand he'd extended to Garfield drop, "thanks for agreeing to meet with us."

"Of course," he said, though the scowl on his face suggested he was thinking better of it now. He looked around the lobby, which teemed with uniformed cops and civilians. "How 'bout we step into my office, huh?"

De Silva took them up an elevator, then down a labyrinth of cramped hallways. Turns out, his offer of an office was sarcastic. His desk was one of many in a detective's bull pen, which was only slightly less cacophonous than the lobby they'd left behind. Once there, he shunted them into a tiny, windowless conference room that looked like it might have been a converted broom closet.

"Sorry about the accommodations," he said. "I'm sure Uncle Sam takes care of you Federals just fine, but us lowly city cops consider it a good day if the AC stays on. Now, what can I do for you?"

Thompson tamped down her irritation at De Silva's tone. Friction with local law enforcement was part and parcel of working for the Bureau—and anyway, she reminded herself, it was Garfield who kicked off this particular pissing contest. She tried a smile. In her current exhausted state, it came out a grimace, and likely did more harm than good.

"I was wondering what you could tell us about the Cruz murder," she said.

"I assume you read my report."

Garfield snorted. "If that's what you wanna call it," he said.

Thompson glared at him. De Silva bristled. "What're you trying to say, *Agent?*"

Garfield leaned back in his chair and showed De Silva his palms. "Just that it was a little slight, is all."

"Through no fault of mine, pal, I can assure you. We traced the shot back to a vehicle, and the vehicle back to a long-term airport parking lot. The owner was at some kinda conference in Reno and had no idea it was even missing. The Crime Scene guys tell me the interior of the vehicle was a bust for prints and DNA, on account of our perp bleached the living shit out of it and wiped down all the surfaces he touched—including his shell casings and gun. And, yeah—the rifle was left behind, but its serial was filed off, so no luck there, either. Somehow every security camera for blocks around went down hours before the shooting, so we've got no footage of either the shot *or* Cruz getting hit, and eyewitnesses were no better. Edgar Morales, the owner of the building, is hiding behind a wall of lawyers—we can't get a straight answer as to whether he was even in the country when the shit went down. We spent hours canvassing the area, and the best we could come up with was a valet for the hotel the shooter's car was parked at who said our suspect was, and I quote, 'a white dude, maybe, in a ball cap, aviators, and a bushy beard.' That beard, by the way, was fake—we found it bleached white in the center console. And when we called around to costume shops in town trying to find out where he got it, we rolled a donut. We worked the trail. The trail ran cold. As simple as that. Whoever killed Cruz knew what he was doing—and my guess is, he's long-ass gone by now."

"Look, Detective, we appreciate your efforts," Thompson said, flashing a glance at Garfield, "and I'm sure my partner didn't mean to imply your investigation was anything less than thorough and professional. In fact, your expertise could prove invaluable to us. If you'd be willing to take us out and walk us through the crime scene, maybe help us track down some known associates of the vic—"

But De Silva cut her off. "Listen, lady, much as I'd just

love to drop everything and help you out, the Cruz case ain't exactly a priority. This whole goddamn state's a war zone. In Miami-Dade alone, we've had fifty-four murders so far this year. Three hundred cases of sexual assault. Well over two *thousand* aggravated assaults. A full third of those cases haven't been cleared yet. Most likely, they never will be. If I had to guess, I'd say your so-called vic Cruz was responsible for a handful of each, so to my thinking, whoever whacked him did me and the decent citizens of this city a favor. You want to poke around, that's your business. But if you want to stand here and gripe that the file's a little thin, feel free to fill it out yourself. I got better things to spend my time on."

De Silva stood, yanking open the conference room door. It slammed against the wall, rattling glass. Then he left, red-faced and fuming.

Thompson fumed as well. If Garfield had played it differently, maybe De Silva would have been more cooperative. She eyed her new partner with distaste, but if Garfield noticed, he sure didn't let on. Instead, he smiled and shook his head, saying to Thompson, "Some fucking detective *he* was. Probably couldn't find his own dick with both hands and a flashlight."

"*Ass,*" Thompson called him.

"Excuse me?" Garfield replied.

Thompson stared at him a sec, an expression of blank innocence honed in many a late-night poker game pasted on her face. And then she said, "What? That's the saying. *Couldn't find his own ass with both hands and a flashlight.*"

"Right," said Garfield, somewhat mollified. "Now whaddaya say we go take a look at that crime scene?"

8.

ENGELMANN, COMFORTABLE despite Miami's heat in a linen suit and woven cowhide loafers, sipped his espresso and watched the two federal agents bicker in the shadow of the Morales Incorporated Building. From his table at a sidewalk café across the street, he'd watched them parade up and down this stretch of Brickell Avenue for the better part of the afternoon, alternately examining the scant physical evidence Cruz's murder had left behind, and sniping at each other like an embittered married couple.

Engelmann spent most of his life observing from a distance. Even as a child, he'd felt set apart from his family, from other children, and from the string of governesses in whose care his parents placed him—and whose emotional states he slowly destroyed with his sadistic manipulations. It was by impulse, rather than design, that he tormented them—an omnipresent itch that he could never truly scratch, an urge to ruin and destroy that could be quieted but never quelled.

It wasn't until he discovered killing that he'd felt truly present in this world.

His first was a pheasant at his family's summer manor, which was nestled in the Inn River Valley in southwest Switzerland. He was ten. The house chef mistook his interest in the process as culinary in nature, and after he'd observed a slaughter without crying, the chef allowed the boy to bleed a bird himself. In that blissful moment when knife parted flesh, and the headless pheasant began to thrash within his grasp, the air had never seemed so crisp, the sky never quite so true a blue. But if the wizened old chef took note of his aroused state—as Engelmann suspected he had, for Anatole never again allowed the boy to partake in the daily slaughter—he never breathed a word of it to anyone.

Engelmann's path had nevertheless been determined. So transformative was the experience, young Engelmann spent the better part of that afternoon traipsing about with hands coated red, only grudgingly washing away the stains when they'd crusted dry, the blood's color fading to rust—and with it, the colors of the world around him. As he watched those flecks of spent iron swirl downstream on the icy waters of the River Inn, he knew they represented the compass by which his heart had been set—a conclusion reinforced weeks later when he took his first human victim, a local farm boy, and experienced an emotional and physical release so thunderous that mere words failed to do it justice.

Today, he watched, as he'd watched the village children decades before, his mind calm and appraising. Of course, he had no intention of harming these investigators. Not that he wouldn't have enjoyed it. The woman was pretty enough, he thought, or at least would be if she gave a damn, and the man had a certain swagger it might be fun to break him of. But he didn't see any utility in it—nor did he expect that they'd discern anything from the crime scene he had not yet himself discerned. He'd arrived in Miami some hours before they did and had already been over every centimeter of the sidewalk and the parking lot, so he knew just how meticulous the hit had been. He elected to stay and watch them not for evidentiary reasons, but because he believed the better he understood his fellow hunters, the better he would understand their common quarry.

Engelmann downed the last grainy bit of his espresso and left a twenty on the table. Ordinarily, he found tipping gauche, a horrid American practice he avoided whenever possible, but today he was in good spirits and thought the mood worth sharing. Then he left the café, and left the investigators to their fruitless examination of the crime scene. His nerves vibrated like a tuning fork from excitement and caffeine, a clarion note of anticipation ringing in his head.

That was fine. Useful, even.

Alexander Engelmann had a busy night ahead of him.

"Pardon me," said Engelmann, "but I was wondering if I might have a word."

It wasn't the man's words that chilled Edgar Morales to his core, nor his polite, well-modulated tone—a tone that implied moneyed good grace and lent an angular quality to his words, a voice suggesting that while he was clearly fluent, this man was not a native English speaker.

What chilled Edgar Morales was the moment itself, for

it was four in the morning, and the words had roused him from sleep. He opened his eyes to find his bedroom dark and still, the security panel on his wall blinking green to indicate all was well. But he hadn't imagined that voice—a voice that signaled to Morales that all his precautions had been for naught and that his life would end tonight.

Ever since Cruz's attempt on Morales's life, Morales had spent his nights in his Bayside Village condo out on Fisher Island. He'd bought the place years ago when his company's value first reached a billion, seduced by the cachet that accompanied the address. What better sign was there you'd made it than living on a man-made resort island that boasted the highest per capita income in the nation? For a kid who grew up poor on a dodgy street in Goulds, the allure of joining Miami's most exclusive community was too great to pass up. It had taken him a while to find a suitable abode, because he'd restricted his search to the city-facing bay side, ignoring Fisher Island's ocean-side properties entirely. After all, what was seeing the sunrise over the Atlantic compared to the glint of the sunrise off the skyscraper that bore his name?

In the days since his mysterious benefactor rid him of his Cruz problem, however, his six-thousand-square-foot condo had taken on a new significance for him, beyond signifying his arrival as a businessman. Situated as it was on the uppermost floor, with views in every direction and every access point monitored by a security system so state-of-the-art the Pentagon couldn't afford it—not to mention the fact that it was on an island with no auto access whatsoever, and ferry access limited to residents and invited guests—it had become his fortress, his island stronghold. The man who saved his life had warned him the Corporation would likely try again, and having witnessed Cruz's grisly demise, he took that warning to heart—even augmenting his already formidable security with a team of trained sentries. His neighbors, no doubt, thought he'd gone off the deep end, another Howard Hughes type unable to handle the pressures of so much wealth. But to hell with his neighbors—better to be a live eccentric than to be thought of well while dead.

"Who...who are you?" he stammered, his voice hoarse from fear.

"Who I am is of little consequence to you," Engelmann replied.

"My guards—"

"Are, at present, indisposed."

"You mean...," Morales began, only to find he could not summon the words.

"If you're asking did I kill them, the answer is no; I've not been paid to kill *them*. I merely rendered them unconscious so you and I would not be interrupted."

"But you *are* here to kill me."

Engelmann smiled. "That depends upon your level of cooperation. You see, I've not been paid to kill *you*, either."

Morales digested the man's words. "If you're not here to kill me, why'd you sneak into my bedroom?"

"I need to ask you some questions. About what happened to one Mr. Javier Cruz."

"You mean the man who died outside my building?" Morales asked. "I don't know; I wasn't there." It was a foolish lie, given the circumstances, but it was a reflex, nothing more. He'd repeated that lie to countless detectives and reporters in the past three days, before instructing his legal team to shut down any further inquiries on the subject.

Engelmann *tsk*ed in the darkness. "Mr. Morales, I think I've thus far treated you with decorum, even respect—I'd appreciate it if you would afford me the same courtesy. I may not have been paid to kill you, but hurting you I'd do for free."

Morales stiffened. He swallowed hard, his mouth dry as sand. "Of course," he rasped, fumbling for the bedside table. "I'm sorry. If I could just turn the light on, so I can take a drink of water—"

"I'm not an *amateur*, Mr. Morales. I removed your firearm from the drawer before I woke you. And I suspect if you think long and hard about it, you'll realize it's in your best interest if you never see my face."

Morales slumped in his bed, defeated.

"Good," Engelmann said, as if something of import had been decided. "Now, Cruz."

"What do you want to know?"

"I want you to tell me how you contacted the man who killed him."

"I—I didn't!"

Morales heard a metallic *sching* as a blade slid free of its scabbard. His heart slammed painfully against the wall of his chest.

"I did caution you against lying, Mr. Morales."

Hands on his face. In his hair. Yanking his head back. Morales cried out—wordless, animal. For a moment, he thrashed against his assailant's grasp, but then he froze as he felt the point of a blade dimple the tender flesh beneath his left eye.

Morales had no idea how the man could be so precise in such utter darkness. The blade's tip did not pierce his skin. It just rested there, so gently that it tickled, but the man's iron grip on the back of his head made it clear it would take little effort to drive that blade into his eye.

"Now," the man said, "I'll ask again. How did you contact the man who killed Cruz?"

Morales tried to withdraw from the blade—by instinct more than volition—but it was no use. "I *told* you," he said, his manner more pleading than correcting, "I didn't—he contacted me!"

Morales braced for the pain to come, but it never did. Instead, the man withdrew, leaving Morales once more alone on the bed, gulping air as he willed his drumroll heart to slow.

"He contacted *you*." It wasn't a question; Engelmann was certain Morales would not have lied to him just then—he had a better sense of self-preservation than that.

"That's right. The guy showed up in my office one day—no appointment, no nothing—and told me there was a bounty on my head."

"Did he say how he knew this to be true?"

"He said he had his sources."

"And you believed him?"

"No, of course not. But he had details—land deals I'd made that weren't yet part of the public record. Communications from the goons in the Cuban Mafia about all the trouble I was causing." He paused, then, wondering if Engelmann would take offense at his thoughtless characterization, but Engelmann said nothing. "He had the when and where, the who and how, and he knew how much this Cruz dude was getting for his trouble. Said for ten times as much, he'd make Cruz go away."

Ten times the price on the target's head. A tidy profit to be sure, Engelmann thought, smiling. The more he learned of his quarry, the more he liked the man. "How did you know he was not conning you? That he wasn't *shaking you down*, as your American mobsters are so fond of saying?"

"I didn't. But he told me I didn't have to decide right away. Said I should sleep on it—as if anyone could sleep when they know there's a price on their head. I hired a PI firm, had them snoop around. It seemed his information was sound."

"How long before the hit did he come to you?"

"Three days."

"Did he give a name?"

Morales shook his head. Even in the dark, Engelmann got the gist. "I don't suppose it would have mattered if he did," he said. "Your building, I assume, is wired for video, is it not?"

"Yeah," Morales said. "It is. Only the thing is, the day this guy showed up there was some kind of glitch in the software, and we lost the whole day's feed."

"Of course you did. Can you describe the man to me?"

Morales thought about it. "Nothing much about the guy stood out, really," he said. "Not too short, and not too tall. Six feet, maybe a little less. Brown hair, short. Muscular, but lean."

"Race?"

"White."

"What about his station?"

"I don't follow," Morales said.

"The way he carried himself. Would you say he sounded moneyed or poor, upper class or lower, educated or uneducated?"

"Uh, I don't know. He came off smart, I guess, but

working-class. The kind of guy if you met him, you'd think he worked with his hands."

Engelmann thought a moment about the description Morales had provided. "Would you say he had a military disposition?"

Now it was Morales's turn to ponder. "Yeah," he said. "I guess I would."

"Excellent. I must say, Mr. Morales, despite a rocky start, you've proven yourself most helpful. So, true to my word, I leave you to the remainder of your night."

"Thank you," Morales blubbered madly, relieved at the realization he'd live to see the sun rise on his building at least once more. "Thank you."

"Think nothing of it," Engelmann said. "Besides, I've no doubt the Corporation will send someone along to kill you once the attention generated by their last attempt dies down. Sleep well, Mr. Morales, while you still can. And if I were you, I'd consider hiring better guards."

Engelmann left as quietly as he'd arrived. Morales listened for a long while to be sure he was really gone. Eventually, Morales climbed out of bed, stepped over the unconscious guard outside his bedroom, and crossed the great room to his wet bar. With shaking hands, he poured himself a hefty belt of scotch. It was a Macallan Fine Oak 30 Year Old, and it had set him back two grand. He'd been saving it for a special occasion.

9.

S O," HENDRICKS SAID, "any chatter?"

He and Lester were sitting at a table toward the back of the Bait Shop's dining room, Hendricks sipping on an Allagash between bites of pastrami on rye, and Lester nursing a club soda with lime. It was a little after noon. The Bait Shop was closed. The blinds were drawn against the light of day, and the bar's lights, save the one above them, were unlit.

"Here and there," Lester replied, sliding a file folder thick with printouts across the table. "Nothing too promising. Family business, mostly. Infighting."

Hendricks opened the folder and flipped through the papers in silence. His line of business wasn't the sort you advertised on Google or in the local Yellow Pages. Any point of contact, physical or electronic, was a potential liability—a chance for an interested party to track his movements and pinpoint his location. Which is why Hendricks insisted on initiating contact with potential clients, rather than the other way around. Half the time, the folks he approached had no idea they'd been marked for death until Hendricks told them. Some refused to believe him. Some believed him but decided to go it alone. Some bought in right away. The ones who declined his services didn't always come to a bad end, but their survival rate was less than stellar. Those who paid fared significantly better. In the three and a half years he'd been doing this, he'd yet to lose a single client.

The key was identifying them early enough to scout the job and make the proper approach. Early on in his career, Hendricks had simply tailed known hitters and identified their targets by hanging back and watching—but that made his margin for error razor thin and damn near got him killed a couple times. One particularly nasty job ended with his client safe, his target dead—but not before the bastard buried an ice pick three inches deep in Hendricks's chest. After four days holed up in an abandoned warehouse, trying to keep the bleeding under control while he waited for the antibiotics he'd boosted from a veterinary clinic to take effect, Hendricks decided it was time for a new approach. That's when he brought Lester in.

Back in Afghanistan, Lester had been the tech-head of the unit. There wasn't a system he couldn't hack, a wire he couldn't tap, a cipher he couldn't crack. And when the grit and wild swings of temperature between heat of day and aching chill of night got the better of their equipment, Lester never failed to jury-rig a fix. A handy talent when you're four days out from your nearest base to resupply— and no less handy if you intend to kill people who kill people for a living.

Every criminal organization on the planet had some kind of underground communications network. The Russians, for example, favored the old classified ad routine, hiding coded messages in Craigslist posts and the tawdry personals you see on the back pages of alternative weeklies. The Armenians buried lines of garbled nonsense in the source codes of various Internet forums they own—a basic substitution cipher any twelve-year-old with a knack for puzzles could solve, if he or she knew where to look. But no twelve-year-old would waste their time right-clicking and combing the HTML of some random muscle-car chat room.

Lester would, though. Or, at least, his systems would.

The Korean network, he identified in weeks. Ditto the street gangs of LA, who were anything but subtle in their messages. The Polish and Lithuanian families—who used anonymous remailers bounced off half a dozen proxy servers around the globe—took longer. But the Holy Grail of mob communications, the toughest nut to crack, had been the Council's. All but the most stubborn or paranoid of their member organizations used it, and why wouldn't they? It was safe, reliable, and damn near impossible to hack—their very own illegal information superhighway.

Take the printout Hendricks was glancing over now, for instance: a set of race results from Northville Downs, a small-time harness track about a half hour west of Detroit. Big winner of the day was a mare named McGurn's Lament.

Only there was no such horse as McGurn's Lament. And if you were to try to make sense of the day's stats, you'd find that they'd resist sense-making. That's because those stats aren't stats at all.

They're a book code.

The Council's member organizations have been passing

messages this way for years. Got their fingers in a half a dozen race sites so they could spread the bogus results around, avoid raising any hackles. They used made-up horses as code names indicating the nature of the message—Brown Beauty if they were moving heroin, Luscious Lady if they were talking whores, and so on—with the pertinent details encrypted in the results that followed.

McGurn's Lament signified a hit. An in-joke of sorts, Hendricks supposed. McGurn had been Capone's chief hitman, the guy responsible for the St. Valentine's Day Massacre. He was gunned down himself a few years later, in the middle of a frame of tenpin. If you saw the name McGurn's Lament, you knew the numbers that followed were code for a target's name—and if you were lucky, an address. Even money said whoever that name belonged to wasn't long for this world.

It worked like this. Say the horse wearing number thirty-eight came in sixth. That meant the sixth letter on the thirty-eighth page was the one you wanted. Big enough block of numbers, you could encode damn near any message you liked. Any message like a name and an address. Any message like *take your time* or *make it look like an accident*. And because nearly every letter of the alphabet appears in dozens of places throughout the course of any book, there's none of the repetition code-breaking programs rely upon to work their mojo. Unless you knew what book the code was referencing—right down to the exact edition—there was no way you were ever going to crack it. At least, that's what Lester kept on telling him once he'd identified the code itself.

Unless you get me the goddamned book, Mikey, he'd told Hendricks, ain't no way we'll break this thing.

So Hendricks got him the book.

Granted, it took him the better part of two years—and if his target hadn't slipped, he might never have discovered it. Said target was a made guy who was picking up a little free-lance wetwork on the side. Hendricks took him alive, and after a couple hours' cajoling—and enough sodium amytal to make half a cell block sing—the guy told him what he wanted to know in return for ending him quick.

Turns out, it was the 1969 first edition of *The Godfather.*

Never let it be said the Mob doesn't have a sense of humor.

After several minutes of poring over Lester's printouts, Hendricks gave up. "You know I'm lousy at reading this stuff," he said. "You want to tell me what exactly I'm look-ing at?"

"The first one's a series of dispatches from the Chicago Outfit. Urgent, by the sound of 'em. Seems they're looking to pop one of their own on the quiet—a capo's nephew. He runs a nightclub the Outfit uses as a front to peddle Molly—but word is, the guy ain't right. He likes cutting on women. They're worried his extracurricular activities put them at risk, and they're sick of cleaning up his messes."

"Pass," Hendricks said. He was no fan of organized crime, but one thing most old-school outfits had going for them was their disdain for crime of the disorganized variety on their turf—even if it was committed by one of their own. Anybody who cut women was a rancid pile of human garbage, and as far as Hendricks was concerned, there was no point saving someone who wasn't worth saving. If Chicago wanted to take out their own trash, it was best to let them do it without a fuss.

"Yup. Good riddance, says I."

Hendricks took a bite of his sandwich—the bread toasted to crunchy perfection, the pastrami juicy and delicious—and washed it down with a sip from his pint. "What else you got?"

"The Los Angeles mob just put a hit out on some gang-banger out of Long Beach. Nobody's accepted the contract yet, so the details are a little light on the ground."

Hendricks ate in silence for a moment. "You got a name on the target?"

"Yeah, and not much more. Born Irving Franklin. Receives mail at his grandma's place. Doesn't seem to have a fixed address."

"Arrest record?"

"Vandalism. Petty theft. Possession with intent. The arresting officer on the latter rolled up a crew of corner boys who call themselves the Savage Prophets, and he was one of 'em."

"Any reason these Savage Prophets would have a beef with the LA family?"

"None that I could find—and anyway, Franklin is the only one they're looking to whack. They're one of the few black gangs in the area not affiliated with the Crips. Could be the Prophets get their product from the LA family, which would make this a supply chain issue."

"How old is he?"

Lester sighed. "Listen, Mikey, I know you, and I know what you're thinking here. But Franklin isn't some scared kid who fell in with a bad crowd—he's a fucking drug dealer."

"How *old*, Les?"

Les hesitated. "He's sixteen."

Sixteen. Jesus. "There a time line on the hit?"

"Nothing solid. Be a few days, at least."

Hendricks finished his beer. Nodded as if something had been decided. "Get me on a flight to Long Beach. I want to give this kid a look."

"You sure you don't wanna sit this one out, Mikey? You've been running yourself ragged lately, and you haven't even been home yet since your last job."

"I'm fine, Les," Hendricks replied. "Book the flight."

"Say for a second that I'm wrong about this Franklin, and he really is a decent guy—there's no way he'd be able to pay your fee. Only way he'd have the money's if he's crooked. You've said yourself you'll never kill for free."

"True. But I can warn him to get clear, at least."

"And if I'm right? If this kid is just another piece of shit drug dealer?"

"If you're right, I let him die."

Lester studied his friend a moment, the lines in Hendricks's face deepened by the angle of the light.

He's looking old, Lester thought. Tired.

Not for the first time, Lester wondered just how long Hendricks could keep this up—and what kind of toll this job was taking on him. Gone was the scrubbed idealist he'd met those many years ago when their unit was first assembled. Then again, apart from him and Hendricks, gone was the whole damn unit. Maybe becoming something cold and hard was the only way to make it through.

Lester'd tried another route. Tried to put the past behind him. After his injury, Lester was of no further use to the military—his very existence a reminder to the current administration of the sins of the past. His discharge had been listed as general, as he knew it would be; regardless of how valiantly their unit served, their actions were covert and could never be acknowledged, so an honorable discharge was never in the cards. Still, after all he gave—and all he lost—it stung. And when his parents died just six months after he returned Stateside, burned alive in his childhood home when his mother fell asleep with a cigarette between her lips, he just gave up. He used his parents' life insurance and his meager disability benefits to buy this bar—an utter shithole at the time—and spent the next year or so behind it, the place closed more often than not as he tried his damnedest to crawl into a bottle and die. He'd lost everything—his friends, his family, his hope, his sense of purpose.

Then one day, Michael walked through that door—back from the dead—and everything changed. Michael gave him hope. Gave him purpose. Gave him some small measure of absolution, as though he'd been sent by God himself to let Lester know the guilt he'd been carrying around for getting his unit killed was too much for any one man to bear. Michael represented both an easing of his burden and someone to help him shoulder the remaining load.

The money didn't hurt, either. Anyone who says it can't buy happiness should do without it for a while. The money he and Michael brought in turned the bar around—turned it into the kind of homey neighborhood place one goes to live a little, instead of just die slowly. And, more important, it got Lester out of the storeroom and into a proper apartment. He'd bought the bar before the market crashed, and by the time Mike found him, he'd been so far underwater he couldn't afford a place to live, so he'd been sleeping on a cot in back. Now the bar was beautiful and so was his apartment, with its stunning view of Portland spreading out below him to the west and nothing but the icy blue Atlantic to the east.

Lester didn't think of what they were doing as killing. The way he saw it, the balance sheet was murder-neutral either way. Either some poor schlub was getting whacked, or a hardened killer was. Hell, you take out a hardened killer, you're probably *saving* lives.

He knew for damned sure they were saving *him*—nothing stronger than club soda'd passed Lester's lips since the day they started on this little crusade.

Michael, though, was another story. For all his bluster, the work ate at him. You could see it in his face. In the slope of his shoulders as he slumped in his chair. Lester may have the luxury of not thinking what they did was killing, but Michael knew better. Michael was out in the field, the muck, the blood—and out there, the truth was harder to avoid.

If it weren't for Evie, Lester wondered if Michael would have lasted this long. Evie'd been everything to him. Walking away from her—regardless of his reasons or his resolve—had devastated him. But he'd never stopped—he *couldn't* stop—taking care of her. It was one more reason Michael needed Lester's skills. Maybe the only reason that mattered.

Even after Michael's supposed death, Evie's parents never forgave her for leaving with him. She—now a nurse practitioner who split her time between three free clinics in her area—was too proud to ask them for help paying back her student loans, her looming mortgage. Michael, with Lester's help, ensured she'd never have to.

She didn't realize who the money came from. Had no idea it was blood money. As far as she knew, the deposits were part of a structured settlement—the result of a bogus class-action lawsuit Lester conjured from thin air, supposedly brought forth by loved ones of war dead who fell victim to faulty body armor. And thanks to Lester's computer chops, that's all anyone who thought to look would ever see.

Lester didn't know if those payments helped Michael sleep at night, but he was pretty sure they kept him rising every morning. Even after all these years—after Evie fell in love with someone else, after she married—he couldn't help but try to take care of her.

Couldn't help but try to make things right, one murder at a time.

10.

THE AFTERNOON SUN streamed through the windows of the dead man's flat—no, *apartment*, Engelmann reminded himself for perhaps the thousandth time, though the Americanism struck him as inaccurate and artless. Cruz's apartment stood apart from nothing, being one of thirty units in the building—a squat, stuccoed box three stories high, from which jutted perfunctory balconies just large enough to place a hibachi and a single chair, and AC units laboring to make tolerable the city's heat.

Cruz's AC unit sat idle, and the windows were all closed. The apartment was oven-hot and stuffy, the air laden with sex and cheap, masculine cologne. As soon as he walked in, Engelmann's face and neck broke into a sweat, and his hands grew sodden and clumsy inside their black nitrile gloves. Had it been this hot in the hallway, Engelmann likely would've taken twice as long to pick Cruz's many locks. As one might expect, Cruz was a cautious man. Though in this case, Engelmann suspected the locks weren't to protect against retaliation for his crimes but to bar entry to his wife.

This apartment was not the home they shared. And though the bedding was mussed and stained—the nightstand topped with oils, candles, and all manner of phallic appliances—Cruz's wife had never seen the inside of its bedroom. Perhaps she suspected the existence of her husband's little love nest, situated just blocks away from their tidy Little Havana bungalow, or perhaps not. Engelmann suspected it was the former—in part because one's wife, he'd discovered in the course of many an interrogation, often knows a good deal more than she lets on, and in part because he'd seen her expression as she stood watching from the lawn as the Feds picked apart her home, one grandchild propped on each wide, matronly hip, another clinging to her legs. Though her neighbors gathered and watched, too, and with them the news crews, and though her youngest granddaughter buried her face in the woman's ample bosom and cried, Cruz's wife's face showed neither shame nor distress.

Instead, her face showed rage.

At first, he'd assumed it was directed toward the agents ransacking her home. Toward the pretty agent in charge of the scene and her swaggering partner—the same agents he'd observed just yesterday investigating the scene of Cruz's murder. But to them she was cordial, polite—even offering them something to eat while they waited for their crew to finish, as if she craved their approval.

As Engelmann watched, one of many in the crowd, he realized it was not their intrusion that vexed her. It was the fact that her husband had brought this intrusion upon her. She spit whenever the agents mentioned him by name; she shook her head in disgust when pressed for details about his work. As if she'd had no idea until his death what he'd done for a living. As if she had no idea what kind of man her husband really was.

Engelmann had seen this a hundred times in his profession. She was content to look the other way when her husband's work bought them a tidy, sunny-yellow Craftsman home, the nicest on the block—tapered stone pillars propping up the clay shingled roof over the covered porch, a well-manicured lawn in front and back for kids to play on, fenced in as if to say to passersby *"MINE"*—but when it came time for her to face the fact that the fruits of his labor were plucked from a forbidden tree, mock horror was her response.

It made her a hypocrite, Engelmann thought—a liar to herself and to the world. Looking around Cruz's spartan apartment, Engelmann knew the teak glider on the porch of his widow's bungalow was not a purchase he would have made on his own, nor was the elaborate landscaping or the darling patio set he'd glimpsed around back.

No, those were his widow's doing. And it seemed to Engelmann if she were so content to spend Cruz's money, perhaps she shouldn't hold his way of making it in such disdain.

No wonder the man had taken a lover. And no wonder he'd taken such pains to keep his wife out of this place. Having seen her reaction to having her husband's earnings outed as blood money, Engelmann could only imagine how livid she'd become if she were confronted with the evidence that she was not the only one on whom he lavished it.

After a brief circuit to take in the gestalt of the apartment, Engelmann searched the dwelling slowly, methodically, without fear of discovery. The Federals knew nothing of this place. It was not leased under Cruz's name, nor under any of his known aliases. In fact, the apartment wasn't leased at all. The rental company's paperwork listed it as vacant, though in ten years it had never once been shown, let alone rented.

The rental company was owned by the Cuban Mafia. The late Mr. Cruz's employer.

All it took for Engelmann to find it was one call to his Council contact. The address was texted to his burner phone in minutes.

Engelmann started in the kitchen. Small and galley style, it stretched along one side of the empty living room. A stack of take-out menus sat on the countertop. The phone jack on the wall was bare and unused. He opened each drawer in turn: empty. Then he removed the drawer boxes from their frames and searched each for false bottoms, or envelopes taped to their undersides. Still nothing. He searched the cupboards. All but one were bare. The cupboard nearest the three-quarter refrigerator contained two juice glasses, a corkscrew, and a box of plastic eating utensils. He dumped the utensils onto the yellowed linoleum floor and let the box fall after them once he saw that there was nothing left inside.

The oven was empty and appeared unused. In the refrigerator he found a half-empty six-pack of Cerveza Cristal and nothing else. In the garbage, a few rancid food wrappers and two empty wine bottles. He emptied the trash can's contents onto the floor, but there was nothing hidden underneath them—nor between the bag and bin.

There was no furniture in the living room. No art. The beige carpet was stained, the window bare of curtains. Beside the window was a sliding-glass door over which hung a set of cheap vertical blinds, louvered open to let in the light. Engelmann grasped the chain that operated them and slid them back and forth. They moved easily on their track. He ran a hand along the top of the track, but felt nothing. And when he poked his head outside, he found the balcony bare.

What he was looking for, he didn't know. Some clue as to how Cruz operated. Some indication as to how his quarry knew Cruz's plans. He didn't know if he would find it here, or even if such evidence existed. But given the attention to detail with which the woman agent conducted the search on Cruz's family home, and the deflated air about her when, after hours of searching, she gave the order to pack up, he was certain there was no such evidence to be found there.

The apartment's bathroom was a collection of dingy offwhites. The cheap faux-marble vanity. The putty-colored toilet—the seat up, the bowl streaked with rust. The yellowed fiberglass tub, blushed with mold at the corners and black from mildew at the edges of the fixtures. The popcorn ceiling was mottled black as well. The whole room smelled of damp.

He checked the vanity. The toilet tank. The hollow inside of the towel rod. Nothing. The fan rattled when he toggled the switch on and off, so he plucked a screwdriver from his pocket tool kit and removed the vented faceplate. Nothing but grimy fan blades.

Engelmann entered the bedroom. One could hardly call it that, for there was no door separating it from the living space—just the suggestion of a doorway as the room narrowed slightly before widening once more. There was nothing in the room but a nightstand, a combination light fixture/ceiling fan, and a mattress resting on a metal frame, draped loosely with unmade sheets of charcoal gray. There weren't even any pillows.

Naturally, he checked the nightstand first. There was no lamp atop it. There was, however, a bottle each of strawberry- and chocolate-scented body oils, an amber prescription bottle half full of Viagra, a hot pink vibrator, and dildos in a variety of shapes and sizes—none of which were likely found in nature. Some were so oddly shaped, Engelmann wondered at their method of use. Then he found the Polaroids in the drawer and wondered no longer.

It seemed when Engelmann assumed Cruz'd taken a lover, he'd underestimated Cruz's appetites. There must have been three dozen photos in the drawer, and at least three times that many partners. Each picture contained no fewer than two people, not counting the person behind the camera—who, by dint of his omission from the collection, must have been Cruz himself—and no two pictures contained the same combination of lovers. They ranged in age from maybe fifteen to twenty-five, and they ranged in gender from male to female to any combination thereof. Most were Hispanic, but many were black, with the occasional Asian thrown into the mix as well. None were white. Cruz apparently drew the line somewhere in his predilections.

Engelmann pored over these images of tangled limbs, toys, and genitalia for quite a while, but it stirred nothing in him. He was simply looking to see if they held some clue that could prove of use to him, but if they did, their secrets were as remote to him as the pleasures of the flesh they depicted. Only killing provided him the satisfaction these hollow images promised.

When he finished with the photos, he tossed them to the floor and returned his attention to the nightstand drawer. There was nothing in it but the old, bulky Polaroid that snapped those pictures, open and empty of film, and a tacky hardback crime novel, which he cast aside after shaking to see if anything fell out. Then he inspected the drawer box as he had the ones in the kitchen, but to no avail.

Engelmann stripped the mattress of its sheets, which were stained, soft from countless bodies, and smelled of sweat. The mattress appeared intact—no openings or hand-stitched seams to suggest Cruz'd hidden anything inside—but Engelmann sliced it open and searched it regardless. Soon the room was littered with springs and batting as well as tawdry photos, but Engelmann was no closer to the clue that he was looking for.

He disassembled the metal bed frame, but that was empty, too. Nothing was taped to the upper surface of the ceiling fan blades, nor stashed inside the glass dome that encased the bulbs. All Engelmann found in the heating vents were mouse droppings, and moving the appliances yielded nothing but dust bunnies and dead roaches.

Engelmann stood shaking with frustration in the center of Cruz's ruined apartment. Filthy and sweat-soaked, he retreated to the refrigerator, yanking open the door, grabbing one of Cruz's beers, and cracking it open. Then he lowered himself stiffly onto the linoleum, letting the chill air from the open refrigerator pour over him as he drank.

His gaze wandered the apartment, dispassionately taking in his handiwork. He found no joy in the mess he'd made—only disappointment. He'd been so certain there was something here to find. And yet.

And yet.

As his eyes lit upon the hardback novel lying spine-up and open on the floor, he felt a rush of discovery, of revelation. The cover, he realized, was in English, though his dossier indicated Cruz held the English language in disdain and would not permit it to be spoken in his home. Perhaps the lack of white lovers indicated he preferred other tongues in his love nest as well. And anyway, the lack of furnishings made it quite clear Cruz didn't spend much time here that wasn't spent in bed.

So why the book?

Engelmann hoisted himself up off the floor and bounded over, his beer and exhaustion both forgotten. He picked up the novel, turned it over in his hand.

It was Mario Puzo's *The Godfather.*

He thumbed through it and found that, here and there, letters were underlined, seemingly at random.

Engelmann smiled and fetched his burner phone from his pocket, fingers clumsy in his sweaty gloves.

That was fine. The Council was on speed dial.

The phone rang once. "Yeah?" his contact answered. Not angry, simply succinct.

"Yes, hello. I believe I've discovered something of interest."

"Yeah? What's that?"

"Nothing you need concern yourself with—I'm working it."

"Then why're you calling *me?*"

"Because you and your constituent organizations have been naughty boys and girls indeed."

"How's that?"

"You've been passing notes in class." Engelmann *tsk*ed. "And I'm afraid I'm going to have to ask to see them."

There was a long pause—so long, Engelmann wondered for a moment if he'd pushed too far, if his contact would simply fail to answer.

Then his contact said: "Our communications are encrypted. Locked down."

"Not so locked down as you might think," Engelmann replied, his self-satisfied smile reflected in his tone.

"You're gonna wanna watch the way you talk to me," his contact spat. "We're not a bunch of fucking morons, and we don't take kindly to people who suggest otherwise."

Engelmann was chastened, his smile dying on his face. "I wouldn't dare suggest—"

But his contact cut him off. "Good. Keep not suggesting." Then he sighed, and when he spoke again, he was once more composed. "If this shitwad's cracked our communications, he's even better than we thought. If I get you the access you want, are you good enough to get this guy?"

"Yes. There's no one better."

"Yeah, that's what they say. But I swear to God, if I find out you're using this information to fuck us over, we'll hire the number two through five guys to hunt your ass down and make you live just long enough to regret it. You get me?"

Engelmann paused before answering. "I do."

"Good. Check your phone. I've forwarded along some links to sites you're gonna wanna take a look at. I'm also gonna put out the word to my organization that our communication network should go dark until you find our man."

"No. That could signal to him that something's amiss. Your communications should remain undisrupted."

The line was silent for a moment. "You understand that's one hell of a big request."

"I do."

"You'd better. Because if I don't plug this leak and any more of our guys die by his hand, it'll be on your head."

"Until today, you were unaware your network had been breached. It would be folly to squander the tactical advantage this discovery affords us."

"All right. I'll give you a week. Then we're changing the locks whether you got the guy or not."

"Understood."

"All right, then. Good luck." And with that, his contact hung up.

No, not good luck, Engelmann thought. Good hunting.

11.

B Y DAY, MacArthur Park seemed safe enough. Sure, it was blanketed in elaborate graffiti and dotted here and there with homeless people, napping in the shade of the park's eucalyptus trees. But people still walked their dogs across the patchy, sun-scorched lawn, and couples brought their kids to kick soccer balls or climb atop the Day-Glo play structure.

Once the sun was doused by the Pacific to the west, though, the tenor of the park—and the Eastside neighborhood of Long Beach in which it sat—changed. Families packed up and left. The indigents retreated to the sidewalks and stoops outside the park, or vanished from the neighborhood altogether. And then the gangs arrived.

They strolled in with cultivated swagger, calculated to intimidate—but they traveled in packs, because numbers meant safety. They were black, mostly, although there were some Hispanics, too, and even one Cambodian crew. There was no intermingling of races within groups. Long Beach may pride itself on its diversity, but it seemed their street gangs weren't so enlightened.

Michael Hendricks watched them with feigned disinterest from his perch across the street. No one paid him any mind. He was nothing more than scenery.

Hendricks had arrived in Long Beach late last night. Lester had booked him into a midrange chain hotel a couple blocks off the water under the name Robert McCall, and supplied him with the corresponding ID and credit cards. Shortly after he arrived, he took a walk down to the beach, a military duffel slung over one shoulder. There, he'd unpacked from the bag a pair of jeans and three shirts—a plain white tee, a heather gray tank top, and a red-and-black checked flannel. The tide was low, polluted water lapping Coca-Cola brown beneath the sodium vapor lights. He walked down to the water's edge, dipped the clothes into the surf, and wrung them out. Then he stuffed them back into the duffel, the dampness bleeding through, and hiked back to his room.

Come morning, the clothes—which he'd hung across the shower rod—had dried. The seawater had discolored them. A saline crust stiffened the fabric. The room smelled like something died in it.

He put them on, layering the shirts—first the tank, then the tee, then the flannel. Then he slipped out a side entrance and hiked inland, stopping at a bike rack to smear grease from the chains into his hair and face and hands. A few blocks later, when he saw a businesswoman's expression flicker distaste as he walked by, he knew he'd achieved his goal; as far as she was concerned, he was one more homeless person in a city full of them.

Irving Franklin's only known address was a modest single-story stucco home belonging to his grandmother. Hendricks settled in on the stoop of a shuttered pawnshop across the street and a few doors down, and watched.

The grandmother was up when he arrived. She tottered back and forth past the windows for hours. Cooking. Cleaning. Tending to two young children—Franklin's brothers, or cousins maybe. But Hendricks didn't lay eyes on Franklin until noon, when he stumbled into the kitchen—his face pillow-creased, his expression sleepy. Hendricks was shocked by how young he looked. Franklin was small-boned, with delicate—almost feminine—features, no visible tattoos, and he stood somewhere shy of five-five. Hendricks couldn't fathom why a major criminal organization would want this poor kid dead.

Hendricks remained outside the house all day, changing looks and position to evade notice. Sitting on the pawnshop stoop, his flannel buttoned up. Propped against a neighbor's fence in his T-shirt. Lying beneath a black acacia tree, tank top showing. He'd hoped for a chance to talk to Franklin alone. But the kid didn't set foot outside until nightfall, when three members of his crew—each older and harder than Franklin, their inked-up necks and knuckles adorned with chunky, ostentatious gold—came by in a tricked-out Civic to pick him up.

On his way out the door, little Franklin gave his grandmother a peck on the cheek.

Hendricks trailed them to the park a few blocks east. Watched them set up with an efficiency born of practice. In the ecosystem of the park, it seemed the Savage Prophets were top dog: they commanded the Day-Glo play structure in the southwest corner, with access to both Warren Avenue and East Anaheim Street. Their drug deals went down like clockwork. Four gangbangers in black hoodies stood at the corners of the playground fence. They were the biggest and scariest of the lot, and their sweatshirts bulged suspiciously at pocket or waist. Two others, one of them Franklin, manned the playground gates. Both appeared to be unarmed. The seventh member of the crew sat beneath the play structure—impossible to make out amid the shadows, save for the glowing ember of his cigarette.

Buyers entered the playground from the southern gate, greeting Franklin with a handshake—no doubt handing him a roll of bills. Then they disappeared into the shadows of the play structure to pick up their bundle. They exited the playground to the north, the lookout there whistling a signal when they were clear. The money transfer and the exchange of drugs were separate transactions. The product remained out of sight at all times. The flow of customers was closely regulated. Anyone who watched their operation for longer than five minutes could tell that they were dealing, but the police would be hard-pressed to capture evidence on camera, or justify a search via probable cause. If the cops rolled up in force, all the Prophets had to do was scatter—the guys with the guns never touched the drugs or money, and vice versa, so the list of offenses any one of them could be charged with was short. And an undercover agent would have to have a death wish to try to make a buy while that outgunned.

That went double for Hendricks approaching Franklin; at least an undercover cop would have some backup. And to the junkies looking to score, Franklin was an afterthought, a means to an end—they barely broke stride as they handed him their cash, and rarely did any of them speak a word to him. If Hendricks were to make his approach under the pretense of making a buy, the Prophets' muscle would be on him before he got five words out—and if Franklin reacted poorly, the situation could go south quick.

Which was a shame, because by the look of the kid, he could use someone like Hendricks in his corner. While his buddies joked and laughed all night, Franklin looked furtive, jumpy, nervous. He was the runt of the litter, more mascot than full-fledged gang member, and—either in spite of his attempts to puff out his chest and project confidence, or because of it—they teased him mercilessly.

Hendricks felt for the kid. Saw shades of his own rough upbringing in Franklin, and remembered all too well how much the path it set him on had cost him. But as long as Franklin was manning that gate, the kid was unapproachable.

There was nothing Hendricks could do but watch and wait.

Engelmann watched and waited, too, not far from where Hendricks lay.

Once his Council contact had forwarded along links to the pertinent race sites and directed him toward those results that signified outstanding hits, Engelmann set to work decoding them. Letter by letter, he'd scratched down messages in his leather-bound Moleskine, alternating his attention between the pixelated sans serif of his burner phone's web browser and the yellowed typeface of Cruz's copy of *The Godfather* until his eyes grew dry and itchy from the strain. The result was a rough sketch of two hits—

incomplete and riddled with misspellings, but sufficiently decoded for Engelmann to grasp the salient details. His Council contact supplied whatever additional background he could, and a little creative Googling filled in the rest. The Internet was such a boon to the business of hunting human prey.

The target of the first hit was one Richard D'Abruzzo. He was the nephew of Monte D'Abruzzo, a capo in the Chicago Outfit, and he ran a nightclub the Outfit used as a front for dealing cocaine and MDMA, among other things. It seemed Richard had a fondness for the product he helped peddle—and an unfortunate propensity, when he was high, for cutting women.

He claimed the first time was an accident. A razor blade across his girlfriend's face while they were showering together. The girl told a different story, but her wound was shallow and didn't require stitches, so a payment in the low five figures was enough to buy her silence.

The second time it happened, his victim—a minor reality TV star of the famous-for-being-famous type—was asleep. She, unlike the first, pressed charges; it took six figures and a binding legal document before she corroborated his story of a late-night snack gone awry.

When a patron of his nightclub turned up with her throat slit in an alley a half-mile from his apartment, the family realized Richard's predilections would be better handled with a payoff of a different kind—this one to a contract killer.

Engelmann had flown from Miami to Chicago with the intent to follow D'Abruzzo until his quarry made his approach, but by the time he landed, D'Abruzzo was already dead. The papers reported his cause of death as an accidental overdose, which made sense. A capo's nephew murdered would have appeared an act of war, and suicide would have besmirched the family name—the D'Abruzzos were Catholic, after all.

Engelmann was disappointed Chicago proved a waste of time, but not disheartened. Instinct told him he was close. Perhaps his quarry had simply been too late getting to D'Abruzzo as well, he thought. Perhaps the second hit on his list would bear fruit.

He flew from Chicago to LAX earlier this afternoon, and drove from there to Long Beach, where the target of the second scheduled hit resided. The line at the rental counter was brief, and the traffic on the 405 southbound was light. By four p.m., his rented Chrysler was staked out in a strip mall across the street from the park the target's gang was known to frequent.

Engelmann surveyed the sun-scorched ghetto before him and waited for the target to arrive. It seemed impossible that, just days ago, he'd felt the cool Lake Geneva breeze on his face—or that these hardscrabble men and women in their vulgar outfits and thumping cars inhabited the same planet as Vian and his guests. The thought brought a smile to his lips. One of the great pleasures of his vocation was that it afforded him a front-row seat to the whole of life's rich pageant—and reminded him that while our journeys may vary greatly, in the end they all converge.

The Savage Prophets arrived shortly after sunset. At first blush, Irving Franklin—the smallest of them by far—came across as a hapless innocent. The impression was heightened by the fact that while the rest of them took languid sips of malt liquor from paper bags, Franklin pounded Red Bull after Red Bull and vibrated with nervous energy.

But—thanks to his Council contact—Engelmann knew better. Franklin's coltish demeanor was not a sign of youth or innocence. It was the external manifestation of Franklin's unbridled ambition. Of his eagerness to prove himself to his compatriots and to the world.

Two weeks ago, Franklin and his cousin—a foot soldier for LA's Hangman Squad—interrupted a transaction between the Los Angeles family's courier and the Savage Prophets' second-in-command, killing both and making off with twenty thousand dollars' worth of heroin and the cash to match. Franklin kept the cash, and his cousin kept the drugs.

Franklin's ineffectual appearance proved an asset. His own gang suspected nothing of his involvement in the heist—they assumed one of their rivals was to blame. But when the Los Angeles family caught someone selling their Black Top branded heroin on their turf without permission, they traced the product back to Franklin's cousin, who—after some persuasion—informed them Franklin was the mastermind behind the plan to steal it. The cousin was now buried at the site of the old Puente Hills Landfill. Franklin's death was to be far more public—a message to the remaining Prophets that any moves against the family by their members, gang-sanctioned or otherwise, would not be tolerated.

As Engelmann watched, he came to realize that Franklin's eyes belied his childlike appearance. They were cunning and suspicious—narrowing at every passerby, darting toward the source of every noise that echoed through the city night. Franklin was a man who expected violence— who saw traces of it everywhere, because it lurked inside his heart.

Worry not, young man, thought Engelmann—violence will find you soon enough. But with luck, my quarry will find you first.

And as those words danced through his mind, Franklin abandoned his post—and the homeless man at the park's edge began to move.

12.

Irving Franklin downed the remainder of his fourth Red Bull and chucked the can into the street. His face felt flushed. His back teeth floated. Caffeine hummed in his veins. When he peeled away from his post at the playground gate, the muscle nearest him called out.

"The fuck you think you're going, Iffy?"

Franklin eyed him up and down. Two hundred pounds of dumb and mean. He wouldn't last long once Franklin was in charge—which would be sooner than he or any of the other Prophets thought. "Ease up, Ty—I gotta take a leak. Ain't nobody coming anyway."

Ty looked up and down the empty street. Shrugged his meaty shoulders beneath his black sweatshirt. "Be quick about it."

Franklin tapped a Newport from his pack and struck a light. Hot smoke and cool menthol filled his lungs, and his racing heart slowed some. This time of night, every business in this stretch of Eastside was closed, and the park's restrooms were in Tiny Rascal territory. Ain't no way he'd risk a bullet to piss indoors when an alley would do just fine. So Franklin exhaled a plume of smoke and set out across East Anaheim, headed toward the narrow service road between the furniture store and the shuttered corner market.

As he did, Hendricks—who'd been slouched beneath a covered entryway with decent sight lines on the park—rose to his feet and followed. Hendricks felt the eyes of the Prophets' enforcers on him as he staggered across the street, so he angled slightly away from Franklin, and fought the urge to glance in the kid's direction. As soon as he could manage, Hendricks ducked down the nearest cross street and out of their line of sight.

Though Hendricks's footfalls had echoed loudly as he'd crossed East Anaheim, feigning drunkenness, his boots were now silent against the stained concrete. He'd been trained to remain undetected in far more challenging environs than these. He sprinted down the sidewalk, buildings blurring to his right as he looked for a way through.

Beyond the second building he passed was a low iron fence—its gate padlocked—barring entrance to a small parking lot. He vaulted the fence in one smooth motion and cut diagonally across the lot toward Franklin.

Maybe I'll save this kid yet, he thought.

Engelmann watched with interest as Franklin crossed the street—and interest blossomed into excitement as he saw the homeless man on the far side of the block stir as well.

The latter had been still so long, Engelmann had forgotten he was there; he felt more like set dressing than person. Rough-sleeping homeless were as much a signifier of Southern California as palm trees and garish murals. One's eyes slid right off them, which made them an inspired disguise for someone trying to blend in.

Unfortunately, the lot in which Engelmann sat faced the park from across the street, which meant both Franklin and the homeless man disappeared from view as soon as they ventured south of Anaheim. He started the car—grateful for the first time since he'd rented it that America's idea of luxury was not performance but serenity; its engine was so quiet, none of the young men in the park noticed. Engelmann slid out of the lot toward the park and took the first left he came to. Then he rolled down the darkened road at five miles per hour, scanning the night for any sign of Franklin—or of his quarry.

Franklin ducked into an alley off the service road. Found a spot halfway out of sight behind a Dumpster. Unzipped. Let loose.

As he did, he saw movement out of the corner of his eye. He turned, startled, midstream.

The glowing ember of his cigarette ruined his night vision, so at first, all he saw was darkness unfolding—resolving into a figure. The cigarette fell from Franklin's lips and hissed when it hit the puddle at his feet. He reached for the gun he'd recently taken to sticking in his waistband, but it wasn't there. It was in his sock drawer at Nana's house because the Prophets didn't like their money guy to carry.

"Hey, Iffy."

"Aisha?" Relief washed over Franklin, followed closely by embarrassment. "Why the fuck did you sneak up on me like that? Shit—I thought I was three seconds from getting ganked in an alley with my dick out." He tucked himself back into his baggy shorts and brushed idly at the front of them.

"I'm sorry, Iffy. I just...wanted to say hey, is all."

Franklin looked her up and down. Stick skinny in ratty clothes. Eyes sunken in deep hollows. Her skin a jaundiced yellow-gray beneath the streetlights. Her forearms pocked with scars from wrist to elbow. "Bullshit, you did. You're looking to score."

Aisha looked at her shoes. "I just need a little to get by until payday."

"You mean until your pimp gives you your take."

"C'mon, Iffy. You and me go back. I could make it worth your while," she said, approaching him and reaching for his open fly.

Franklin shoved her. She went down hard. Whimpered as she hit the ground. "Get the fuck off me, bitch. I ain't the same little nickel-bag nigger who used to float you shit back in the day. I'm big weight now, hear? I'm *better* than you. Don't come around no more with your whiny bullshit—the shape you're in, I wouldn't let you suck a stolen dick."

He cocked his leg back to kick the girl. She squealed and covered her face with her arms, but didn't move to stop him. From somewhere nearby, Franklin heard a cough. When he raised his head to look, a homeless man stood at the alley's mouth, silhouetted by the streetlights.

Franklin, momentarily chastened by the audience, lowered his foot.

When the blow she was expecting didn't come, Aisha peeked between her forearms, eyes widening when they lighted on her unlikely savior.

The homeless man said, "Go."

Aisha scrabbled wordlessly to her feet, tears streaming down her cheeks, and ran. Franklin looked from the homeless man to her, wondering if he should maybe give chase and teach that bitch a lesson.

The homeless man took a step toward Franklin. "I wouldn't."

Franklin stayed put. Though he'd never admit it, even to himself, something in the man's tone frightened him.

They stood that way—an uneasy détente—until the sounds of Aisha's hurried footfalls were swallowed by the night. Then Franklin puffed out his chest in an attempt to repair his wounded pride. "The fuck are you still looking at?" he asked, trying to force some edge into his voice.

"Nothing," the man replied. "Nothing at all."

And then he disappeared into the shadows.

Engelmann was rolling slowly westward on 11th when a young black woman burst from the alley to his left and bounced, crying, off the fender of his car. He slammed the brakes and peered back the way she came. He spotted Franklin fifty yards up the alley, zipping his fly in the shadows of a nearby Dumpster, alone. When Franklin finished, he looked around, and then hiked back toward the park.

Engelmann circled the block, but the homeless man was nowhere to be found. He did another circuit for good measure, and then slid the Chrysler back into his chosen parking lot. Apparently, this poor young woman was the reason Franklin had abandoned his post, and the timing of the homeless man's awakening was no more than an unfortunate coincidence.

For two more days, he trailed the boy. For two more days, no one approached him. On the third day, two large men of Italian extraction dragged Franklin from his grandmother's home while she begged for them to stop and shot him in the street—two taps, head and heart, like the professionals they were.

Irving Franklin was a dead end.

13.

McKay Pond was still as glass in the chill morning air, a fine mist rising off it and shrouding the reflected image of Mount Washington that graced its surface. It looked to Michael Hendricks like a Japanese landscape painting hung upside down.

Hendricks checked his GPS and nodded slightly to himself. This was the place. He scanned the dense New Hampshire forest, its massive pines so tall they appeared slender from a distance—the needled branches jutting from their trunks suggesting feather more than Christmas tree. But up close, those trunks were big enough that a grown man couldn't wrap his arms around them if he tried. Hendricks drank in their scent and smiled at the thought that these trees had stood for centuries, yet may never have been seen by anyone but him. And as his eyes followed one trunk upward, spotting the dull glint of fiber-optic camera hidden in its branches some twenty feet off the ground, he hoped they never would be.

Though it was barely six a.m., Hendricks had been up for hours, hiking the length of the perimeter he'd set up around the cabin he called home since he'd returned from Afghanistan—checking pressure sensors, ensuring his cameras were still hidden. It was a ritual of his—something he did whenever he came home from a job. He told himself it was a necessity. That his line of work made him a target. But the truth was far simpler than that. The truth was, those days spent in the woods quieted his mind—allowed him to leave the baggage of the job outside the cabin.

He followed the sight line of the camera to the spot that he was looking for—his footfalls silent on the thick mat of needles below. The cameras were too numerous for him to remember their precise placement; he'd hung two hundred of them in a perimeter that stretched for five square miles of forest. So instead, he relied on GPS and instinct. Locating them was simply a matter of assessing the landscape and determining the optimal placement. Invariably, that was where he'd placed them.

Hendricks was as competent as he was consistent. He had his Uncle Sam to thank for that.

Fresh tracks pitted the earth all around. Fresh, but not human. Hendricks knelt and ran his fingers through the churned up loam.

There. The broken wire, just as he'd suspected.

He removed a tool kit from his belt, and set to work stripping, splicing, and re-shielding the wire. When he was finished, he covered it over with a thin layer of soil and pine needles, and took a big step forward—over the wire.

Instantly, the satellite phone on his belt began to buzz.

Hendricks waved at the camera in the tree, so small as to be nearly invisible. He knew when he returned to the cabin, there'd be a video of that wave waiting for him.

The wire led from the camera to a series of pressure-sensing mats, one of several he had wired up throughout the forest. They didn't span the full circumference of the perimeter—that would have been too great an undertaking, even for Hendricks—but as far as he was concerned, they didn't need to. New Hampshire's White Mountains provided ample protection in the form of treacherous terrain; Hendricks's sensors simply monitored the most likely ingress points, the spots anyone with any tactical training might identify as attractive for an approach. Step on a mat, activate a camera—and give Hendricks fair warning that you're coming.

In the three and a half years he'd been living out in Evie's abandoned family cabin, though, any protection the system afforded was merely psychological. All his cameras ever captured were wildlife. Take today, for example: a mother moose and calf strolling through the woods set off the camera overhead, then bolted suddenly just before the feed cut out. The scene was worrisome enough to Hendricks that he packed a firearm for the hike—something had startled them into flight, after all—but it appeared his worry was unfounded. The tracks suggested they'd been startled by a black bear, and the absence of blood at the scene indicated they'd parted ways without incident.

The thought pleased Hendricks. He'd never been much of a hunter. He didn't care to see animals suffer.

Hendricks's stomach grumbled. He realized he'd been up for hours without food, that he'd hiked for miles without pause. Pushing himself a little harder than was typical. Usually, his post-job rounds were leisurely, leaving his mind refreshed and his body loose, relaxed, responsive. Today, though, all he felt was a knot of tension between his shoulders that made breathing an effort. He wondered not altogether idly if that tension was the result of the Long Beach trip proving so unsatisfactory—or if it had more to do with seeing Evie pregnant by another man.

The throbbing in his temples at the latter thought was answer enough to that.

No point dwelling, Hendricks thought. You made your choice—now you have to live with it.

The problem was, in some deep, self-pitying corner of his mind, he didn't believe it.

Didn't believe he'd been given any choice.

Or that you could call this living.

The faint ozone scent of the gas burner gave way to smoke and salty rendered fat as the bacon in Hendricks's skillet began to sizzle. Three rashers—thick-cut, uncured—from a smokehouse just north of Ossipee. Once they were cooked just shy of burnt, he moved them to a paper towel, then cracked a pair of fresh eggs from a local farm stand into the hot grease. Whites bubbled as they hit the bacon fat, and the eggs cooked up quickly. As soon as the whites set, he transferred each egg onto a fat slice of tomato from his plot out back, then set the skillet in the sink to cool.

Hendricks ate standing at the butcher-block kitchen island, washing down his country breakfast with two cups of French-pressed coffee, black. The cabin—a sprawling post-and-beam log home with heart-pine floors, vaulted ceilings, and an open floor plan centered around an enormous stone hearth—was quiet and still, but to Hendricks, every corner of it echoed with memories of his fiancée. The kitchen where she'd fumbled her way through dinner after lousy dinner, playing grown-up and conjuring suspect recipes from the canned food her parents had stocked the cupboards with years before. The sleeping loft where he'd fumbled, too, unskilled and impatient—until her body, once so mysterious and unfamiliar, became an extension of his own, their rhythms synching as they began to understand each other. The hearth they'd huddled around, their only source of light and heat as autumn descended upon the mountains and they found themselves too poor to afford propane for the baseboard heaters or gas for the generator. Even his rusted old Chevy outside seemed to hold on to her scent—impossible, Hendricks knew, but still true enough in his own mind for him to keep it after all these years. He'd stash it in a public parking lot when he left for a job so that it would be waiting to carry him back home, and swap its plates with some other rust bucket's every couple of months.

Back home. A funny way of thinking about a place he had no rightful claim to—a place owned by two people who hated him so much they disavowed their daughter just for taking up with him. A place where happy memories were just that, a literal lifetime away for the woman who filled them.

Yet it was the only place Hendricks had ever been that felt like home to him.

And so he haunted it as surely as if that roadside bomb had really killed him.

When he was here, surrounded by the echoes of his past, so close yet so out of reach, he could half-believe it had.

* * *

"Hey, pal—how's life at the villa? I hear Tuscany's lovely this time of year."

Hendricks smiled. Though Lester was his closest friend—a title that sounded like faint praise from a man who had no others—he hadn't the faintest idea where Hendricks hung his hat. It was a security measure, like the panic buttons Lester'd rigged up at his bar and his apartment to warn Hendricks via text if anyone came looking for him. They were Lester's way of ensuring he could never compromise Hendricks's safety—even under duress. Lester had no intention of harming a member of his unit ever again if it could be avoided, and he'd seen too much during his tours of duty to think he could hold out indefinitely if tortured—he'd seen too many true believers sell out God, country, family, and anything else they could just to end the pain. When pundits tell you torture doesn't work, they're only half right. It's not that people can withstand it. It's that they'll tell you literally anything they can—true or not—to make it stop.

Les was not without a sense of humor, though. He teased Michael mercilessly for having a secret lair. Lately, he'd taken to guessing its location when Hendricks called. As Lester's guesses went, Tuscan villa was kind of tame. Last time, it was an arctic Fortress of Solitude. Time before that: moon base.

"Overrated. All I can get delivered is Italian."

"Yeah," said Lester, "sounds awful."

"It is when you've got a hankering for lo mein."

"Ain't it a little early in the day for lo mein?" It was barely nine a.m.

"Not in Tuscany, it's not," Hendricks said. Lester laughed. "You got anything for me?"

"Yeah," he said. "Some rumblings about a gig that may prove up your alley. We clear to talk?"

Hendricks tapped a couple keys on his laptop, and a diagnostic screen came up. Lester'd built the laptop for him from scratch. It looked like a cheap off-the-shelf Dell. Its insides were anything but. "Clear on my end. No signs our encryption's been compromised, and I swept the place for bugs this morning. I assume we're clean on your end?"

"No, we're not, on account of I was born just yesterday on the back of a turnip truck."

"Okay then, smart-ass—what's the job?"

The target was a guy by the name of Eric Purkhiser. From what Les could gather via the Council's coded communiqués, Purkhiser was the Atlanta Outfit's very own IT guy—at least until he took them for a cool twenty-eight mil in some kind of computerized wire-transfer scheme and then turned stoolie for the Feds, decimating their operation in the process.

The bounty for the hit was $25K. The instructions were to make it as public and as messy as possible—and they wanted Purkhiser dead by the weekend. Guess the Atlanta mob wanted to discourage the employees of their so-called legitimate business interests from pilfering the office supplies—or ratting them out to the FBI. They get so touchy about that.

"You get the name of the hitter they're sending?"

"Yeah. Leonwood. You heard of him?"

"Doesn't ring a bell. See what you can dig up on him—pics, also-knowns, MO."

"Will do."

"They know where this Purkhiser is?" Hendricks asked.

"Yup. Missouri."

"How'd they find him?"

"Dumb fucking luck," Les said. "As in Purkhiser ain't got none. Check your e-mail."

Lester had forwarded along an attachment that proved to be a scan of Purkhiser's Georgia driver's license, now long expired, as well as a URL. The URL led to a piece in the Springfield, Missouri, *News-Leader*, dated yesterday, about a local Gadget Shack employee named Eddie Palomera who'd hit the jackpot playing slots at a Kansas City casino to the tune of over six million dollars. Article asked him how he felt. "Lucky" was his reply.

Only Eddie Palomera of Springfield, Missouri, didn't seem so lucky to Hendricks. Because Eddie Palomera's stupid mug was smiling back at him from his computer screen, and he looked an awful lot like a stoolie IT guy named Eric Purkhiser.

Hendricks guessed WITSEC figured if they stashed a guy in a town called Springfield, even if somebody let it slip, the bad guys'd have to search every Springfield in the country before they found the right one.

Then again, maybe Purkhiser *was* lucky. After all, between what he stole from the Atlanta Outfit and what he won playing the slots, he had enough money to cover Hendricks's fee sixty times over.

Which meant he might live long enough to spend the rest.

14.

HENDRICKS HAD spent some time in bombed-out villages. Weathered snowstorms in drafty mountain caves. Holed up for days in squat concrete bunkers full of frightened, unwashed soldiers. But he didn't think he'd ever been anywhere more depressing than Westlake Plaza on a Monday afternoon.

The old mall was ten minutes outside of Springfield, Missouri, an ugly splotch of asphalt and yellow brick amid the farmland west of Lake Springfield. When they built it in the early eighties, they must have figured folks from town would be eager to make the scenic drive. But most weren't, and eventually, Westlake Plaza was supplanted by more modern facilities closer to the city center. Now it was a tired, old collection of tired, old stores whose staff and customers came and went more out of reluctant habit than any real desire.

Hendricks eyed the elderly mall-walkers, suburban housewives, and Hot Topic goths with an anthropologist's detachment. Most weren't shopping so much as passing time. He wondered why they'd chosen to hang out here instead of the much larger, sleeker Battlefield Mall a few miles north. Maybe they found some comfort in the faded glory of a time gone by. Maybe they simply preferred the quiet. Hendricks could relate to that, at least—but in their place, he would have chosen the lakeside park instead.

Hendricks wasn't here to shop or to kill time. He was here to find his new client.

He'd tried Purkhiser's home address first, of course—a drab split-level in a neighborhood full of them—but the driveway was empty, the garage piled high with junk. He considered breaking in and waiting, but the schedule for this hit was tight—he couldn't afford to waste time sitting around, waiting for his potential client to show up.

That's what he told himself, at least.

The truth was, seeing Evie pregnant with Stuart's child had rattled Hendricks, and calling off the Long Beach job had left him antsy. What he needed was distraction, not time alone with his thoughts.

What he needed was to work.

The Gadget Shack wasn't busy. No Gadget Shack Hendricks had ever been in was. There were two guys behind the counter, dressed identically in store-branded polo shirts and khakis. One was a rumpled teenager, pudgy and long-haired, with a thin wisp of peach fuzz on his upper lip. The other was older, neater, and fussier—a manager, by the look of him. Neither of them was Purkhiser. Hendricks wasn't surprised. If he'd just won six million bucks, he wouldn't be caught dead peddling RC cars and Y-adapters, either.

But home address and job were all Hendricks had on the man, so he figured he'd come here anyway and shake the tree.

"Can I help you?" the manager asked. Chad, according to his name tag.

Hendricks flashed him a smile. "Maybe—is Eddie around?"

Chad's eyes narrowed. "Palomera? What do you want with *him?*"

"He helped me out big-time a few weeks back. I was in the neighborhood, so I thought I'd swing by and tell him thanks."

"If he helped you out, you'd be the first. Guy was the worst employee I've ever had," he said, casting a sidelong glance at the teenager standing next to him. "And that's saying something."

"Was?"

"He up and quit a couple days ago. Didn't even think to tell me. I found out when I called to ask him why he didn't show up for his shift."

"So you don't know where I could find him, then?"

"Don't know. Don't care. Now, if you'll excuse me," he said brusquely, and drifted off toward the only other customer, a woman eyeing a display of smartphones. Apparently, a friend of Eddie's was no friend of his.

"What a douche," the kid behind the counter muttered. His name tag read Brody and had a faded sticker of the Punisher logo affixed to one corner.

Hendricks sized him up—a little shaggy, a little nerdy, with a woven-hemp necklace and sly, heavy-lidded eyes. When Hendricks bounced that off the image of Purkhiser that Lester's file had painted, he decided Brody and

Purkhiser were probably friendly, if not friends. "You ain't kidding. Any chance you know where Eddie is?"

"Seems like you wanna find him pretty bad—how come?"

Hendricks made a show of looking left and right, then dropped his voice. "He told me how to splice into my neighbor's cable. Made it sound so easy, I figured it was too good to be true. So he bet me twenty bucks that it'd work. It did, and now I'm trying to make good."

Brody laughed. "That sounds like Eddie, all right—but he doesn't need your twenty. He hit it big last week at the casino. That's why he quit. Said fuck this job—he didn't need it anymore."

"Still," Hendricks said, "a deal's a deal. I'll throw in a twenty for you, too, if you can point me in the right direction."

The Starlite Arcade was adjacent to the food court. The place wasn't vintage or retro or hipster-ironic, just old—a relic from another time. Black lights shone down from a water-stained drop ceiling. At the center of the room was an air hockey table, glowing beneath the lights. On the far wall was a bank of Skee-Ball lanes. Beside them, a claw machine was piled high with stuffed animals. Everywhere else, arcade games blipped and emitted random bursts of stilted dialogue all by themselves.

An unshaven man with an Atari T-shirt stretched across his beer gut and a quarter dispenser on his belt was nodding off atop a stool inside the entrance, his back propped against the wall, one arm resting on a Jimmy Fund gumball machine. It wasn't hard to see why he was bored. The arcade only had one customer.

Eric Purkhiser was in his early thirties—wiry and slouch-shouldered in a bowling shirt and skinny jeans. His rockabilly pompadour and wallet chain glinted in the black light. His face was lit by the glow of the Galaga cabinet he was hunched over.

Purkhiser was a rarity among Hendricks's would-be clients. He'd testified against the Mob, which meant he knew damn well there were people out there who wanted him dead. Hendricks figured that'd make him a little jumpy. But Purkhiser didn't even glance at him when he sidled up to watch him play.

Purkhiser's eyes flitted across the screen as he piloted his spaceship left and right, shooting teeming swarms of pixelated insects. The speed at which they came at him was astonishing, and Purkhiser's score was climbing steadily toward one million—he must have been playing awhile.

"That's a hell of a score," Hendricks said.

"Shhh," Purkhiser hissed. He slammed the joystick hard left and smacked the fire button repeatedly, to no avail. His ship exploded. Purkhiser cursed.

The game prompted him to enter his initials. It appeared he'd taken second place. First place read KNH. Once Purkhiser put in his initials, second through eighth read ELP. "Thanks, asshole—you just cost me my high score! It's the last one in the whole joint I don't hold."

Hendricks glanced at the machine beside him—some Technicolor monstrosity called Mr. Do! Sure enough, the top score was held by ELP. "I'm sure you'll get it next time," he said mildly.

"Maybe—but I'm running out of next times," Purkhiser replied. "Come Friday, I'm leaving Springfield and never looking back. Onward and upward. Sayonara and good rid-dance. I just hope I beat this fucking thing before I go."

"Why?"

"A fella's gotta leave his mark somehow. Ain't no point floating through life like a ghost." Purkhiser took a quarter from his pocket and rolled it idly up and down his knuck-les. The move looked more practiced than cool. "Wait—why're you so interested in me and my high score? You're not KNH, are you?"

"No, Eric—I'm not KNH. But I am here to talk to you."

At the mention of his real name, Purkhiser blanched. The quarter fell from his hand.

"What did you call me?"

"You heard me fine the first time."

"My name's not Eric, it's Eddie. You must have me con-fused with someone else."

"I don't. Now, listen: you're in danger. I'm here to help you get back out of it. I can explain more once we're some-where safe. But you have to come with me right now, okay?"

Purkhiser swallowed hard. Nodded slowly.

Then he shoved Hendricks and bolted.

Hendricks sighed. Fine, he thought—we'll play it your way.

At the sound of Purkhiser fleeing the arcade, the sole employee jerked awake and rose, startled, from his stool. Purkhiser grabbed him by the shoulders and propelled him toward Hendricks with all he had. He threw the stool at Hendricks, too, and knocked down the gumball machine on his way out of the arcade. The former sailed wide and slammed into a Donkey Kong machine. The latter shattered when it hit the floor, scattering shards of glass and gumballs everywhere.

Hendricks caught the stunned arcade employee, steadying him before he toppled over. Then he took off after Purkhiser at a sprint, gumballs crunching underfoot.

Purkhiser cut across the food court, climbing tables and knocking over chairs—anything to separate himself from Hendricks. When he peeked back over his shoulder, he slammed into a man in an apron, sending a tray of Panda Express samples flying. Both men went down, but Purkhiser bounced back up like he was spring-loaded. He winged the empty tray in Hendricks's direction and took off down the hall toward Westlake Plaza's main concourse.

Hendricks closed the gap between them, ignoring shouts of anger and alarm from those he passed. He ignored the mall's security cameras, too; they were hardwired to the security booth—a dated system—and he'd cut their feed as soon as he'd arrived. But if he didn't calm Purkhiser down soon, mall security was going to be an issue. Even if they were armed, they didn't pose much of a threat, but if he had to hurt one of them it would no doubt make the evening news.

Purkhiser dodged his way down the broad hall—trying his best to put as many people between him and Hendricks as he could. Hendricks juked around an old man on a Rascal scooter and leapt over a stroller when a panicked mother froze.

He caught a break when Purkhiser reached the mall's main atrium and tried to head up the down escalator. As he struggled against the tide of people and stairs, Hendricks hopped on the up escalator and glided past. Then he planted a hand in between the escalators, and vaulted onto the down one, three steps ahead of Purkhiser. Purkhiser pirouetted, flashing Muppet eyes at Hendricks, and took off down the escalator—but not before Hendricks got a hold of a fistful of his hair—pomade greasy in his hand. Eric screamed as Hendricks yanked him backward.

"Calm down, Eric—I'm trying to *help* you!"

"My name's not Eric!" Purkhiser replied. He threw a wild elbow that caught Hendricks in the eye, and wriggled free. Then he burst off the escalator and tore across the atrium—splashing straight into its massive, rust-stained central water fountain.

Hendricks gave chase for a moment, and then stopped.

Mall security ringed the atrium, their Tasers drawn.

Hendricks raised his hands above his head.

Purkhiser, dripping wet and panting at the center of the fountain, smiled.

"You boys want to tell me what the problem is?" The man speaking was in his late fifties. Decent shape. Bushy mustache. Brush cut beneath his uniform cap. No wannabe, this guy, Hendricks thought; he looked like a cop who went private once he put in his twenty.

"Yeah, asshole," said Purkhiser. "How about you tell the nice man why you're chasing me?"

"Sure," Hendricks said. His expression was neutral, his voice calm. "Officer, this no-good greaser stole my wallet."

Purkhiser laughed. "I *what?*"

"Eddie," the mall cop said, "is this true?"

"True? It's goddamn ridiculous, is what it is. Why would I take some random dude's wallet?"

"I don't know *why* he took it, but he took it," Hendricks said. "Search his pockets if you don't believe me."

"C'mon out of there," the mall cop said. Purkhiser

sloshed to the edge of the fountain and stepped out. "Now empty your pockets."

"Gladly," Purkhiser replied. But when he reached into his right front pocket, his face dropped—and his hand came out with an unfamiliar wallet.

"You son of a bitch," Purkhiser said.

Hendricks didn't react—but inside, he was all smiles. He'd seen the guards approaching during his ride on the escalator and planted the wallet when he and Purkhiser tussled seconds later, as insurance against this very eventuality.

"Let me see the wallet, son."

Purkhiser reluctantly handed it to the mall cop. The mall cop glanced inside, and then gave it to Hendricks. "Well, Mr. Allard, it seems you're telling the truth. Although I wish you'd simply notified security instead of chasing this idiot around my mall."

"Please, Officer, call me Kent," Hendricks replied. "And you're right—I wasn't thinking."

"Would you like to press charges?"

"No," Hendricks said, fixing Purkhiser with his gaze. "I think he's learned his lesson."

"I suppose he has, at that. C'mon, Eddie—you and me are going to go fill out an incident report. And when we're done, you won't be welcome back here anymore. I hope you got that high score of yours this morning."

Purkhiser's expression curdled. Hendricks blinked flatly back at him.

"So I'm free to go?" Hendricks asked.

"Yes, Mr. Allard, you're free to go."

15.

P URKHISER SPENT an hour trying to convince security he
was innocent, shivering in his wet clothes all the while.
He explained that he'd been set up. That this Allard dude
was after him. He'd even gone so far as to ask them to re-
view the security footage—he was sure it would exonerate
him. But apparently, there was some kind of mall-wide security camera outage, so he had no choice but to back away
from his claims. Without evidence—or disclosing the fact
that he was in hiding from the Mob—even Purkhiser was
forced to admit he sounded like a loon.

Eventually, they released him—two guards escorting
Purkhiser from the building and into the falling dusk. The
mall parking lot was nearly empty. Most of its lights had
yet to turn on, although a couple early risers flickered to
life as night descended. Only three cars were in sight.
Purkhiser's rusted-out Buick Skylark sat a ways out from

the other two, its windows reflecting the sky's fading orange.

Purkhiser stood there for a moment—watching, waiting, looking for any sign of Allard. He was sure the name was an alias, but he had nothing else to call the guy. He told himself the parking lot was too big for one man to keep track of. That loads of cars had come and gone since he'd been detained. That there was no reason to think Allard knew which one was his. But he still sprinted to the car like a runner stealing home and unlocked it with jittering hands—peering wildly around the lot the whole time.

He ducked inside, slammed the door, and jammed the key into the ignition. As he turned the key, he closed his eyes, half-expecting the car to explode.

It didn't.

It didn't turn over, though, either.

"Yeah, sorry about that," came a voice from the backseat, "but after your freak-out in the mall, I didn't want you gunning the engine and crashing us both into a light pole before we had a chance to talk."

Purkhiser went for the door handle. Didn't realize he'd put his seat belt on. Hendricks reached forward with his left hand and locked the door—and with his right, he grabbed the shoulder strap of Purkhiser's seat belt and yanked. The lap belt tightened, pinning Purkhiser to his seat.

"Relax, Eric," Hendricks said. "I'm not here to kill you."

"I *told* you," he said, thrashing against the seat belt like a trapped animal, "my name's not Eric—it's *Eddie*. Eddie Palomera. You've got the wrong guy."

"No, I don't—and the sooner you stop trying to bullshit

me, the better this will go for the both of us. See, while *I'm* not here to kill you, there are others close behind who mean to—and they're doubtless good at what they do. If you want me to, I'll let you go right now and disappear from your life forever—just say the word. But understand that if you do, you're on your own. I won't be able to protect you."

Purkhiser stopped struggling while he digested what Hendricks had said. His eyes met Hendricks's through the Buick's rearview. "You're here to *protect* me?"

"That's right."

"Are you with WITSEC?"

"No," Hendricks replied. "I'm not with WITSEC."

Purkhiser laughed then, black and bitter as old coffee. " 'Course not. I figured maybe they saw my picture in the paper and sent you to keep an eye on me, but I shoulda known those ass weasels don't give a damn about me anymore."

"You're no longer in the program?"

"Nope. I told those fuckers to take a hike about a year back. Always keeping tabs. Checking up on me. Poking 'round my business. I couldn't get at a dime of the dough I socked away—"

"Stole, you mean."

"—with them looking over my shoulder all the time. So I dropped out. Told 'em I was fine. And I woulda been, too, if it wasn't for that fucking picture. That *is* what brought you here, ain't it?"

"Yeah," Hendricks said. "That's what brought me here. Honestly, Eric, what the fuck were you thinking letting them print it?"

Purkhiser shrugged. "I didn't have a choice. The casino made me sign a bunch of shit that said I'd do whatever publicity they wanted or I wouldn't get my goddamn winnings. So I figured what the hell—it's just some tiny local rag. Probably nobody'd even see it."

"*I* saw it. And I'm not the only one."

"So if you ain't with WITSEC, who the hell *are* you? All I know for sure's your name ain't Allard."

"You don't need to know who I am. All you need to know is who I work for."

"Okay, then—who do you work for?"

"You, actually. Or, rather, I *will*, for the bargain-basement rate of a quarter million dollars."

"A quarter million dollars."

"That's right."

"Which gets me what, exactly?"

"You know those guys coming to kill you?"

"Yeah?"

"I kill them first."

"Shit—you're like some kind of hitman entrepreneur? Now I've fucking heard *everything*. But seriously, dude, don't you think a quarter mil's a little steep?"

"Hey, that's your call to make. But I would've thought a guy with damn near thirty million of the Atlanta Outfit's dollars in the bank would have no trouble forking over a paltry quarter mil to avoid his own grisly murder."

"You've seen my car, dude, and the shithole I've been working in these past two years. Do I look like I got thirty mil to you?"

Purkhiser had a point. Hendricks told him so.

"Damn right. See, the Marshals Service took it personal when I kicked 'em to the curb. Guess once I did they figured out I wasn't square with them when I told 'em I didn't know shit 'bout all the money that went missing. Next thing I know, I got a federal prosecutor sniffing around, asking all kinds of questions about unreported income and wondering if maybe I had any back taxes needed filing."

"Wow. Bad break."

"You're fucking telling me. I ain't been near my stash since, for fear they'd bust my ass. I don't have to tell you that if they locked me up, I'd be shanked within the week—and no pile of money's worth that. I was gonna skip the country and wire my money to a new account once I was clear, but those assholes revoked my passport. So instead, I decided it was time to get some dough that I could actually use. Hence my trip to the casino."

"A six mil payout goes a long way toward putting you back in the upper class," Hendricks said. "Picture in the paper aside, that was quite a stroke of luck."

"Luck? You think that shit was *luck?* Took me eight months to write a program that could get through the casino's firewall and hack those slots. I earned every fucking *dime* of that money."

"And now that you have it, you'll have no trouble paying me."

"Yeah, only that's just it—I don't *have* it yet. Maybe Vegas does it different, but a two-bit slot joint in KC don't exactly hand over that kind of coin right on the spot. I gotta go back Thursday to pick it up."

A puzzle-piece clicked into place, and suddenly, Hendricks saw the whole picture. The instructions in Lester's decoded communiqué said to make the hit as public and messy as possible. "Let me guess," he said, "big crowd, oversized novelty check—that sort of deal?"

"That's right," he said. "Not ideal for a guy on the lam,

I know—but I figure nobody's got better security than a casino, and once I get my money I can disappear for good."

"Be careful what you wish for. I'm pretty sure that's where they're going to hit you."

Purkhiser made a little whining noise in the back of his throat. "Why? What makes you so sure?"

"Their instructions were to make a show of it. Their goal is to make sure no one ever tries to burn them like you did again. What better way to make their point than to take you down in front of God and everyone during your supposed moment of triumph?"

Even in the dim light of the Skylark, Hendricks saw Purkhiser go pale. "Fuck," he muttered. "Fuckity fuck fuck fuck." Then he brightened. "But you said that you could stop 'em, right?"

"I said if you *paid* me, I could stop them."

"Right, but if you stop 'em, I can get my money, and then I'll have more than enough to pay you."

Hendricks shook his head. "I don't work that way. I get my money up front or no deal."

"I dunno, dude—that sounds pretty fucking hinky to me. If you're as good as you're puttin' on, why's it matter if I pay you after?"

"Well, for one, there's no guarantee you ever would, in which case I'd have to kill you—and that makes *two* jobs I don't get paid for. And for two, an attempt on your life is going to attract all kinds of attention from the authorities, which will help keep you safe from subsequent attacks if you hire me to do my thing, but it *also* makes any subsequent transfer of funds a whole lot riskier than it would have been beforehand. But all of that pales in comparison to the fact that I don't kill without good reason. No money, no reason. So take it or leave it, but my offer's nonnegotiable."

"Everything's negotiable, dude."

"Not this."

"So, what, then?" Purkhiser said. "You're just gonna let me *die?*"

"That's up to you," Hendricks said. "You've got a choice to make. Today's Monday, which means if I'm right about the timing of the hit, you've got three days. You can choose to run—to leave this place tonight—and if you do, who knows? Maybe you'll manage to disappear again. Maybe they'll hunt you down and kill you. Or you can choose to spend the next three days getting my fee together. There's a slip of paper in your glove compartment. On it is a phone number. Once you're ready to pay my fee, call me at that number, and you have my word no harm will come to you."

Hendricks released his grip on Purkhiser's seat belt and climbed out of the car. Purkhiser leaned heavily against the wheel.

With one hand resting on the open door, Hendricks said, "You'll find your spark plugs in your glove compartment, too. They'll come in handy getting home."

Then he shut the door and walked away, leaving Purkhiser with his thoughts.

16.

LEON LEONWOOD was a burly, rough-hewn man of fifty in a plaid flannel shirt tucked into off-brand jeans, a pair of steel-toed work boots on his feet. His considerable heft—he was six foot four if he was an inch, and tipped the scales north of two-sixty—gave him the appearance of an athlete gone to seed. His clothes, bushy mustache, and ruddy features suggested a man who worked with his hands: a contractor, or a plumber perhaps. But, bar brawls aside, Leon had never been one for athletics—and though he did, indeed, work with his hands, it was not drywall in which he specialized.

Leon lumbered down the airplane's narrow aisle and wedged himself into his seat. If the scant crowd at the gate was any indication, his flight from Logan to St. Louis International wouldn't be too crowded, and for that, Leon was grateful. A guy his size didn't fit so well in coach.

Leon had built up a decent stake in his time as a contract killer, but he still couldn't bring himself to pay for an upgrade to business class or better. While on assignment, Leon had imagined his own death a thousand times, picturing all the ways a job could go bad in a heartbeat—but he'd spent too much of his life barely scraping by to let a bunch of fat-cat airline execs nickel-and-dime him to death.

The oldest of seven siblings, Leon grew up in squats and tenements all over Boston's Southie neighborhood, catching as catch can to put food on the table and clothes on his brothers' and sisters' backs. He learned early on that if you wanted something, you had to go after it—to take it, if need be. His pop—a petty thief and an even pettier man, who spent his time bouncing back and forth between the bars of Southie and those of the Suffolk County lockup—taught him that. In Leon's estimation, instilling that fundamental truth in Leon was the one good thing that piece of shit ever did. The only other thing his father ever taught him was how to take a punch.

Well, that, and the basic dos and don'ts of a body dump. One fateful day in '82, Leon bashed the fucker's head in with an ashtray when he made a move on Leon's eldest sister, Margaret. The old man had been drunk and said Margaret looked just like her mother "before the bitch let herself go." It was Leon's first kill—just shy of his eighteenth birthday. Later that night, Leon tossed his old man's body into Boston Harbor with a pair of ten-pound barbells tied to his feet. He was sure the body would never be found. But two weeks later, his pop's ankle joints separated and his bloated corpse washed ashore on Deer Island a few feet from the sewage treatment plant.

Leon figured it was a fitting resting place for him, at least.

Boston PD had liked Leon for the crime but couldn't prove a thing. Only Leon and Margaret knew for certain what had happened, and Leon's father had enough shady associates to create reasonable doubt a thousand times over. Leon was pretty sure his mother—a sad, dead-eyed woman who'd spent her life turning a blind eye to her husband's many transgressions—suspected the truth.

His next kill had been an accident. A drunken bar fight gone awry. Leon couldn't for the life of him remember what set it off. It hardly mattered—desperate men and drink are ingredients enough for any tussle. Leon's opponent —a grizzled ex-con who, upon reflection, reminded Leon of his father—pulled a knife.

Leon took it.

Used it.

Seventeen times, if the police reports were to be believed. Leon would have guessed he hadn't stabbed the guy more than twice—his memory of the night's events was hazy to this day. Blood like warm silk spraying his hands and face and clothes. The looks of shock and horror on the faces of the bar's other patrons—hard men all, or so Leon had thought. Cops arriving as if from nowhere, seconds it seemed after the fracas ended, though Leon later learned nearly ten minutes had elapsed.

That night marked the only time to date Leon took a fall. He served three years (of a ten-year sentence—God bless overcrowding) for manslaughter in the Massachusetts Correctional Institution at Concord, during which he racked up kills three through seven—most for money, and all without getting fingered. By the time he left, he'd amassed a mental Rolodex of people who needed people killed, and had a résumé to match.

Leon specialized in high-risk, high-pay jobs, or those his fellow hitters found distasteful—women and children and the like. Leon told himself he gravitated toward those kinds of jobs because he was still that scrappy kid from Southie, willing to do whatever it took to get ahead, but that was only partly true. If he were still that scrappy kid from Southie, he'd be more likely to stand up for women and children than to lay them out on metal slabs. But then, he'd had to watch as Margaret grew up into the same brand of glazed, hollow woman as their mother. Margaret's poison was Oxy, not booze, but the trajectory of her life had been the same.

Killing women didn't bother Leon none. And he thought killing kids might be a mercy. This world's no place for innocents.

His current job looked to be a cakewalk compared to most of his gigs. Wouldn't even be the sort of job the Outfit usually tapped him for, if it weren't for the fact they wanted it to be messy. The target was some Federal snitch who'd stuck his head out of his hidey-hole when he shoulda stayed buried. Purkhiser, his name had been, though now he went by Palomera. Seemed he hit it big at some Kansas City casino—so big it made the papers. Those same papers said Palomera'd be given his award at a ceremony this coming Thursday, which is where Leon intended to pop him. Leon swore the next time Purkhiser was buried, it'd be for good.

As the plane filled, a baby toward the back began to wail. Leon cast a scowling glance over his shoulder that softened slightly as he saw the child's mother—wan and sunken-eyed in a stained T-shirt and sweatpants, her un-washed hair in a hasty bun—trying to calm him to no avail. He turned around, and a nearby flight attendant—Felicia, according to her name tag—caught his eye. Felicia was a dark-skinned, curvy black woman in her midthirties who shared his pained expression at the racket. Leon thought she wasn't bad-looking—though he coulda done without the ghetto braids or the tiny stud in her nose. He flashed her a smile and said, "Any way I could convince you to get that kid a muzzle? He's giving me one hell of a headache."

She returned his smile. "Believe me, darlin'," she said, low and conspiratorial, "I wish I could."

"Well, then, I guess I'll have to settle for a drink."

"Sad to say I can't help you there, either—at least, not until we're in the air. Airline policy."

"Thing is," he said, his smile vanishing, "I wasn't asking."

Felicia's smile faltered as well as she tried to determine whether he was joking. Her hand rested on the seat back in front of Leon. He put his own hand atop it. His fingers wrapped around her wrist and squeezed. Not enough to hurt her—to a casual viewer, the contact might have seemed no more than an escalation of their flirtation—but enough to suggest he easily could.

Felicia's eyes went wide. She tried to withdraw her hand, but Leon held her fast. And when she glanced around the cabin for backup, she realized no one was paying them any mind. The plane was too empty. The crew otherwise occupied.

Leon's grip tightened as if to chastise her for seeking help. Her gaze met his once more. His expression was dark amusement now, like a schoolyard bully's. He felt her pulse quicken in her wrist and noted with satisfaction the sheen of sweat that had broken out across her brow.

"I want you to go get me two bottles of Jack Daniel's and two cups—one with ice, one without. Not one bottle, and not one cup. And don't go pouring for me—I wanna get the ratio of booze to ice just right. Can you do that for me, Felicia?"

Felicia nodded. Leon's expression darkened, and the pressure of his grip increased once more. It hurt. He knew it. "I want to hear you say it."

"Y-yes," Felicia said. "I can do that."

"Atta girl," Leon said, releasing her, a smile upon his face once more. "That wasn't so hard now, was it?"

Felicia shook her head and took off trembling down the aisle to fetch his drink.

"Oh, and Felicia?" he called, cheery as could be.

Felicia turned.

"Fetch me one a them neck pillows while you're at it."

17.

"Yo, Chazz," said Hank Garfield from the open doorway of Charlie Thompson's file-strewn, overstuffed office, nestled deep inside the concrete monstrosity of the J. Edgar Hoover Building in DC. "You got a sec? I got something you oughta see."

Thompson wasn't wild about her partner's new nickname for her—or the fact that he'd waited until she was on the phone to interrupt her—and she was pretty sure he knew it. But she didn't get as far as she had in the Bureau by letting pricks like Garfield push her buttons, so instead of giving him the satisfaction of correcting him, she told Jess she'd call her back and then asked Garfield, "Is this about my ghost?"

"Sorry to disappoint," he scoffed, "but not all roads lead back to your little pet obsession. As you may or may not know, there are one or two other bad guys in the country the FBI's been tasked with nabbing."

Shit. It'd been nearly a week since the trail in Miami ran cold, but Thompson had been holding out hope some of the feelers they'd put out among their community of confidential informants would pay off. She felt sure someone had to be helping this guy—funding him, arming him, issuing his marching orders. And any organization brazen enough to order the hits they had—not to mention powerful enough to pull them off—had to leave a footprint of some kind. But there wasn't one. It was so damned maddening she was starting to half-believe Garfield's gibes that she was hunting Batman.

She extended a hand toward the manila folder Garfield was holding and curled her fingers twice in a gimme sign. "What've you got?"

He handed her the file. It contained a photocopy of a commercial airline's passenger manifest and a series of grainy, black-and-white security-cam photos of a burly, mustachioed man walking through an airport concourse with the sort of hunched, furtive demeanor that suggested he knew damn well he was on camera—and that he didn't like it one bit.

"Fella you're looking at is a hitter by the name of Leon Leonwood," Garfield said. "TSA forwarded along the passenger list when one of his aliases popped."

"I know the name," said Thompson. "This guy's got one hell of a nasty reputation. How come he's not no-fly?"

"Rep aside, we've got nothing on him. He's suspected in no fewer than a dozen hits in the past five years alone, but as bloody as he leaves his vics, he never leaves us much to go on by way of evidence. But if he's on the move, maybe we can catch him in the act."

"Where were these pictures taken?"

"Saint Louis International. He landed an hour ago."

"Any idea who the target is?"

"Nothing yet. I figure he's got a job lined up in town. I've got Atwood and Prescott looking into it."

Thompson shook her head. "The hit won't be in St. Louis. Leonwood's a pro—he'd never fly into the city the job's in. My guess is, the hit's someplace close, but not too close. Have Atwood and Prescott comb through the chatter out of Kansas City, Louisville, Nashville, Memphis, Chicago—anywhere we've got ears out within a day's drive. And have our agents on the ground circulate these pics at every rental car company in town, with special attention to the ones near—but not *in*—the airport. He'll be looking to break up his trail, and my bet is, he won't want to run the risk of a cabbie remembering him, which means he'll leave the airport on foot. Get them a complete list of Leonwood's aliases, too—he's gonna switch up now that he's on the ground."

"Anything else, *boss?*" Garfield asked, both annoyed by his partner's marching orders and embarrassed he hadn't gotten there on his own.

Thompson thought a moment, her gaze passing over the stacks of unread files and unfinished reports on her desk—all awaiting her attention, and a good three-quarters of them unworthy of it. "Yeah," she said, finally. "Two things, actually. Thing one: book us on the next flight to St. Louis. You and me are gonna track Leonwood from the ground."

"Okay—what's thing two?"

"Thing two, *Henry,* is if you call me anything other than Charlie, Charlotte, or Special Agent Thompson again, me and my trusty sidearm are gonna make sure the only thing the boys around here ever call you is One Ball, *com-prende?*"

Garfield gulped. "You got it, b— Special Agent Thompson."

"Good," she said, smiling sweetly. "Now get moving. We've got a bad guy to catch."

18.

ERIC PURKHISER'S stomach churned as he frantically stuffed clothes into a duffel bag. He was dizzy and light-headed. Acid scratched at the back of his throat.

He should have known the whiskey was a bad idea.

He'd taken a swig straight from the bottle as soon as he got home from Westlake Plaza. He thought that it would calm his nerves. Instead, it came back up immediately, along with what was left of his lunch.

He tried to tell himself the dude who braced him at the mall this afternoon was running some kind of con—that he was a petty lowlife who'd stumbled across the story on Purkhiser's big win and figured he could shake him down for some quick cash. But he didn't really believe that. The guy'd been too skilled, too steady—too clearly practiced in this sort of meeting for it to've been a one-off. Planting his wallet in Purkhiser's pocket without him noticing?

Knocking out the security feeds? Talking his way out of an armed standoff with mall security? That shit screamed pro. And the fact that the dude didn't bite when Purkhiser offered to pay his fee out of the casino winnings further suggested this was no shakedown.

Which meant the dude was telling the truth.

Which meant the Atlanta Outfit had found him.

Problem was, Purkhiser was skint. Strapped. Flat-ass broke, to own the truth. There was no way he was gonna come up with a quarter mil in just three days. He was no holdup artist; he was a computer geek. It took him the better part of a year to plan and run his little casino scam—and anyway, it was that selfsame scam that put him on the Outfit's radar in the first place.

That left running.

Clueless. Blind.

He knew he didn't stand a chance. Didn't have the skill set to make himself disappear at the drop of a hat. Given time—time and money—he could set something up, finesse a new ID out of the ether, and set up a series of blind trusts on which to live; that was his plan once he got his six-mil payout, after all. But when it came to running balls-out, to Bourne-style evasion and ass-kickery, he was as ill-prepared as any career cubicle-dweller in America. Which is, of course, essentially what he had been before he turned stoolie and his whole life went to shit.

Purkhiser ducked under the bed, reaching for the shoe box full of cash he'd stashed there in case of emergencies. Well, more like a quarter full. He'd blown most of his emergency stash on Papa John's, Xbox games, and handles of Jim Beam. Fat lot of good those did him now.

"Mr. Purkhiser," came a voice, lightly accented, from

behind him. Purkhiser started when he heard it and slammed the back of his head against his bed's wooden support slat. His vision dimmed momentarily, but he remained conscious. Given that he assumed whoever that voice belonged to was here to kill him, he wasn't convinced that was a good thing.

That son of a bitch, he thought. He said I had three days.

Purkhiser withdrew his head from under the bed—moving carefully, this time—and rolled over to face the man who stood just feet away inside his bedroom. The man wore a pair of khaki trousers over burnished leather oxfords the color of cognac, and a starched blue button-down with a white collar and French cuffs. His sandy blond hair framed an aristocratic face, and he wore kid gloves on his hands despite the fact that the day's warmth had yet to bleed off into the night sky.

In one hand was a silenced gun.

When Purkhiser saw the gun, he quailed and covered his face, waiting for the shot to come.

"My apologies," said the man, who made no move to raise the gun from where it hung at his side. "I didn't mean to startle you."

Purkhiser peeked at him from between parted fingers. When nothing happened for a couple beats, he said, "Are you fucking kidding me?"

"I assure you, I am not."

"Are you going to kill me?"

The man smiled. "Not so long as you do as I request. I've no interest in your petty squabbles with whosoever wants you dead."

Purkhiser smiled—an unhinged expression that wouldn't

have appeared out of place in a psych ward lockdown. "Anything! Just name it, and it's yours!"

"I came here looking for a man. A man who I assume, given your sudden urge to take a holiday, has recently visited you. A man whose services I suspect you've recently turned down. Do you know the man of whom I speak?"

Purkhiser nodded with crazed enthusiasm.

"And am I correct in my assumption that you elected not to employ him?"

Again, Purkhiser nodded, not trusting himself to speak.

"I see. Now—and understand, this next question's an important one, with nothing short of your continued existence riding upon your response—did he give you any method by which to contact him?"

"Yes!" Purkhiser exclaimed. "He gave me his phone number! He said if I changed my mind, I should give him a call."

"Excellent. That's precisely the answer I was looking for. I'm going to need that number, of course—and one other thing, as well."

"What's that?"

"I'm going to need you to call him and tell him you've changed your mind."

"B-b-but I can't afford to pay him!"

"Oh, I'm sure you'll think of something," said the man. "You've proven quite resourceful in the past. And it goes without saying that I'll be watching your every move, so I assure you, fleeing is not a viable option."

"You trying to trap this guy or something?"

The man smiled. "Yes, or something."

"If I hire him, you'll let me live?"

"You have my word I will not harm you."

"No—I mean, *thanks*, but... what I meant was, will you let him do his job before you whack him? Take out the guy who's coming to kill me, I mean."

The man appeared to think about that for a moment. Then he shrugged and said, "Oh, why not? It seems you've caught me in a charitable mood."

"Okay then," said Purkhiser, "you've got a deal."

"Wonderful. I'm glad we could reach an accord. It bears mentioning that if you breathe a word of our agreement to our mutual friend—or anyone else, for that matter—said agreement is null and void, and so are you. Once I tire of watching you writhe in agony, that is—and believe me when I tell you, I do not tire easily."

At that last, Purkhiser imagined himself an insect pinned to a collector's board, limbs flapping.

"Oh, and one last thing," said the man. "I don't suppose he was so kind as to give you his name, was he?"

Purkhiser shook his head, and the man's face fell—theatrically, as if for Purkhiser's benefit. "Ah, well. One can't have everything, now, can one?"

Purkhiser looked at the bag on the bed, half-full of clothes and wasted hope. All he'd wanted was his dough back—a second chance at the good life he thought a man of his ingenuity deserved, but of which the Feds had seen fit to strip him.

Instead, what he'd gotten for his trouble was a heaping ton of shit—one he might not be able to claw out of alive. Which left him pining for the depressing, quotidian life he'd so callously tossed aside.

So can one, in fact, have everything?

No, he thought. One very fucking *can't*.

*   *   *

Meeting adjourned, Alexander Engelmann returned to his temporary accommodations—a foreclosed split-level ranch across the street and three doors down from Purkhiser's, painted a horrid combination of white and salmon pink but nonetheless affording from its master bedroom a smashing view of Purkhiser's mirror image of a home. Engelmann had employed countersurveillance tactics on his brief trip back here, walking a good ten blocks with many an abrupt reversal of direction to travel three, but—his own satisfaction at a job well done aside—he knew it was for naught. Partly because he was an astute enough student of human nature to see Purkhiser was too frightened to dare follow him, and partly because he could hear Purkhiser pacing his living room via the sound-activated bugs Engelmann had planted throughout the man's home.

The bugs transmitted to a receiver in the living room of Engelmann's squat. When he returned from Purkhiser's, he cranked the volume on the unit until Purkhiser's every footstep—his every breath—echoed through the empty house. As Engelmann listened, he wandered the house, his eyes half closed—to the kitchen, to the bedroom, to the master bath. His movements mirrored Purkhiser's, their footsteps ringing out in time. For a moment, as their breathing synched, he felt that he and Purkhiser were one—and in that moment, he was sure his plan would work.

Though Engelmann would scarcely admit it to himself, he was relieved his intuition regarding his quarry's use of the Council's book code had finally borne fruit. Since his discovery of Cruz's cipher, it had yielded nothing. After

Chicago, he was mildly concerned. But when Long Beach failed to pay off, too, he began to doubt the veracity of his lead. He'd been forced to consider the notion that his quarry identified his clients by means other than the Council book code.

Then again, he realized, perhaps there was another conclusion to be made by the fact that he'd elected not to help either Franklin or D'Abruzzo: it was possible he considered protecting violent criminals beneath him.

Could it be his quarry fancied himself a moral man?

When Engelmann revisited his quarry's file, that question in his mind, a pattern emerged. His clients were all relative innocents. Like Morales. Like Purkhiser.

It appeared Engelmann had arrived in Springfield just too late to lay eyes on his quarry. He'd driven directly from the airport to Purkhiser's home, hoping that by staking it out, he might witness his target's approach, and then follow him until a time to strike presented itself. Instead, what he found was a panicked Purkhiser preparing to flee, and so he made do as best he could.

Engelmann refused to grant the possibility that Purkhiser would fail as a lure. He was now certain his quarry believed himself a good person and was therefore predisposed toward helping this pathetic wretch.

Such burdensome things, consciences. Engelmann was relieved not to be afflicted with one.

Of course, there was another reason Engelmann refused to entertain the possibility that Purkhiser would fail in his task. The week Engelmann's contact had promised him was almost up, which meant the Council would soon halt all communications via their old book code, their old race sites. The Purkhiser job would likely be the last one posted—which made it Engelmann's last chance to bag his man.

And it was clear to Engelmann the Council was losing patience with him. He heard it in his contact's tone when they spoke over the phone. He saw it in the resources the Council offered by way of assistance—once unlimited but now often withheld. He was certain the only additional rope they'd be giving him would be used to bind his hands and feet before they killed him should he fail.

No matter, he thought. Such maudlin concern got him nowhere. And besides, he was right about Purkhiser and his quarry both—he *knew* he was.

And though he assured himself of exactly that a thousand times in the musty stillness of the abandoned house, Engelmann relaxed perceptibly when he heard Purkhiser pick up the phone and dial.

Hendricks's burner phone rang long-short-long. That meant Purkhiser. The only other person who had Hendricks's number—as far as Hendricks knew—was Lester, and his ringtone was set to an ascending scale, four trilling tones from low to high.

Hendricks wasn't surprised when Purkhiser called. In the years he'd been at the job, they nearly always did. What he hadn't figured on is what Purkhiser would say.

"You get my money?" Hendricks asked without preamble.

A hesitation. "Not exactly," Purkhiser replied.

"Then this conversation is over."

"Wait—don't hang up!"

In spite of his own better judgment, Hendricks didn't hang up. "I'm listening," he said.

"I want you to take it all."

"Excuse me?"

"The whole six mil. Every fucking penny. Just get these guys off my ass long enough for me to rabbit, and it's yours."

Six million dollars.

Six *million* dollars.

It was more than Hendricks could make in three jobs— in *five*. All he had to do for it was pop some low-life Outfit button man.

A six-million-dollar payout would ensure neither Evie nor Lester would ever need to worry about money again. It meant that someday, once Hendricks had finally made his penance, there might be an end to this violent life he led.

But Purkhiser didn't need to know any of that. So Hendricks played it calm, cool.

"And how do you propose to get me this money?" he said.

"That's the beauty part," replied Purkhiser, relief apparent in his tone. "We just have the casino give it straight to you. See, that big check is just for show—I'm supposed to give 'em my account info ahead of time so they can transfer the funds directly once their dog-and-pony show is over. But I figure a big-shot hitman like you has probably got a numbered account somewhere, all nice and anonymous-like, am I right? So who's to say for the purpose of this transaction that account ain't mine?"

Hendricks should have said no. Should have realized that the Purkhiser he'd met a few hours ago would never have parted so easily with so large a sum. He should have sensed that something wasn't right—should have up and walked away.

But six million dollars buys a lot of bad decisions.

So what he said instead was: "You try to screw me, and I'll kill you—you know that, right?"

Purkhiser, hopeful: "That mean we got a deal?"

Six. Million. Dollars.

"Yeah, we got a deal."

"Cool—let me grab a pen."

19.

PENDLETON'S RESORT and Casino was a tacky riverboat-themed complex overlooking the Missouri River from an industrial park just north of Kansas City proper. The approach was like pulling into an airport—a confusing tangle of roads peeling off toward various parking lots, some of them vast asphalt plains dotted by sodium vapor lights resembling bare husks of long-dead trees, and some multilevel concrete structures, open on all sides. Sleek black shuttle buses ferried people to and fro, their mirrored windows a false promise of debauchery within. The fact was, Pendleton's was more a family place. Their shows tended toward the squeaky clean, mostly traveling productions of Broadway staples, and their upscale steak house and French-inspired fine-dining restaurant sat shoulder-to-shoulder with a dinosaur-themed rib joint and a NASCAR-branded bar and grill.

Michael Hendricks left his rental car in one of the outermost satellite lots, opting to hoof it rather than hitch a ride in the shuttle bus. The sun blazed orange as it touched the western horizon, streaking the cirrus clouds that stretched across the evening sky. The lights of the casino glinted like a mirage in the distance. It was seven p.m. Tuesday—twenty hours and change since Purkhiser had hired Hendricks, and less than two days from Leonwood's planned hit. Hendricks had spent the morning on the phone with Lester, who'd worked his digital mojo to put together a dossier on Purkhiser's would-be assassin, Leonwood, which he read to Hendricks in its entirety. Hendricks never traveled with his laptop, because it contained no shortage of incriminating evidence, and he refused to download anything that might later implicate him to his cheap, unencrypted burner phone.

Lester's dossier painted a picture of a seasoned hitter with a rep for high-risk, high-stakes jobs—public figures, law enforcement, you name it—and his MO seemed to be the nastier, the better. Rumor was, Leonwood was the one responsible for stringing up that First Circuit Court of Appeals judge on Boston's Zakim Bridge after he ruled against the Winter Hill Gang back in '04. If the Outfit wanted Purkhiser's death to be messy, they'd sure as hell hired the right guy.

Once Hendricks had memorized the salient details, he made the drive from Springfield to Kansas City—just under three hours at a sensible five miles per hour over the speed limit. He made a stop at the FedEx shop in Belton—a sprawling suburb south of town—where Lester'd sent along a package to be held for pickup by one Steven Rogers.

The contents of the package were listed as "Cookies," and the sender as "Grandma Rogers." Inside the box was a tin containing one thousand dollars cash (all the excuse one ever needed to be in a casino); a ceramic knife, which was invisible to metal detectors and twice as sharp as steel, with a pebbled grip designed to thwart fingerprinting; a functional penlight that doubled as a single-shot zip gun, loaded with a jacketed 9mm hollow-point round; a mug shot of a young, fresh-faced Leon Leonwood, taken decades ago when he was arrested for manslaughter, but hopefully bearing enough resemblance to the man he'd grown into for Hendricks to ID him; and four oatmeal raisin cookies.

The mug shot and weaponry, Hendricks stashed inside his rental's spare tire, protection against the unlikely event the car was searched. Today's mission was one of reconnaissance, not violence, and carrying weapons—even ones as unlikely to be detected as these—would potentially create as many complications as it would guard against. Once his scouting was complete, if Hendricks decided more firepower—such as handguns, rifles, or small explosives—was required, he'd acquire it locally; it was foolish to travel with such items when they were so readily available, so unwise to hold on to, and so easily discarded.

Lester's cookies, as ever, were delicious.

Hendricks's boot leather creaked as he ambled along the sidewalk that ran parallel to the casino's main drive. A job like this, the key was blending in, so he'd decked himself out as a full-on gambling cliché. A red-and-white checked cowboy shirt with white trim. Dark-blue boot-cut jeans over alligator cowboy boots. An off-white Stetson on his head, a pair of BluBlockers hiding his eyes, and as much of a horseshoe mustache as he could muster from three days' stubble. Even his walk was affected: a slouching, duck-footed swagger that took two inches off his height. He looked ridiculous—but it was precisely the same sort of ridiculous as half the gamblers in attendance, the sort of ridiculous that caused one's gaze to slide right by.

Hendricks was greeted at the casino entrance by a smiling bellhop. An old-timey marquee awash in the light of a thousand bulbs gave way to an interior whose decor was as loud and jarring as the din rising from its endless banks of clanking slots.

Purkhiser's ceremony was supposed to take place in a banquet hall just off the gaming floor called the Fountain Room. Today, the Fountain Room featured two performances by a ventriloquist—lunch and dinner, complete with buffet. Later tonight, it hosted a country act Hendricks had never heard of.

Hendricks bought a ticket to the ventriloquist's buffet—fifteen dollars, food included. The clink of flatware on glasses filled the hall as he entered, and the tables—round and draped in coarse white linens—were about three-quarters full. Though the show had yet to begin, the buffet'd been open twenty minutes by the time he arrived, so the line was short. The buffet ran half the length of the room along the left-hand side. Hendricks got in line—a good excuse to walk the length of the room and scan the crowd.

The room was big and dimly lit, with plush carpeting of green and red and floor-to-ceiling curtains on each wall. The stage was small, set up at the far end of the room from the main entrance. There was a bar in the corner to the right of the stage, people crowded all around. The only points of entry were the main doors through which Hendricks had arrived and two emergency exits, one on the right-hand wall and another behind the stage. At each of the emergency exits was a security guard—husky, uniformed, armed. Another two security guards stood offstage at either side.

Hendricks didn't like it.

Assuming the setup on Thursday was the same, the hall was too full—of people and furniture both. It had too few exits and too much security. Not to mention the half-domes of tinted plastic that protruded downward at regular intervals from the ceiling—security cameras, watching every inch of the place.

But like it or not, he had six million reasons to make it work.

So he fixed himself a plate and grabbed a seat up near the front, where a corner table was vacant by virtue of the fact that it afforded an awkward view of the stage. Fine by him. He didn't care to see the performance, and from his perch in the nine-o'clock position at the table, he had sight lines on the bar; the crowd seated at the tables; the room's main entrance; and, in the reflection of the chromed water pitcher on his table, the buffet patrons behind him.

As Hendricks settled into his seat and draped his napkin across his lap, the overhead lights dimmed, signaling that the show was about to begin. Hendricks didn't pay any mind to the tired old man who took the stage with his dummy.

He had a job to do.

Albert Tuschbaum was having a lousy day.

For one, his throat was killing him. Thirty shows in thirty days will do that to you. Well, that and the sinus infection he'd picked up somewhere between here and

San Antonio. He'd spent the last month snaking upward through the country on Greyhound after Greyhound: north on I-35 to Austin, Fort Worth, Dallas, and Oklahoma City, then east on 44 to Tulsa and Joplin. To get to the gig in Branson, he got stuck on a local bus instead of an express, which meant stops every other mile it seemed, and damn near twice the travel time—all while wedged between a grubby, ponytailed biker-type too long since his last shower, and a woman whose snot-crusted toddler kept coughing like he had the plague. On the leg from Branson to Springfield, they'd lost his dummy, Mickey—though they claimed they'd loaded him into the luggage compartment before departing, he wasn't there when they arrived—which meant he had to go onstage with the backup dummy he kept stuffed into the bottom of his other suitcase, whose threadbare clothes and chipping paint seemed to mirror Albert's own sorry state. And from Springfield to his Pendleton's gigs, his bus's toilet had backed up, meaning that he not only couldn't pee—his cholesterol meds made him piss like a racehorse—but he also couldn't eat, the foul stench of human waste ensuring the lunch he bought at the station went untouched. Hell, he'd been in town for hours now, and still he felt as though the awful reek of chemical toilet clung to his clothes, his hair, his skin.

Then again, maybe that was the smell of his career.

How could he have let it come to this? Time was, he played the Vegas strip, warming up the sold-out crowds for acts like Tom Jones and Neil Diamond. Twice, he'd appeared on Carson, once even getting invited over to the couch. But that was years ago—decades. Two divorces and countless hip flasks of Canadian Club. The booze had eaten through his stomach, his marriage, and his reputation, etching its mark deep into the lines of his face, into the broken corpuscles draped like lace across his nose and cheeks. It drove away his wife and friends, and left his children flinching every time the phone rang, not knowing if the voice at the other end would be that of their maudlin old man, or the inevitable rote sympathy of some faraway police officer, informing them they needn't flinch any longer.

Then Grace came and changed everything.

Five weeks early, she showed up. Her lungs were weak, her body bruised from the trauma of early labor and a breech presentation. Ultimately, the doctors were forced to perform an emergency Cesarean on Albert's daughter Rachel—herself the baby of the family. In the end, mother and daughter were fine, though the first few days were touch-and-go for both. And though Albert's ex managed to put aside years of heartache and resentment to wire him money for an airline ticket so he could be there should both or neither wake, Albert wasn't man enough to make the trip—the thought of losing both his daughter and his grandchild in one fell swoop proved too much. He stopped off at some shitty cocktail lounge on his way to the airport for one steadying drink and woke up days later in a flea-ridden motel, the rumble of landing aircraft shaking the four empty bottles on his nightstand, with no memory of what had transpired in the interim—without even knowing if his child and grandchild had survived.

That's when he decided to get clean.

The first month was the worst—the shakes, the sweats, the horrid clarity that ensured each unendurable minute proceeded directly to the next, with no fast-forward, no blissful blackout time-jump. Gone was the soft amber whiskey filter through which he experienced his life, and all he was left with was the cold reality of the pathetic existence it had become.

So he resolved to change it. To make amends. To glue back together what he'd broken, as best he could.

Now he peddled his dying art in two-bit rooms in two-bit towns, to crowds who didn't give a shit if he moved his lips or not, let alone said anything funny. But he didn't do it for the laughs, or the accolades, or even for himself. He did it for Grace. Albert was determined that when she was old enough to look at him with any kind of understanding, it would be love he saw reflected there, not pity or disappointment.

It was a damn good thing he didn't do it for himself. Because these assholes in the crowd wouldn't know talent if it got up in front of them and sang "It's a Long Way to Tipperary" while gargling a glass of water.

Take the fellow stage right, for example. The wannabe cowboy in the Stetson and the BluBlockers, sitting to one side of an otherwise empty table and pointedly ignoring him. Guy'd barely even glanced his way when Albert took the stage—and he'd spent the whole time since staring at the rest of the audience. Apparently, every other person here was more interesting than Albert's set.

Then there was the old-timer who'd fallen asleep in his mashed potatoes, a rail-thin guy with a wispy horseshoe of too-long white hair and a week's dusting of white stubble. Albert saw him swaying gently as if to music only he could hear as Albert was going into his knot/not riff on "Who's on First?" Then his eyes closed, and down he went. Albert was inclined to give that guy a pass—it was doubtless drink and not boredom that knocked him out, and as the six-month chip in Albert's front pocket reminded him, drink was one thing over which some folks had little control.

The prick at the bar was another matter.

He'd come in twenty minutes into the set, long after everyone else was seated. The banquet hall's main double doors had been closed at the start of his performance, but this flannel-clad oaf banged them open and headed straight for the bar. There, he got into an argument with the bartender regarding the proper ratio of ice to Jack Daniel's—loudly enough that Albert could hear the dropped *R*s and nasal *A*s of his Masshole accent.

And Albert wasn't the only person who noticed. A good quarter of the crowd was now training their attention on this blowhard idiot instead of Albert—including, it dismayed him to discover, Stetson-and-BluBlockers on the far side of the room. Apparently, a skilled rendition of a classic vaudevillian act in the vein of Bergen and Winchell wasn't enough to interest him, but a boorish oaf berating the waitstaff was downright riveting.

That was it. Albert had had enough. Family show or not, it was time to teach this man—and this crowd—some manners.

"Hey, pal! Yeah, you at the bar!" It was not Albert who spoke, but his backup dummy, Rickey. "Is this guy's act bothering you? 'Cause I could ask him to cool it for a sec while you get this business with the barkeep figured out!" Rickey always was a bit of a dick.

The crowd responded with titters of discomfort. It was always that way when a comic first engaged a heckler; they never knew which horse to back. But Albert wasn't some novice. He knew how to handle himself in front of hostile audiences. The fact was, he hadn't felt this alive in decades.

The big man turned his attention from the bar to the stage, flushing with anger but saying nothing.

"Whatsamatter, Tons-of-Fun," continued Rickey, "*fat got your tongue?*"

That drew a bigger laugh. The man's fists balled at his sides, and he seemed to shrink a bit from the attention of the crowd, but still he remained silent.

"Come on now, Rickey," Albert said, good cop to his dummy's bad. "Give the man a break. He's just trying to get a drink."

"Oh, sure. Take his side," Rickey replied, and then baited the hook: "Hey, barkeep, what's his poison?"

The bartender looked at the man, and then the crowd, and then at Albert. After a moment's hesitation, she said, shaky-voiced from nerves, "J-jack Daniel's."

Rickey continued: "Tell you what—how 'bout you give it to him on old Albert here. 'Cause without the Jack, he'd just be an ass."

The crowd went nuts. Albert smiled. And for just a moment, as he stepped closer to the stage, the man smiled, too, but it was a feral smile—a wild animal baring its teeth in warning. Albert's stomach clenched at the sight.

When he was a few feet from the stage, the man spoke, low enough so that only Albert could hear. "You're lucky I'm working, old man, or I swear to Christ I'd shove that doll a yours so far down your fucking throat you'd hafta clench your asshole to make his mouth move. And you can keep your goddamn drink."

Albert blinked at him, paralyzed in the no-man's-land between pride and fear. The casino security guards who flanked the stage weren't quite close enough to hear, but they got the gist and closed in to defuse the situation. But before they reached the man, he shrugged them off, turning toward the exit and storming out. One of the guards spoke briefly into his walkie.

As the crowd settled down, and Albert resumed his set, the man in the Stetson and BluBlockers rose and followed.

20.

ALEXANDER ENGELMANN stood at a roulette table outside the Fountain Room, alternating bets of red and black. Engelmann was not much of a gambler; he chose this game both because its odds were such that one could play for quite some time without requiring additional chips— roughly forty-seven percent on any red or black bet—and because it afforded him an unobstructed view of the entrance to the ballroom in which Purkhiser was to be killed. Engelmann was certain his quarry would reconnoiter the room—but he'd not yet seen anyone who matched the description Morales had given him.

Still, he thought, that did not mean his quarry was not here.

Engelmann absently fingered the cell phone in his pocket. He was tempted to dial his quarry's burner phone, to see if he could hear it ring nearby—but he knew the potential upside to so brazen an act was too slight, and the downside too great. Cell-phone usage was forbidden on the gaming floor, to discourage cheating; it would be difficult to use his here without running afoul of casino security. And by every indication, Engelmann's quarry was a cautious man—it was doubtful he would make so egregious an error as to leave his ringer on while on a job. But mostly, Engelmann could not because to do so might tip his quarry to the fact that something was amiss.

"Thirty-five," called the croupier as the ball rattled to a stop. Engelmann's fellow players sighed with disappointment—the corresponding patch of felt was empty. "Nobody home."

A flurry of betting as the wheel was spun again; Engelmann slid one chip, the table minimum, onto red. Then the croupier waved his hand over the table and said, "No more bets."

That was fine by Engelmann. He was eager for the real games to begin.

When Leonwood burst, red-faced, out of the Fountain Room, Engelmann raised an eyebrow. For a moment it looked like Leonwood was headed straight toward him, and though Engelmann understood rationally that Leonwood knew nothing of his existence or of his mission, a jolt of adrenaline pricked at his limbs at the perceived threat. But then Leonwood veered left toward the casino's main entrance, and the moment passed.

Four security guards materialized as if from the cardinal points of the lobby's inlaid compass rose, flanking Leonwood but not engaging. Leonwood tried to duck past them, but one stepped in front of him, hands raised in a placating gesture. The guard said something to Leonwood, but his words were lost to Engelmann thanks to the clamor of the gaming floor. Leonwood responded angrily. Engelmann drifted away from the roulette table to better hear their exchange.

"Sir—" the croupier objected because the ball was still in play, but Engelmann ignored him. Anger blossomed in his mind. Anger, and a hint of fear. He couldn't fathom what this stupid hunk of flannel-draped beef was thinking, making such a spectacle of himself, and he was all too aware that if Leonwood was thrown out, his last-gasp effort to eliminate the Council's pest was as dead as Engelmann himself would be once the Council got wind that he had failed.

"Sir, I understand you're upset," said the guard as Engelmann got within earshot.

"You're goddamn *right* I'm upset," growled Leonwood. "All I wanted was a fucking drink before dinner, and that creepy guy with the dummy started heckling me! What kinda establishment are you running here?"

"Please realize, sir, that the views expressed by Mr. Tuschbaum do not in any way reflect those of Pendleton's or her employees. I'm very sorry if he offended—"

"*If?*" Leonwood interrupted.

"—and, if you'll just calm down, we'd like to make this right, so we could avoid any further unpleasantness."

"Make this right *how?*" Dubious. Interested.

"You mentioned you hadn't eaten dinner yet?"

"That's right."

"Then perhaps we could arrange for you a table at Gasparini's, where I suspect the steak will be to your liking. We will of course refund the cost of the buffet, and tonight's dinner will be on the house."

Leonwood's expression softened. "I suppose that'd be all right," he said.

The guard led Leonwood to the concierge's desk. Engelmann—satisfied that his plan hadn't been derailed—turned back toward the gaming floor, only to run into a ridiculous Roy Rogers of a man in sunglasses, a silly mustache, and a garishly outsized Stetson.

"Pardon me," said the man, a hint of drawl to his voice. "Just lookin' for the head. Any chance you could point me in the right direction?"

That drawl was more Virginia South than Western cowboy twang, but Engelmann was unaware of the difference. "I'm afraid not," Engelmann replied, and continued on his way.

The cowboy lingered a moment, watching Leonwood, the guard, and the concierge converse. Leonwood, ever the professional hitter, scanned the crowd surreptitiously a time or two while they spoke, and by suspicion or mere happenstance, his gaze settled briefly on the cowboy.

Then he turned his attention back to the concierge, flashing a polite smile at some solicitous, unfunny joke—and when he glanced up again, the cowboy was gone.

21.

A VOICE IN his ear, crackly and delayed—the telephone con-
nection terrible. Henry Garfield strained to hear over the
clamor of the FBI's St. Louis field office on Market Street.
Then his eyes went wide. "You serious?" he asked. "Hell
yeah, I'll wait." He covered the mouthpiece of the office-
issue landline and shouted to his partner, one cubicle away:
"Hey, Thompson—you're not gonna fuckin' believe this."

Charlie Thompson wearily removed her glasses and
closed her eyes, but the ghostly image of the traffic camera
footage she'd been staring at remained. She massaged at
the knot of tension where nose met forehead that had
twisted her handsome features into a scowl, but it did nothing to relieve the march of her headache. "Garfield," she
said, "I swear to God, if you're calling me over there to see
another sleazeball bang some floozy in an alley, I'm going
to put a bullet through your monitor. Or you."

"Right," Garfield said, "like there's two guys in one day that lucky in all of Saint Louis. Look around—the lucky people in this town have done moved out. I never seen a city this big this empty."

About that, at least, Garfield was right. The population of St. Louis had declined by two-thirds since its peak. The results were broad sidewalks and multilane arterials that sat empty, or damn near. Which, theoretically, should have made their current task easier, but in practice made it dull enough to render it unbearable.

Thompson and Garfield were looking for a late-model metallic blue Nissan Versa sedan, rented Monday evening from Reliant Auto Rental—less than a mile's walk from the airport—by a Mr. Lawrence Landry. Landry was one of Leonwood's go-to aliases. They'd been at it for going on twenty-four hours—since midday Tuesday, when the footage from the traffic cams, ATMs, and private security feeds started rolling in. Reliant, like most auto rental companies across the country, didn't bother placing tracking systems inside their compacts or economies—just their luxury options. Paying monthly premiums to track a fleet of low-rent cars unlikely to be stolen wasn't worth the cost. And either Leonwood was wise to the fact or he was just a tightwad, because moose of a man that he was, when it came time to rent a ride, he opted to cram himself into a compact rather than fork over the dough for something he might actually fit into. And that left Thompson and Garfield hoping somebody somewhere had eyes on him, so they could figure out where he was headed. Even in a town as sparsely populated as St. Louis, it was like trying to find a needle in a pile of other needles—and the St. Louis field office was understaffed, so they were on their own sifting through the literally thousands of hours of video and reams of digital stills. With twenty trained agents, it might have been doable. With two, it was a waste of time.

"So what have you got?" Thompson said.

"What I've *got* is a call from our office in KC. They got a nibble on the pic of Leonwood we've been circulating. Seems ol' Leon got himself into an argument with a fucking ventriloquist of all things at some cheap-ass casino buffet, and security had to step in to talk him down."

Thompson stood, rising all the way to her tiptoes so she could peer over the cubicle wall. Her cell phone vibrated—a text from Jess—and her headache intensified. She was too busy for family drama right now. "They sure it was our guy?"

"Sure enough to call it in. I'm on hold with KC while they call the casino back to see if they can e-mail me a still from their security cameras."

"He's not still *there*, is he?" Thompson asked.

"No," Garfield replied. "The place's got a hotel, but he wasn't registered. They comped him a dinner to shut him up, and he left just after."

"Wait—he wasn't registered? That mean he gave them a name when they talked to him?"

"Yeah," Garfield said: "Smith."

Figures, Thompson thought. If he'd used a known alias, they'd have him pegged. But Smith was almost as damning. In fact... "Son of a bitch," she said, plopping back into her chair and swiveling once more toward her computer.

"What?"

"What's the name of the casino?"

"Pendleton's—why?"

Thompson googled, brought up their website. Her cell

phone vibrated again, but she ignored it. "That's where his hit is going down."

"How can you be so sure? We don't even know it's *him* yet." Garfield's e-mail chirped, indicating a new message. A quick click to open it, and another to open the attached image, and he said, "Scratch that—it's him. But you can't know that's where it's gonna go down. I mean, he'd be crazy to whack a guy with that much security around, wouldn't he?"

"Leonwood specializes in crazy," Thompson said. "Besides, when's the last time *you* flew halfway across the country to see a ventriloquist?"

"Fair point," Garfield conceded. "Still, it's pretty thin. Maybe he's just killing time until killing time."

"Cute," Thompson said, "but I don't buy it. If he was staying there, I might grant the possibility he just wandered down and plopped himself in whatever show was going on to kill the hours. But he's *not* staying there, and he didn't even dare to drop one of his common aliases. Ergo, he was casing the place."

Thompson thought she heard Garfield scoff at her *ergo*, but he had the sense at least not to put words to his derision. Nice to know her threats of violence were starting to pay off. She fired off an e-mail and heard the electronic chirp from Garfield's cubicle as it arrived.

"What's this?" he asked.

"The Pendleton's event schedule for the month. I need you to talk to someone on their end and find out which of these events are scheduled for the same room the ventriloquist is in for, say, the next three days. If nothing pops, then make it seven." But she knew something would pop— Leonwood wasn't the type for loads of careful prep.

"You want me to alert their security to the threat?"

"And run the risk they'll spook him?" she asked. "No. Leonwood's too slippery. We have to do this right. Tell them to let us know if he comes through again, but don't tip them that he's dangerous; make up something white-collar if you have to. Tell them we have agents on the way. And whatever you tell them, make sure they buy it, or you'll cause a panic, and Leonwood will disappear. If they blow this collar on us, I'll hold you personally responsible."

"And what're you gonna be doing while I tackle all your scut work?"

"I'm going to get us on the next shuttle to KC, and then I'm going to get on the horn with our KC office and make sure their SWAT team's good to go. Be ready in five."

"But all my shit's at the hotel!"

"Which is where you'll find it when you get back," she said. "No time to pack a bag, pretty boy—whatever's going down is going down soon."

22.

Eric Purkhiser wiped his palms on his thrift-store dress pants and watched the Missouri countryside roll by as the limo Pendleton's sent for him drove north on Route 13. It was his first time in a limousine. He'd always thought that they'd be nicer; they looked so swanky from the outside. But the interior was dated—black lacquer trimmed in pink and purple. The air inside reeked of cheap air freshener. There wasn't even any booze—just two bottles of off-brand water where the bar should be.

Not that Purkhiser would have poured himself a drink. His stomach was a wreck already. The collar of his dress shirt felt like it was slowly tightening around his neck. He tugged at it with one finger and forced himself to take deep breaths. For what felt like the hundredth time, he ran through the plan his mystery savior had laid out yesterday and told himself he'd be just fine.

* * *

"Talk me through it one more time," Hendricks had said.

"Dude, we've been through this five times already!" Purkhiser whined. "What more do you need to know?"

"I need to know you're up for this. I need to know that come tomorrow, you'll play your part. And I need to know you haven't forgotten any detail that'll get us both killed. Now talk me through it one more time."

They'd been going around like this for the better part of an hour—Purkhiser sitting at his kitchen table and sipping from a can of Bud, Hendricks pacing back and forth across the yellowed linoleum.

"The limo will be here to pick me up at one p.m. They offered to pick me up earlier and comp my lunch—but as instructed, I declined. Thanks a fucking bunch, by the way—I mean, why would I want all the four-star cuisine I can eat when I got a fridge full of mustard and batteries right here?"

Hendricks doubted the Pendleton's restaurants were anyone's idea of four-star cuisine, but he held his tongue on that count, instead saying, "The Outfit's instructions weren't to whack you at your ceremony—they were to make it public. Lunch at a fancy restaurant might strike the guy who's here to kill you as plenty public, and a hell of a lot easier to pull off than in a banquet room that'll likely be full of guards."

"All right, all right," he said, showing Hendricks his hands. "No lunch."

"What happens after you arrive?"

"I arrive no later than four p.m. They bring me in via the employee entrance and take me through the service corridor that serves as backstage for the banquet hall."

168

"Then?" prompted Hendricks.

"The head of the casino does his little jerk-off dog-and-pony show, they roll an it-could-happen-to-you video that ends with me hitting the jackpot—can you believe they built that fucking slot machine with a camera to capture the big moment?—and then they bring out the big check. I get up, accept it, and then there's gonna be a balloon drop. I hear-tell there's gonna be a bunch of giveaways hidden in the balloons—free meals, concert tickets, fifty bucks in chips, even a coupon for a weekend stay in the Mark Twain Suite—their way of guaranteeing the seats get filled. People are gonna go apeshit once those babies drop."

"That's when the Outfit's goon will make his move. Given that they want to make a scene, and there's no screening on the way into the casino, we have to assume the worst, which in this case would be a fully automatic firearm, likely stowed in a briefcase or piece of luggage to blend in with the hotel crowd. Once they drop the balloons, you're to get down and stay down, understand? I'll try to neutralize the guy before he ever gets a shot off, but better safe than sorry."

"I still don't understand why I'm not wearing a bullet-proof vest," said Purkhiser.

"Well, for one, Eric, you don't need one—you've got me," replied Hendricks. Purkhiser frowned—not entirely certain he believed that. "And for two, any pro worth his salt would spot its bulk a mile away, in which case he'd just scotch his plans to hit you then, and whack you later."

"Eddie," he halfheartedly corrected. "And I'm just saying, this don't seem right to me. Maybe we should call the whole thing off—hole up somewhere and let the bastard come to us."

"Eddie," Hendricks echoed. "Right. Believe me when I tell you, *Eddie*, it's a hell of a lot easier to keep you upright if we know where and when your killer's gonna strike. You take that away from me—restore his element of surprise—and it's a coin toss whether you live or die. But hey, you're the gambler—you wanna roll the dice?"

"Jesus, dude," said Purkhiser sullenly, "I was just askin'. No need to be a dick about it."

"You didn't pay me to be nice," Hendricks said. "In fact, you haven't paid me yet at all. You get the transfer paperwork I requested?"

Purkhiser fished a crookedly folded piece of paper from his back pocket. Four pieces, actually, of that translucent too-thin onionskin paper that's pulled from stacks of carbon-transfer duplicates. Hendricks thumbed through them: all fine print and Purkhiser's initials, the last page signed, dated, and featuring the number to one of Hendricks's accounts in the Seychelles, listed here as Purkhiser's own. Well, Palomera's, according to the paperwork—not that it mattered. What *did* matter is that by the close of business Thursday, the day of Purkhiser's ceremony, six million dollars—less taxes—would be transferred to Hendricks's account.

"Looks like this is all in order," Hendricks said. "Which means as long as you do as I've said, everything is going to be just fine. You have my word."

The limo bypassed the casino's main entrance and pulled into the employee garage around back. The driver opened the rear door, but a sense of impending doom kept Purkhiser in his seat.

"Sir?" the driver said. "We're here."

Purkhiser swallowed hard and clenched his jaw, and then he stepped out of the car.

23.

THURSDAY AFTERNOON, and the Fountain Room was packed. Gone was the buffet, replaced by a smattering of additional tables and a waitstaff circulating trays of hors d'oeuvres. The bar was flush with drunks and compulsive gamblers taking advantage of the free food and drink offered to anyone willing to attend Purkhiser's big event. The casino'd been handing out tickets for hours, and though no one gave a damn about Purkhiser or his enormous jackpot, the room was vibrating with anticipation of the impending balloon drop, and the promise of prizes contained therein.

To one side of the stage, a local news anchor was filming an intro segment. Crews from other TV stations were setting up in the back of the room. Pendleton's was dropping some serious coin on Purkhiser's big win, and they were going to milk it for every ounce of publicity they could.

Special Agent Charlie Thompson scanned the room from just inside the massive double doors, but if Leonwood was here, she couldn't see him. The chatter on her earpiece indicated that Pendleton's security team—and Garfield, monitoring the CCTV feeds from the casino's surveillance room—was faring no better. Of course, looking for a specific burly, red-faced man at a Kansas City casino was something of a losing proposition, and anyway, the balloon-filled netting rigged to the ceiling was obstructing the camera coverage. Thompson wondered if she'd been wrong to mislead casino security about the severity of the threat—as far as they knew, she was here to take down a fugitive hedge-fund manager on the run from an insider-trading rap.

She hadn't anticipated the environment would be so uncontrolled. Plus, there was the matter of not knowing who the target was. Four people were expected to take the stage. There was Norville Rogers Pendleton, majority owner of the casino and grandson of the namesake Pendleton, whose money—after a protracted legal battle between his many heirs—was used to build the casino complex. Ditto Bernie Liederkrantz, Pendleton's longtime pit boss and—word had it—former mob enforcer out of Las Vegas who'd burned some bridges when he went legit. Ken Carson, mayor of Kansas City (KC for KC read the signs leading up to Election Day) and scourge of the local crime community thanks to his crackdown on prescription narcotics dealing, would be up there, too. And then there was the guest of honor, one Edward Palomera of Springfield, Missouri. Of the four of them, Palomera was the only one she could safely say wasn't Leonwood's likely target—he was a lower-middle-class wage slave with no sheet, no enemies, and no ties to organized crime. The guy didn't so much as have a speeding ticket to his name.

Of course, Alexander Engelmann knew otherwise. He loitered on the left-hand side of the room halfway between the main entrance and the stage, his elbow propped against the chair rail, an untouched gin and tonic in his hand. He wore a white button-down with a periwinkle check and a pair of charcoal slacks that terminated over suede chukka boots the color of putty.

Engelmann had taken full advantage of the casino's lack of metal detectors in suiting up today; he was determined to be prepared when he finally met his quarry face-to-face. His button-down hid beneath it a concealment shirt—a formfitting wicking tee into which was stitched two heavy-duty nylon holsters, one beneath each arm. The holster beneath his left arm was stocked with a Ruger LC9 compact 9mm pistol he'd purchased from a prison-inked neo-Nazi at a paramilitary compound west of town. The Ruger held seven rounds in the magazine and one in the chamber. He carried two spare magazines in the holster beneath his right arm. That meant he had twenty-two rounds in total. He hoped not to use a one of them.

Strapped to Engelmann's right thigh was a knife sheath containing a Blackhawk double-edged combat blade, also courtesy of his new Aryan friend. He'd removed the interior of his trousers' right pocket for easy access. His left pocket contained a garrote of his own making, comprising a low E acoustic guitar string and two wooden trowel handles. It had taken him a half hour to track down the necessary components and mere minutes to construct, and cost him eleven dollars.

He had no intention of using those, either.

No, Engelmann thought the ice pick hidden in his sleeve would suffice.

It was not affixed, instead held in place by the cuff of his sleeve, and by the angle at which he held his wrist. It sat point down, its handle resting against the meat of his forearm. He'd practiced deploying it in his hotel room—a flick of the wrist and it slid down his arm, its point passing through his fingers, its handle just clearing his cuff and dropping into the palm of his hand. He pictured driving it sewing-machine fast into his quarry's back—*snick snick snick snick snick*—puncturing his renal artery so often and so quickly he would scarcely have a moment to react before his heart filled his abdominal cavity with blood. The narrow bore of the ice pick ensured little external bleeding, which meant that Engelmann should have time to guide his quarry into a chair and walk out of the casino before anyone was the wiser. Now all that remained was to identify his quarry, and he would fulfill his Council contract. Such identification required nothing more now than patience and a keen eye—because unlike the Feds or casino security, Engelmann had Leonwood in sight, having followed him since he'd left Pendleton's on Tuesday.

Hendricks had Leonwood in sight as well. It was no surprise the authorities had yet to spot him; the close call with casino security had forced Leonwood into altering his appearance. He'd shaved his stubble and his mustache, and tamed his unkempt hair—now wearing it slicked into a severe part, which made it look dark as well. He'd traded his flannel and work boots for an off-the-rack suit of checkered gray, worn tieless over a cheap, shiny blue oxford. Though the suit was ill-fitting, the jacket did wonders to hide his gut, and the overall effect was to transform Leonwood from the rough-hewn redneck security'd encountered into one of the many low-rent traveling businessmen that filled the casino, blowing their per diems at the blackjack tables.

Leonwood sat a few tables back from the stage. With a bottle of beer in front of him and his carry-on at his feet, he looked like a guy whiling away the hours between checkout and flight. But his carry-on contained a compact, fully automatic Heckler & Koch MP5K Personal Defense Weapon with collapsible stock—capable of delivering nine hundred rounds per minute—as well as four magazines of thirty rounds each and a large, cylindrical suppressor. The suppressor was not—as movie silencers would lead you to believe—enough to dampen the sound of the gun's report entirely, but enough to dull it such that folks might mistake the shots for balloon pops long enough for Leonwood to make his escape.

Hendricks was once more in his cowboy getup, though this time a faded snap-button chambray shirt stood in for his flashier red check, and weathered jeans replaced his ink-dark ones. He wasn't as heavily armed as either Leonwood or Engelmann. He carried only the ceramic knife and penlight zip gun Lester'd sent him. The zip gun jutted from his shirt pocket. The knife he wore in a jury-rigged belly sheath of Ace bandages and duct tape; he'd left the third button of his shirt unsnapped and could draw the knife at a moment's notice.

Despite what he'd told Purkhiser, Hendricks had hoped to tail Leonwood from the moment he entered the casino and kill him long before the ceremony started. He only led Purkhiser to believe it would happen during the balloon drop to keep him occupied, so he didn't get any ideas about changing the routing on Hendricks's millions. The threat of death does wonders for keeping people on the straight and narrow.

But Leonwood hadn't entered the casino through the main lobby—he slipped in through one of the restaurants with both exterior and interior entrances, no doubt wishing to avoid being recognized by the concierge. Hendricks didn't spot Leonwood until he was walking into the banquet hall—only recognizing him in his new getup because he looked as fresh-faced as his childhood mug shot—and the man hadn't budged since claiming a table. That meant plan B.

Plan B was to feign drunkenness, staggering through the crowd of tables and stumbling into Leonwood right before the ceremony began. Before Leonwood ever had a chance to open fire, Hendricks would sever his femoral artery with the ceramic knife and let him bleed out where he sat, all evidence of the crime obscured by the dim lights and floor-length table linens.

24.

H ENDRICKS CUT THROUGH the crowd, approaching from his target's seven o'clock, his eyes locked on Leonwood. The big man was no more than forty feet away, a thicket of spectators between. As the lights dimmed, Hendricks focused on navigating the darkened space—on readying himself. He didn't notice that to his right, a lithe blond man was tracking his approach.

Leonwood peered intently at the stage, where a cluster of presenters and security sporadically obscured his line of sight to Purkhiser, who sat waiting in the wings. He never saw Hendricks coming. He *did*, however, see the Pendleton's security guard surveying the crowd from the stage linger a hair too long on him before his gaze continued past—and likewise noticed that same guard mutter into his shoulder mic a moment later. The guard was a pro—he'd only paused on Leonwood for a second, and he'd waited a beat, all casual-like, before reporting in—but Leonwood was a pro, too. He knew he'd been made.

He'd hoped to bide his time until the balloon drop, spray the stage with bullets—his suppressor blunting the worst of his gun's report—and slip out before the popping of the prize-hungry casino patrons died down. But that plan went out the window the second he was spotted. If he was gonna take out Purkhiser, he was going to have to do it now.

Just inside the entrance to the banquet hall, Charlie Thompson's earpiece crackled. "We got something," Garfield said to her from his perch in the Pendleton's surveillance room. "One of the casino's guys spotted Leonwood. Says he's seated three tables back from the stage."

"You got eyes on him?" she asked.

"Wish I did," Garfield replied. "The cameras ain't picking up a thing but balloons and netting."

The impending balloon drop, thought Thompson—her chittering heart rate registering what her instincts were telling her seconds before her brain caught up. An obscured line of fire created by security and bystanders both. Leonwood's position in the middle of the crowd—too close and too exposed for a precision rifle shot, but too far away to count on the limited accuracy of a handgun. A picture of carnage took shape in her mind.

"Could their guy see his hands?" she asked.

"What?" Garfield replied, perplexed.

"His *hands*. Could their guy see Leonwood's hands, or were they under the table?"

An electronic crackle as Garfield broke the line, a pause as he conferred with casino security, and then he broke back in. "Under the table. What're you thinking?"

Thompson's stomach lurched. She unsnapped the thumb break on her holster and drew her sidearm. "I'm thinking he's assembling an automatic weapon. I'm thinking he means to open fire. We need to put him down, and quick."

Thompson moved along the right-hand wall of the room, her arms down and gun held ready, scanning the crowd for any sign of Leonwood. There were too many people still milling around for her to see. Too many bodies. She probed the crowd's edge here and there—standing on tiptoe, or shoving folks aside—but he was lost to her. All she succeeded in doing was scaring anyone close enough to see she had a gun.

Tension seemed to ripple out through the crowd. The volume rose. And there was still no sign of Leonwood. Thompson broke out in a sweat. She was running out of time.

Leonwood's hands worked frantically under the table: locking the hinged gunstock of his MP5K into place, inserting the magazine with a satisfying *click*, threading the suppressor onto its truncated barrel. Hendricks noted from Leonwood's outline his flurry of activity beneath the table and realized that the time line for the hit had shifted. He lengthened his stride and reached for the knife inside his shirt. Engelmann saw Hendricks put on the speed, and did the same.

Hendricks closed the gap between him and Leonwood: ten yards, five. He threaded through the crowd like a running back—a quick sidestep, a glancing blow—receiving dirty looks and muttered epithets along the way. Engelmann cut through the crowd as well—like a dancer, or a knife through silk. The ballroom thrummed with agitation. The folks onstage could sense the crowd's distress but didn't know the cause—they stood awkwardly waiting for their cue, sweating through their fineries beneath the stage lights. Leonwood, heart racing as he too sensed the sea change in the crowd, completed assembly of his weapon and began to rise.

Hendricks never saw the waitress coming. He was three feet behind his intended target, who stood in an awkward half-crouch, his hands still hidden, as if waiting for the proper stage alignment to open fire. Hendricks drew his knife, knowing in that moment a stealthy end to Leonwood was no longer in the cards. He had to do something—even if it meant blowing his cover.

The waitress had been serving a group of men to Hendricks's left from a silver platter of crudités and cheese. As Hendricks darted by, she wheeled, and they collided.

An upturned tray. A pretty face, eyes wide with surprise. Crudités everywhere. Dip smearing down the waitress's shirt. Hendricks's training kicked in, and—muscle memory guiding him—he spun away from her and caught the tray before it hit the floor.

That waitress—and that tray—saved Hendricks's life.

He'd grabbed at it with one fluid motion, snatching it from the air like a Frisbee and carrying the motion through while he pivoted around the waitress. The sudden turn brought him momentarily face-to-face with Alexander Engelmann. Engelmann lashed out with the agility of a puff adder—five strikes with his ice pick in the blink of an eye. But he hadn't counted on Hendricks catching the serving tray. The ice pick left behind five dimples in the silver and drove the tray into Hendricks's chest, a far cry from the killing blow Engelmann intended.

Hendricks stumbled backward, confused and off-balance. He took a clumsy swipe at Engelmann with his ceramic knife. The crowd around them tried to scatter, but chairs and tables got in the way.

Leonwood's system jolted with the queasy, invigorating prickle of adrenaline as the fight broke out behind him. Before he could react, Hendricks staggered into him, driving him downward onto the tabletop. But Hendricks couldn't take advantage of the situation—he and Leonwood were back-to-back, and his immediate threat was the man before him with the ice pick.

Which, to the great misfortune of everyone in the room, gave Leonwood a chance to think.

Leonwood had no idea what the fuck the fight behind him was all about. Near as he could tell, it had nothing to do with him. For a moment he even entertained the notion that the guy onstage hadn't spotted him at all, but had instead been reacting to these two brawling shitbags. Then he realized it didn't matter—casino security was gonna be on high alert now either way. Which meant if he wanted to get out of here alive, he'd have to shoot his way out. And that was gonna be one hell of a lot easier before security could lock down the perimeter.

Leonwood might not have been the smartest man, but he was cunning, and good at what he did. He knew his odds of walking out of here weren't stellar. And he also knew deep down that another fall wasn't an option for him. He'd made a lot of enemies over the years—and at his age, he'd no longer be the toughest, meanest bastard on the cell block.

So okay then, he decided: freedom or a bullet—preferably the former. But either way, he thought, I'm putting Purkhiser in the ground.

When Engelmann and Hendricks engaged, Thompson could sense something in the room had changed—but the details of what was happening were unclear thanks to the sound and fury of the frightened crowd.

"The hell's going on down there?" chirped Garfield through her earpiece. "Our guy onstage says there's some kind of scuffle."

"Honestly, I have no goddamn idea," said Thompson. "You still in the dark up there?"

"Yup—we can't see shit past these balloons."

Thompson heard mounting worry in Garfield's tone. Worry and helplessness. She peered over the heads of the scrambling, fleeing crowd, trying to figure out what the hell was going on. She saw the arc of Leonwood's table being upturned, the swing of an elongated barrel brought to bear. Too late, she realized what was happening.

"FBI—everybody on the floor!" she shouted, though in their mounting terror, few listened. Then, to Garfield: "What's above me?"

"What?"

"In the casino—what's above this room?"

Someone on Garfield's end barked an answer, which he relayed. "Nothing. The hotel's over the gaming floor itself. Why?"

Thompson shot twice into the air—deafening in the enclosed space—and suddenly all eyes were on her. "I said everybody on the floor—*now!*" she yelled. This time, some listened. Thompson caught a glimpse of what looked like two men grappling, and Leonwood pressing his gunstock tight to his shoulder—its barrel aimed not toward her but toward the frozen men onstage.

In the fleeting seconds between Engelmann's first strike and Thompson's warning shots, Hendricks and Engelmann were locked in a battle as well-matched as it proved brief. Rare is the knife fight that lasts more than thirty seconds, and even rarer is the knife fight that doesn't leave both participants bloodied.

This fight, despite the skill of its participants, was not so rare as either.

As Hendricks stumbled into Leonwood and rebounded, the silver tray clattering to the floor, Engelmann struck once more. It was his only play, but not a good one. He hoped to take advantage of his quarry's forward momentum, to impale him on the ice pick. But Hendricks kept his head. He blocked Engelmann's jab with an openhanded slap to the rounded side of the pick's steel spike, knocking his opponent's arm wide.

The inside of Engelmann's elbow exposed, Hendricks slashed downward with his ceramic knife, hoping to sever Engelmann's distal biceps tendon and render his attack arm useless. But Engelmann anticipated the attack and blocked it, his left forearm slamming upward into Hendricks's in a white-hot flare of bone-jolting pain.

His arms open, his chest vulnerable, Hendricks was exposed. Engelmann released his ice pick and grabbed at Hendricks's knife hand, held aloft as he tried to drive the knife down against the resistance of Engelmann's block. Engelmann's fingers closed around Hendricks's wrist, and he twisted with all he had, spinning Hendricks around and wrenching his hand upward into a hammerlock.

Hendricks's shoulder dislocated with the sickly pop of a drumstick separating from a turkey, and he screamed. His knife clattered to the floor as his hand went slack.

Engelmann forced Hendricks facedown onto a nearby table, trapping Hendricks's good arm beneath him. He kept pressure on Hendricks's injured shoulder with one hand and held him fast by driving his knee to the small of Hendricks's back. With his free hand, he reached through the open-bottomed pocket of his trousers and slipped his combat blade from its leg sheath.

Engelmann released Hendricks's wrist and grabbed a fistful of Hendricks's hair, yanking back his head. His blade dimpled the tender flesh of Hendricks's neck, its stinging pressure against his Adam's apple heralding the killing blow Hendricks had expected—even, on occasion, wished for—for so long. In that moment, Hendricks realized he'd been mistaken. Much as he'd loathed himself for the things he'd done in the name of God and country, he didn't want to die. Not without balancing his accounts. Not without saving more lives than he had ruined. It was ironic, he thought, that such a revelation only came—maybe only could come—in the instant his demise was certain.

"Goodbye, Cowboy," Engelmann said.

Then, as he began to draw his blade across Hendricks's neck, Thompson fired into the ceiling, and everything Engelmann had worked for went to shit.

25.

W HEN ENGELMANN heard Thompson's warning shots, he tensed. His knife bit at Hendricks's neck, spilling blood across the tablecloth, but neither severing arteries nor puncturing windpipe. Engelmann's head jerked toward the sound, and Hendricks made his move, twisting his body beneath Engelmann and using Engelmann's startled reaction against him. Momentum rolled Engelmann sideways, and he fell backward—one leg still on the floor, the other flashing shoe-tread Hendricks's way.

Hendricks flopped over onto his back, and planted a sharp kick on the side of Engelmann's load-bearing knee. Something snapped, and Engelmann crumpled. As Engelmann headed for the floor, Hendricks snatched a rocks glass from the table with his good arm. Scotch, soda, and chipped ice sprayed a comet trail behind as Hendricks swung the glass with all he had at Engelmann's stunned face. Engelmann tried to throw his hands up to protect himself, but the trajectory of his fall carried his face toward the glass, and his flailing limbs failed to cooperate.

The base of the glass smashed into Engelmann's left eye with a crack of glass and bone. Blood gushed from his eye socket. Hendricks's hand welled red as well, the glass shattering in his grip. Engelmann's one good eye showed nothing but white, and he went down, dead or unconscious, Hendricks didn't know.

That's when Leonwood opened fire.

Thompson heard the muffled *pop pop pop pop pop* of Leonwood's suppressed automatic, and hit the floor. The podium exploded into a thousand wooden shards. The heavy drapes along the wall behind it were sprayed with blood. The crowd—which had instinctively contracted when Thompson fired into the ceiling—now struggled to get away from Leonwood, pushing in every direction but his.

The guard who'd ID'd Leonwood went for his weapon. Leonwood cut him down. The civilians onstage who were too slow or too stunned to hit the deck took rounds to their heads, their chests, their necks. The two guards who flanked the stage tried to draw on Leonwood, too. Both were dead before their guns cleared their holsters. His magazine was empty before the first shell hit the ground.

Her senses alive, Thompson heard the thud of Leonwood releasing his spent magazine, and then a click as he replaced it with a new one. Her nostrils prickled with the smell of the thick carpet scorching beneath the ejected casings.

"Jesus, Thompson—what the hell is going on down there?" Garfield said, worried. "We can't see a goddamned thing!"

"Leonwood just opened fire!" came Thompson's shouted reply.

"You got a shot?"

Thompson crawled toward the nearest table. Its floor-length tablecloth hid her from view but would do nothing to protect her from gunfire if she were spotted. She peered over the tabletop at the melee beyond: the upturned furniture, the broken bodies and shattered glassware, the writhing mass of people trying to flee. She couldn't even *see* Leonwood from where she hid.

"No," she said, despondent. "I've got nothing."

"I'm trying to clear the stage," Garfield said, the strain evident in his voice, "but there's no response on the comm." He shouted to someone off-mic, and then said: "Local SWAT is five minutes out. Hold tight. Stay safe. Help is on its way."

Thompson cringed as Leonwood loosed another volley of gunfire. "These people are sitting ducks," she said.

"Hang on," Garfield replied. "I've got an idea."

Thompson's mind flashed back to North Philly, to the flash-bang grenade. He'd gotten lucky that day.

"Garfield, whatever you're thinking, don't—"

"Relax," Garfield interjected. "I got this."

And then two thousand balloons in every color of the rainbow descended from the sky, blanketing the destruction below.

26.

LEON LEONWOOD hadn't the faintest idea if he'd hit Purkhiser or not. He knew he'd put the three guards down—not the only ones in the room, but the only ones with a line of sight on him, and therefore his biggest threats—and through the bouncing mass of multicolored balloons, he could see a couple bodies facedown on the stage, but he couldn't swear any of them were his target. Which meant he'd have to check.

He had two mags left. Sixty rounds, plus the nine in the throwaway pistol he wore tucked into his pants at the small of his back—a dinky little .25-caliber eight-plus-one that was handy in a pinch but worth shit in a firefight. Suddenly, what seemed before like overkill now threatened to fall short. At this point, a standoff seemed likely—if not inevitable.

He ejected his empty magazine and slid another into

place. Then he toggled his weapon to semiautomatic. Sixty rounds shot one at a time would last way longer than the same count sprayed indiscriminately across the room—long enough to finish Purkhiser, maybe get himself out of here alive.

The balloons were nearly waist-high, or would have been, if they had stayed put. They lighted on furniture and one another, only to take flight once more thanks to the flailing of the frightened and wounded beneath them. They bounced off Leonwood with his every movement as he headed toward the stage, and reduced his visibility to inches. All around him he heard movement—a shift of fabric, a sharp intake of breath. Those fleeing him, he ignored. But some, by either confusion or design, shuffled ever closer or maneuvered themselves directly between him and the stage. Problem was, thanks to the balloons, he couldn't tell if they were security or bystanders until he was right on top of them—and if they proved to be the former, that was too late to react. He'd be caught or killed for sure.

So—his heart thudding and acrid flop sweat beading on his meaty, furrowed brow—Leonwood decided he'd just have to shoot them all.

Michael Hendricks had no idea what the fuck was going on. Last time he saw a mission go so FUBAR so fast, he lost his squad, his fiancée, his whole damn life.

He collapsed, exhausted and bleeding under a layer of balloons, trying to catch his breath. His right shoulder rang with pain, his left hand bled. His face smarted from getting slammed into the tabletop. He tried to put together what the hell had just transpired, but the edges of the pieces didn't seem to match. He'd had Leonwood in his sights.

He'd been blindsided, attacked. That smacked of a setup—but if that's the case, who the fuck discharged their firearm into the ceiling?

And he had *no* idea what to make of the balloon drop.

So where did that leave him? His assailant hadn't stirred since Hendricks had taken the guy down, but that didn't mean he'd stay down; from where Hendricks lay, he couldn't see him past all the damn balloons. He knew he should finish the guy—eliminate the threat, in the parlance of his former military life. But Leonwood was still on the loose. And the place would soon be surrounded by local PD and Feds, if it hadn't been already. God only knew if Purkhiser was still breathing.

Hendricks heard two quick pops—powerful but dulled, an assault rifle with a suppressor. They sounded as though they came from somewhere between his position and the stage. That meant Leonwood was on the move—that he was trying to finish the job.

Purkhiser, Hendricks thought, must still be alive.

That fact shouldn't have mattered to him. If he were half as cold-blooded as he thought he was, it wouldn't have. Even if Hendricks could stop Leonwood from killing Purkhiser, there wasn't a chance in hell he'd ever see a dime of the six million he'd been promised. He'd be lucky if he didn't leave Pendleton's in shackles—or a body bag.

But he'd given his word. So, exhausted and bleeding, Hendricks heaved himself up off the table. He clenched his teeth, and with a sharp intake of breath, he closed his left hand around his right wrist and yanked his shoulder back into place. The effort—and the subsequent solar flare of pain—damn near made him faint.

Once he could bring himself to move again—once he

trusted his trembling legs to hold him up—he began scanning the floor for his knife, willing himself to focus despite the chaos around him. By some miracle, he found it, then picked it up and began pushing through the balloons, heading toward the muffled sounds of Leonwood's continued gunfire.

Eric Purkhiser's mind was blank with terror. His mouth moved in silent prayer. Shredded bodies lay across the stage. The avuncular local politician was frozen midsmile, his blood hot and sticky on Purkhiser's hands and clothes. The burly, dark-skinned security guard with the crew cut was missing half of his head. The weasel-faced casino owner remained relatively unscathed, having taken refuge behind the first wave of the fallen. His pit boss had survived as well, though the bullet wound in his thigh spurted crimson with every beat of his heart, so without help, he likely wouldn't last much longer.

Eric himself had taken some shrapnel when the podium exploded, but had somehow avoided getting shot—possibly because, despite both Hendricks's and Engelmann's assurances, he'd remained tensed for this eventuality since long before he actually took the stage. He'd taken every opportunity to keep the other people onstage between him and the crowd, and he'd hit the ground at the first sign of trouble—which turned out to be Engelmann and Hendricks engaging. It was only in the silence after Leonwood emptied his first magazine that Purkhiser realized he'd survived the initial onslaught—and when that silence was once more punctured by the sounds of gunfire, he realized he had to move.

Still, he couldn't force his mutinous limbs to do his bidding until he saw the sea of balloons that lapped lazily at the shore of the stage part around the grim, determined visage of Leon Leonwood, approaching slowly but with purpose. Somewhere in the distance, law enforcement shouted, and through the flickering of the damaged lights above, Purkhiser saw armored officers positioning themselves on either side of the banquet hall's entrance. But they were too careful to simply storm the room, too concerned at the prospect of spooking a gunman whom they couldn't see. That meant they'd be too slow to save him.

Eric Purkhiser began to crawl.

He made his way across the stage toward the entrance to the service corridors. Leonwood's grease-slicked hair was a shark's fin, parting the balloons as he passed. Occasionally, that hair would halt and a single shot would ring out, silencing some poor soul's cries.

Purkhiser reached the stage door and panicked. Just beside it was a square panel of black plastic, an LED embedded in it shining red. A proximity sensor for an ID badge, to prevent those without badge access from entering the corridor. Purkhiser had no such badge and no such access.

But he knew one of the bodies onstage must.

The casino owner was sure to have one, he thought, but as he scanned the stage for him the man slithered off the edge on the far side, disappearing beneath the balloons and leaving a trail of blood behind.

That left the pit boss and the dead guard. The pit boss was in the center of the stage, maybe ten feet from where Purkhiser lay, propped against the back curtain. The dead guard was closer but lay at the front of the stage, toward Leonwood.

Still on his belly, Purkhiser waved his arms madly, trying

to catch the pit boss's attention. "Hey!" he whispered, as loudly as he dared. "Over here!"

The pit boss's head lolled to one side, and his glassy eyes met Purkhiser's.

"Can you move? With your badge, you and me could get outta here!"

The pit boss removed his hand from the wound on his leg and placed his index finger to his lips. "Shhhh...," he said. Absent pressure, his leg gushed blood. His eyes fluttered, and he was gone.

A scream. A pop. Purkhiser looked up and realized the gunman had nearly reached the stage. Purkhiser scrabbled on all fours to the fresh corpse of the pit boss. He grabbed the man by his lapels and violently patted him down. He checked the outer patch pocket on his suit coat's breast, and the inside pocket as well: nothing. The breast pocket of his oxford contained only a hard pack of Camels and a disposable Bic lighter.

Okay, Purkhiser thought, if it's not in his jacket, then it's got to be in his pants.

He tipped the dead man to one side to check his pants pockets. There—clipped to his belt loop. A retractable key reel, from which the card dangled.

He snatched at it. His hopes fell.

The card was in tatters, a bullet hole clean through it.

He tore it from the man's belt loop anyway, key reel and all. There was a chance it might still work.

Purkhiser found his feet and sprinted for the stage door.

Balloons parted at the foot of the stage, and from them Leonwood's hulking form emerged. His once-slicked-down hair was now half-wild—greasy parentheses framing his sweaty face.

Purkhiser reached the door. Leonwood clambered onto the stage. The former moved with the twitchy panic of a trapped animal, the latter with an almost lackadaisical certainty. He bore Purkhiser no malice—or, at least, no more malice than that which he bore the world. It was simply a matter of fact in his mind that Purkhiser had to die, and he was the one who was going to kill him. So he didn't rush. He didn't fret. He didn't even raise his weapon in threat to halt Purkhiser. He just kept coming.

Purkhiser waved the damaged badge in front of the proximity sensor, the fingers of his free hand lighting on the doorknob so that he could yank it open the second the lock disengaged.

The lock held.

He tried again, more frantically. The light on the sensor stayed red. A third time, with exaggerated care. Still nothing happened. He slapped the badge against the sensor, but it was no use. The card was ruined.

Purkhiser leaned heavily against the door. His legs failed him, and he slid down its cold, steel surface. He saw a blur of checkered gray, the blended fabric taking on a sickly sheen beneath the stage lights, and then Leonwood's shadow fell across him.

Purkhiser closed his eyes. Hot steel pressed against his temple, searing a brand into his skin, but still, he did not move.

"Jesus fucking Christ, have you been a pain in my ass," Leonwood said. A hysterical laugh escaped Purkhiser's lips—he could think of no better eulogy from the universe than that. His bladder emptied. He quaked with fear the likes of which he'd never felt before. It hit him with the force of a seizure.

The barrel tightened against his temple as Leonwood's arm tensed for the shot.

A keening wail rose in Purkhiser's throat.

And then, nearby, a woman said: "Leon, I wouldn't do that if I were you."

27.

THE PRESSURE of the barrel against Purkhiser's temple lessened but didn't disappear. Purkhiser opened one eye—cautious, wary. The woman's words were flint against the last small measure of steel in his heart, sparking hope. She stood just off the right-hand corner of the stage, gun drawn. Given her suit, her expression, and the way she held her gun, she was law. She looked the type to shoot if called upon to do so. She looked as if she wouldn't likely miss.

Leon saw that in her, too, but where Purkhiser found cause for hope, Leonwood found only irritation.

"Bitch, can't you see I'm working?" He turned to face her, his automatic still pressed to Purkhiser's head. His free hand inched toward the .25 at the small of his back.

"Ah, ah, ah," Thompson said. "Keep your hands where I can see them."

Leonwood laughed, and drew the .25 on her. Thompson

flinched but didn't fire—she couldn't risk Leonwood clenching when the bullet hit and killing Purkhiser. "Or what," he said. "You'll shoot? I ain't some fucking moron—I know the only leverage I got is this poor bastard right here, and the fact you know I'll paint the wall with his brain if you try to pop me. So how 'bout we cut the shit?"

"Leon," Thompson said, her voice as measured as she could manage. "You don't want to do this. No one else has to die today. Let's talk this through."

"Lady, maybe you ain't been keeping score, but what I done today no talking's gonna fix." He glanced toward the entrance of the banquet hall, where armored SWAT slinked like living shadows toward the stage. "Hey, you wanna tell your buddies to pull back? That is, unless you'd prefer being carried outta here."

Thompson frowned. "Uh, Garfield—I'm assuming you heard that, right?"

"Loud and clear," rang her earpiece. "And I wish I had better news for you, but our snipers haven't set up yet—they were waiting for the entry team to clear a line."

"Right," she said. Shit. She hoped they had a shot—that they could end this standoff from afar. "Tell our boys to pull back, then."

Garfield gave the order. The shadows receded. Leonwood watched them go, though the barrel of his .25 never faltered—it remained trained on the bridge of Thompson's nose.

When the SWAT team had exited the hall, Leonwood nodded almost imperceptibly, and said to Thompson, "The door." She gave the order, and it swung closed. "Good," he said. "Now lower your weapon."

"You think I'm nuts?"

"Listen, bitch, the only way you're walking out of here is if you put down your fucking weapon. Me and Eric here—"

"Eddie," Purkhiser muttered weakly, only to squeal under the renewed pressure from Leonwood's suppressed barrel.

"As I was saying, me and *Eric* here are going through that door—which, by the way, you're gonna have unlocked for me." He waited a second, staring at the light on the proximity card-reader, which glared red. "Uh, *now?*"

"Unlock the stage door," said Thompson through gritted teeth. The light went green.

"Good," said Leonwood. "Now, what's gonna happen is, you're gonna put down your gun. If you don't, I shoot you both. You and me and Eric are going for a little walk. Unless I'm mistaken—and I'm not—past the kitchens, there's a loading dock. I want a car waiting for us—keys in, engine running. Your people lock us in, I shoot you both. I see any more coppers, I shoot you both. If the car's fucked with in any way, I shoot you both. You get me?"

"Yeah," Thompson said. "I get you."

"Good. Now be a doll and put down your fucking gun."

Reluctantly, Thompson complied. She didn't have much choice. Her best play was to keep him moving, keep him talking, get him out into the open so her people could find their shot.

"Good girl," he cooed. "Only, you wanna know a secret?"

"What's that?"

Leonwood pulled the trigger on the MP5K. A report like a firecracker, and every muscle in Purkhiser's prostrate form contracted at once, then slackened. Blood and brain misted across the heavy backstage door.

As the life left Purkhiser's body, Leonwood swung his miniature assault rifle toward Thompson, now unarmed. When Leonwood had pulled the trigger, she'd nearly gone for her gun, but his pistol—and his gaze—never left her. And now it was too late.

"I know full well you ain't gonna let me walk outta here—and I sure as hell ain't going back to prison. Which means, like it or not, neither of us are ever gonna leave this room."

"Well," said Hendricks, emerging from the balloons to the left of the stage, "you're half right."

By the time he'd spoken the words, the ceramic knife had already left Hendricks's hands. Leonwood wheeled toward him, as Hendricks knew he would. Hendricks's throw was true: the point of the knife caught Leonwood in the Adam's apple, driving hilt-deep before Leonwood could so much as blink.

Hendricks had hoped to sever Leonwood's spine. Hoped, but didn't count on it. That shot would have been one in a million—slipping between or driving through his vertebrae—and Hendricks wasn't quite that lucky. Spewing blood as he fell backward from the force of the blow, Leonwood raised both the MP5K and the .25 at Hendricks and squeezed off a few rounds. Hendricks didn't even flinch. He knew Leonwood's shots would go wide.

Thompson didn't know what to think. She hit the deck, face to floor. As she fell she saw the stranger mount the stage with ease and close the gap between him and Leonwood in three quick strides.

When Leonwood slammed into the stage, he dropped his weapons and grasped weakly at the knife jutting from his throat, blood surging between his fingers. Hendricks crouched over him and watched the light in his eyes die.

"Happy travels, Leon. Maybe we'll meet again in hell."

The whole encounter had taken maybe twenty seconds. Thompson listened, still as death, where she lay. She feared if she moved, she might make herself a target. But when she heard Leonwood's assailant rise and turn to flee, she scrambled over to her gun, which lay to her left. She snatched it off the floor and rolled, meaning to draw down on the new man—the new threat.

But by the time she did, the man was gone.

28.

THE SERVICE HALL was long and bright, with off-white painted cinder-block walls glaring beneath the cheap fluorescent lighting and emergency lights strobing all around. Nice of Leonwood to have the Feds unlock the door for me, Hendricks thought.

There were no cameras that he could see, but all the doors had card-swipes like the door he'd used to escape into the hallway, the lights on their card-readers red. No doubt the female agent's doing, Hendricks thought. Trapping him backstage was a pretty lousy thank-you for saving her life.

Finding the stairwell door among his twenty-odd choices was a breeze: it was the only one marked with an exit sign. Its swipe pad indicated it was locked like all the others. Hendricks dug his fingernails into the seam between the unit's wall-mounted base and the plastic cover protecting its guts, and pried the cover off. Inside was a tangled mess of leads and wires. Lester probably could've hacked the thing in seconds. Hendricks, however, could work at it for an hour with the best tools money can buy, and all he'd likely get for his trouble was electrocuted.

Lucky for Hendricks, there was more than one way through a door.

The door and frame were painted steel. Busting through was not an option. The door handle was a heavy-duty lever-style, not unlike the one he'd just come through. Hendricks examined the brushed nickel plate into which the lever was set, hoping to separate it from the door and expose the mechanism within, but it was flush and well-affixed.

That meant the lever was the weakest link.

Hendricks looked around for something to break it with—a fire ax or an extinguisher. But the hall was bare, the only fire-suppression tools in sight the sprinklers in the ceiling. He considered trotting the length of the hall to see if there was anything of use around the corner, but then they cut the lights, and he knew there wasn't time. He had seconds, not minutes, to make his move.

As he was plunged into darkness, the hall's only illumination the faint, hellish glow of the LEDs reflecting off the glossy walls, Hendricks's hand went instinctively toward the only weapon left in his possession—his penlight zip gun. Some help this'll be, he thought. Not that he had any intention of putting any members of the SWAT team in the ground, but the fact was, if he had a gun, he'd have more plays to make. The threat of violence is often more powerful a persuasion than violence itself—and anyway, a well-placed shot square in the center of a flak jacket might provide him just the opening he needed, while leaving its recipient with nothing more than a couple cracked ribs. But just try to threaten violence with a fucking penlight. The very thing that seemed so clever when Lester built it—the fact that no one would ever suspect it was a weapon—was suddenly threatening to get Hendricks killed.

And then it hit him.

The zip gun might make for a lousy deterrent in the face of imminent violence, but it—and the hollow-point round inside whose raison d'être was to maximize internal damage—might make for a half-decent key.

Hendricks pressed the penlight to the door lever and fired. The shot was deafening in the empty hallway. The handle fell from either side of the door with a metallic *thunk*.

Hendricks was in the stairwell.

It was a narrow old affair, designed for evacuations in the case of fire and the like—poured concrete steps rimmed at the edges with rusted metal, the metal handrail rusted red as well. The air inside the stairwell was kiln-hot and smelled of oxidation.

One landing down, there was an air vent, its cover held fast by two rusted screws—top left and bottom right. The other two holes sat empty, the screws either long gone or never installed in the first place. Hendricks yanked the cover off the vent and tossed it onto the center of the landing. He disturbed the dust and rat shit just inside the vent with both hands and tossed his cowboy hat as far into the ductwork as he could. Then he turned around and headed up the stairs—ignoring the down-arrowed exit signs and their false promise of daylight, of liberation.

Hendricks knew the Feds' playbook in situations such

as these. They'd expect him to panic—to flee. To get as far from the scene as he could before they locked the county down. And they'd respond accordingly. So let them give chase, he thought—as long as it wasn't actually him they were chasing.

Sometimes you survived by the bullet, or by the blade. Sometimes you survived by tradecraft, spotting tails and squashing bugs. But sometimes, survival came down to nothing more than swagger—bluffing big and playing it to the hilt. Problem is, you go all-in on a bluff and someone calls it, you go bust. Which ain't so comforting when it's your life that's on the line.

Hendricks knew he was in deep shit. What he didn't know yet was how deep. He'd been set up—of that much he was sure. The timing of his assailant's attack suggested he hadn't ID'd Hendricks until today—otherwise, why try to take him out in so public a venue? And it seemed clear that Leonwood wasn't in on the scam. A good sign. It suggested that whoever was behind this was operating alone, rather than marshaling the full resources of the Council, who—given that this gig fell into his lap after intercepting their communiqués—were no doubt the ones behind the hit. The fact that his assailant was keeping his cards close to his vest pointed to a freelancer; he was hoarding intel to preserve his value to the organization and ensure they couldn't take care of Hendricks themselves and then kill him, too.

Problem was, Hendricks had no idea who the hell this guy was, or how to find him. And until he did, he remained exposed. Every job would offer his guy another opportunity to bag him. Every communication, every contact point, would place whomever Hendricks was talking to—friends and clients both—at risk.

And that was just the half of it. It wouldn't be long before the Feds found out who Purkhiser really was—if they didn't know already—and looked into his supposed Seychelles account. Hendricks never intended to leave Purkhiser's money in that account. Lester had set it up to automatically transfer to several of Hendricks's other accounts within seconds of deposit, after which he'd close the one that Purkhiser had access to—a fail-safe against Purkhiser double-crossing him. Hendricks had no idea how fast the Feds might chase down that first account, or whether they could trace it to the others. Which meant he'd have to sever ties with *all* his Seychelles accounts—and forfeit any funds within. So not only was there no fucking way he'd see a dime of today's payday, this shit-show of a job actually *cost* him dough.

Wait—today's payday. The result of a surprise reversal on Purkhiser's part, and too big a number for Hendricks to've resisted.

That weasely bastard, Hendricks thought. Purkhiser *knew* that son of a bitch was gunning for me. Purkhiser helped the fucker set me up.

It took the edge off failing to prevent his death, at least.

Now all that was left was getting out of Pendleton's alive.

The hotel's upstairs hallway looked like a high school twenty minutes past the final summer bell: doors left swinging open, detritus scattered about—clothing, bits of trash, a half a turkey club. An ice bucket lay overturned beside one room, ice water bleeding into the carpet, a stack of food-caked plates beside it. Hendricks watched through the wire-crossed safety glass of the fire door for a hundred-count—his cowboy boots in his hands, the concrete warm beneath his stocking feet—before he eased the door open just enough to slip out. He counted another hundred before he actually did so, easing the door closed so it wouldn't echo down the stairwell. He knew SWAT would typically take their time breaching the hallway in which they assumed he was trapped—letting him sweat awhile in the dark to keep him off-balance—but he couldn't discount the possibility that by discharging his zip gun, he'd accelerated their time line. If that had happened, there was a chance they were peering into his decoy ductwork at this very moment and reconnoitering the landings up and down from there as well. He didn't want to give them any reason to turn their cursory search up the stairwell into anything more aggressive. Subterfuge was his only ally in getting out of here.

Hendricks was on the seventh floor. The hotel portion of the Pendleton's casino complex stretched twelve stories high. Hendricks chose the seventh floor for two reasons. One, he knew any systematic search of the building would begin at top and bottom, meeting somewhere between four and nine depending on occupancy, so the middle floors afforded him the most leeway with regard to time. And two, Pendleton's had dome cameras mounted at the end of every hall—not a problem to his left, because the hallway jagged around a corner four rooms down, but a huge problem to his right, where the camera at the end of each hall had a clear shot of the fire door. Everywhere but the seventh floor, that is. On the seventh floor, some member of the cleaning staff had left the utility room door open in his or her haste to flee—even though the shooting downstairs had lasted only minutes, word spread quickly through the

Pendleton's complex, sending patrons and employees alike into hysteria—and the door, prevented from closing by an abandoned cleaning cart, now blocked the camera's sight line to the fire door.

Hendricks had half a mind to leave a tip.

He padded silently through the abandoned hallway— neither slinking nor hurrying, and affecting a look of fright and worry in case anyone was watching his progress through the peepholes in their doors. A good quarter of the doors were open—some wide, some kept ajar by the brass-plated ovals of the interior door latches, protruding from the door frames like bookmarks—but many were still closed, and Hendricks had no way of knowing how many of those rooms were actually occupied.

Hendricks snatched the ice bucket up from the hall, scooping as much of its spilled contents back in as he could manage. He popped his head into every open door he passed, examining at a glance the open closet space in- side like some hard-boiled Goldilocks. Too big. Too small. Too showy. In one case, the dimensions were about right, but he thought the odds of him walking out unspotted in this enormous woman's pink chiffon dress unlikely.

Then, finally, he hit pay dirt.

Once he'd found what he was looking for, he closed the door behind him and threw the bolt. He removed the wad of cash Lester'd sent him—rolled tight and rubber- banded—from his pocket and set it on the nightstand. Then he stripped naked, folding his clothes as flat as he could and placing them between the mattress and box spring.

The room belonged to Norm and Patty Gunderson of Parker, South Dakota. Hendricks knew this because of the

tags on their luggage and the printed Google driving directions on the nightstand. They must have skedaddled in a
hurry, because the TV was still tuned to KMBC's coverage
of the shooting. As Hendricks riffled through their belong-
ings, he couldn't help but feel sorry for them. The suitcase
was filled with patterned polos, iron-creased denims, and
wrinkle-free blouses in a cascade of Easter pastels. The
closet held two pairs of khakis and two dresses as appro-
priate for Sunday service as dinner out. Below them on the
floor was a pair of boat shoes—a little small for Hendricks,
but they'd have to do—and a pair of sensible, low-heeled
pumps. There were no ties, sport coats, or any other indica-
tions of business-wear to be seen.

The Gundersons were on vacation.

Hendricks wondered if they'd ever take another one.

Hendricks padded naked to the bathroom and eyed
himself in the mirror. Nothing I can't work with, he
thought. Sure, his shoulder hurt like hell, and his body was
a road map of bruises, but apart from the cuts drying sticky-
red on his left hand, a half-inch-long knife wound across his
Adam's apple—bleeding, but superficial—and some slight
swelling on his right cheek, his injuries weren't the sort
most folks would notice.

Pawing through Patty Gunderson's dopp kit, Hendricks
found a pair of tweezers. He ran his left hand under the
bathroom tap, rinsing away the drying blood, and found
that although he'd been cut multiple times by the shattered rocks glass, none of the cuts were deep. Carefully, he
tweezed free what few shards of glass remained, dropping
each of them into the trash.

That done, he grabbed a hand towel and filled it with
ice, pressing it to his swollen face until the worst of the

puffiness had receded. A faint dusky smudge streaked below his right eye, riding the tangent of his orbital socket's curve across the meat of his cheek, and would likely darken in the hours and days to come. If that proved the worst of his problems, Hendricks would consider it a win.

The shower stung like needles against his skin, and ran pink from clotting undone. Hendricks scrubbed himself clean and then stood beneath the water until it ran clear. When he was finished, he toweled off gently and disinfected his hand with a goodly helping of ol' Norman's Aqua Velva. It smelled like Hendricks's first foster father— a hard, mean man—and it burned like perdition, but it made a fine disinfectant.

Hendricks filled the sink basin and, with Norm's disposable Gillette, removed the ratty bristle of horseshoe mustache he'd sculpted from his stubble for the job. He used Patty's tweezers again, this time to thin his eyebrows some and change their shape, softening his standard frown from one of determination to one of worry. He eyed his handiwork for a moment and then picked up the razor once more, using it to take his sideburns up to an unfashionable forty-five-degree angle. The end result was a man who looked little like the cocky cowboy who'd sauntered into the casino this morning. A dab of Patty's concealer on the bruise beneath his eye, and his transformation was complete.

All that was left to his plan was to wait. So he sat down on the edge of the tub, a bathrobe tied around his frame, to do just that.

He wasn't waiting long.

The rapping was loud and sharp. Seven in a row, meant not to be ignored.

"That you, Patricia?" Hendricks called, dropping the drawl he'd been affecting in favor of a tone more broadcast-neutral. "Don't tell me you forgot your key again! Well, hold your horses—I'm in the bathroom!"

He splashed some water on his face—avoiding his makeup job as best he could—and grabbed the razor from the vanity. Then he headed for the door. Hendricks had scarcely disengaged the interior lock before the electronic lock buzzed—unlocked from the outside—and the door swung in toward him. Outside was a blazered, khakied mound of flesh with a buzz cut and spiral-wired earpiece—Pendleton's security—and a more compact but no less intimidating man in full-on body armor aiming an automatic rifle at him—FBI SWAT. For a millisecond, Hendricks calculated the odds of taking them grab the SWAT guy's barrel, force the gunstock into his throat, turn the weapon on his cohort once he crumples and releases it—but he dismissed the thought as soon as it flitted through his consciousness. Fighting wasn't going to get him out of here.

So instead, he threw his hands in the air, the razor clattering to the floor, and he let out a not entirely manful scream, cowering at the sight of the gun.

"It's all right, sir—but I'm going to have to ask you to calm down while I search your room. Are you aware, sir, that you're bleeding?"

"What? I—" The security guard gestured to his own neck, and Hendricks echoed his movement as if uncomprehendingly. He touched the knife wound on his neck and acted surprised when his fingers came back bloody. "Oh!" he said. "Oh, my! I was shaving when you two—and then the knocking startled me, and…wait—what do you *mean* you have to search my room? What the heck is going on here?"

The two men shared a glance, and the security guard said, frowning, "There's been an incident. A shooting just off the gaming floor. Can you tell me, sir, who's registered in this room?"

Hendricks backed away from the doorway, feigning terror. "Me and—I mean, N-n-norm and Patty Gunderson," he said. "You think the shooter is up here?"

Another glance at each other, a confirmatory nod, and their features softened. "No," said the SWAT agent. "The shooter's down. But we think he may have had an accomplice. We're just covering our bases," he added, in what he seemed to think was an encouraging tone.

"Was anyone hurt?" Hendricks asked.

No reply. Instead, the two men fanned out inside the room. They checked inside the shower. Under the bed. Behind the heavy curtains.

"Oh, God," Hendricks said, allowing a note of hysteria to creep into his voice, "was anyone killed?"

"Clear," said Security.

"Here, too," SWAT replied. Both acted as though Hendricks wasn't even there.

"Please, you have to tell me—my Patricia is down there! Patricia Gunderson? She—we..." Hendricks made a show of marshaling his wits, and started over. "I had a little too much to drink with dinner last night—my stomach can't handle whiskey like it used to—so Patty thought she'd let me sleep it off awhile while she tried her hand at craps. I prefer cards to dice, myself, and she's got this thing about this being our vacation, like she can't leave my side for more than a trip to the can, you know? I kept telling her, you want to play, go play, but she never listens to me…"

"Uh, sir?" SWAT said, trying to nudge Hendricks back on track.

"Yes. Right. Anyway, I was feeling lousy, so she let me sleep in and headed downstairs herself. Six hours ago, this must've been. You don't think she's hurt, do you? You don't think she's…"

At that, Hendricks began to cry.

"Sir," said Security, "I'm sure your wife is fine. We're going to need you to lock your door and sit tight awhile, okay?"

"Sit tight? *Sit tight?* How do you expect me to sit tight while Patty could be bleeding to death God knows where?" Then, with no small measure of steel: "You have to take me to her. You have to take me downstairs."

"I'm afraid that's not possible, sir." This from SWAT. "We've got a job to do. You wanna help, you're gonna have to stay put until we complete our search."

"*No.*"

A pause. "No?" said SWAT, incredulous. "Are you aware you're defying an officer of the law?"

"So arrest me," Hendricks said. "Shoot me if you want. But please, for the love of God, take me downstairs to find Patty." Though SWAT was resolute, Hendricks saw doubt in Security's eyes and redoubled his efforts. "If you don't, I swear I'll follow you the whole way. You'll be putting me in danger, and Lord knows, I'll slow you down."

That did the trick. Security piped up. "Ah, hell, Cy, what's the harm? Let me take this guy downstairs to find his wife."

SWAT was unconvinced. "You can't abandon me up

here—I need you to open the doors. My team's spread thin enough as it is."

"It's a fucking card key, for God's sake. I think you can manage."

The SWAT agent stepped into the hall and radioed down to his commander. They conversed a second—muttering punctuated by bursts of static. When he returned to Hendricks's borrowed room, he looked irritated. "Fine," he said to the security guard. "Straight down. Straight back." And then, to Hendricks: "Report directly to the holding area—they've set up triage for the victims there, and they're taking a head count of all evacuees. If your wife's been injured or"—he swallowed, searching for the proper euphemism—"otherwise accounted for, they'll know it."

Hendricks's features showed relief. Under the circumstances, it wasn't hard to muster. "Thank you—thank you both so much! I can't tell you how much this means to me." He made for the door, all puppy-dog enthusiasm. The security guard stopped him with a hand to the chest.

"Uh, sir?"

"Yes?"

The guard and agent shared a look, both grinning at the kind if ineffectual man standing before them in nothing but a bathrobe. "Don't you think you ought to put on some clothes first?"

In that moment, Hendricks knew his cover was cemented. These men would pose no problem for him now.

"Clothes! Right!" he said, flashing them a wan smile. He grabbed a pair of underwear, a blue polo with red and white stripes, and a pair of jeans from the Gundersons' suitcase. He hooked the boat shoes with a finger in each shoe back and tossed them and his clothes onto the bed. Then turned his attention to the two armed men. "Uh, fellas? You mind giving me a little privacy?"

The two men turned around, their gazes trailing toward the ceiling. Hendricks dropped his robe and dressed quickly, mindful of the many bruises that blossomed across his taut, scarred warrior's frame. If they'd glanced back, or caught his reflection in the mirror on the wall beside them, all his subterfuge would be for naught.

But they didn't look back. And clothes on—pinching shoes and all—he was Norm Gunderson once more. Loving husband. Hapless guest.

He snatched up his bankroll off the nightstand and stuffed it in his jeans pocket. Then, leaving the SWAT agent to canvass the seventh floor alone, Hendricks and his escort headed toward the elevators.

Toward freedom.

29.

"AGENT GARFIELD? You might wanna get over here. This guy's got some information you're gonna wanna hear."

The triage tent was bustling with activity, makeshift cots overflowing with the dying, injured, and just plain terrified—first responders flitting back and forth like flies among them. Garfield wended his way through it toward the woman who called to him—a cute twenty-something paramedic. A half an hour had passed since the SWAT team had declared the ballroom clear. Nearly an hour since Leon Leonwood was executed by Thompson's so-called ghost— for she and Garfield were certain that's who it was.

Thompson was rattled by her experience in the banquet hall, of course, as well she should've been, having faced down what she thought was certain death. Garfield didn't need the phantom throb of his long-healed bullet wound— a parting present from the Mara chapter he'd worked so hard to infiltrate—to remind him what that was like. He saw it in the worry lines around his eyes every morning in the mirror. He felt it gnawing at his insides every time he went into the field.

The MS-13 Task Force he'd worked for had placed him with the LAPD, posing as a dirty cop with a taste for blow and Salvadoran women, since being useful and corruptible was the only way into Mara for those who weren't full-blooded Salvadoran. Turns out he didn't pose well enough. Even now, six months after the shooting— his wounds healed and the coke habit he'd developed in the line of duty kicked quietly on the Bureau's dime—he felt empty, a hollowed-out version of the man he'd been before.

He had to hand it to his partner, Thompson—she might come across a ballbuster, but even facing down the barrel of a gun today, she kept her wits enough about her to render a full account of what was said, as well as a half-decent description of her ghost. Seemed he fancied himself a cowboy. Anyway, he wouldn't be free to roam the prairie long—word was, SWAT had chased him into the ventilation system and had every access point covered. If he made a move, they'd nab him—and if he didn't, they'd gas him unconscious and go in after him.

Problem was, he only half-believed it. It seemed too pat. Too easy. Not that he could put the feeling into words. But the way his guts were twisted up, it didn't feel like anticipation of the collar. It felt like worry. Like watching the sky for a big-ass second shoe.

Garfield looked the paramedic up and down. Slight, small-boned, dark-skinned: Hispanic or Latina or whatever. Damn pretty, too—nice body, high cheekbones, doe eyes.

She coulda used a touch of makeup, maybe, but then again, she was on the job.

"Special," he said, with as much charm as he could muster.

"Excuse me?" she said.

"The title's *Special* Agent Garfield," he said.

"Special. Right." The look on her face suggested she found him anything but.

Garfield heaved a weary sigh and shifted into business mode. There was a time, before the shooting, when he had game—a cocksure swagger women tended to respond to. But ever since, it was like whatever it was they were responding to had atrophied. "All right, then, whaddaya got?"

"White male, forty-five. Illinois license under the name of Alan L'Engle. Claims he tangled with your perp."

"Leonwood, you mean?"

She flashed him a stern look, as if to say, *No, asshole—I know how to read a fucking memo.* "Not him, the other one. The guy who got away."

"Did he, now. So this fellow's what—some kind of ninja? Because he'd have to be, to go toe-to-toe with a guy like that and just walk away. Unless, of course, he's just some attention-craving whack-job intent on wasting our time."

A long pause—the woman's pretty face unsure. Her tone unsure as well: "Actually, he says he's a librarian." Then she mustered up a fresh helping of confidence and added: "But he didn't just walk away. He got beat up pretty bad. His leg's been splinted, and his face is a swollen mess. I can't say for sure without a doctor checking him out—and some imaging to boot—but my guess is, his ACL is blown, and his orbital socket's cracked, at least."

"Jesus," said Garfield.

"You're not kidding. I spent the last ten minutes picking glass shards out of his cheek—he says your perp hit him with a cocktail glass. He's lucky his eye is still intact—he could have lost it."

"He say why the guy attacked him?"

"No. In fact, the picture he painted, I think it was the other way around."

"Come again?"

"He claims he started it."

Garfield shook his head in disbelief. "Okay, sweetheart, I'm sold—take me to him. No way I'm passing up a chance to meet a librarian who picked a fight with a goddamn assassin."

The woman bristled at his chosen pet name. "My *name's* Sofia. You'd do well to remember it." Then she turned on one heel and set off through the teeming crowd.

"I don't understand," said Engelmann, all furrowed brow and tortured innocence, to the arrogant FBI agent he'd last laid eyes on back in Miami. Frankly, he was surprised to find the man here so soon—it meant they'd had some foreknowledge of today's events. Perhaps he and his partner were more competent than he'd given them credit for, and they had tracked his quarry's movements. Or perhaps that boorish oaf Leonwood had slipped up somewhere along the way, and it was he they'd followed. Either way, Engelmann was glad of this development. After all, he'd failed to complete his mission, and he suspected that despite the Bureau's best efforts, the man might yet escape. Best to enact a backup plan immediately. "Have I done something wrong? I was only trying to help."

"No, of course not, Mr. L'Engle—"

"Doctor," Engelmann corrected for his own amusement. "But please, call me Alan."

"Alan. Sure. As I was saying, Alan, you've done nothing wrong as far as I'm aware—we're simply trying to construct a fuller picture of the day's events. So if you wouldn't mind walking me through what happened..."

"But I already told my tale to the lovely young woman who patched me up," he protested weakly. Engelmann knew this man would be more apt to believe his story if he was forced to work for it.

"And now I'd like you to tell it to me," Garfield insisted.

Engelmann raised his hands in acquiescence. The hook was set. "As you wish."

As Garfield listened rapt, Engelmann wove the tale of Alan L'Engle, reluctant hero—an elaborate braid of half-truths and outright lies. Alan L'Engle, it seems, was in town on business—what business, he never said—and had stopped in at the casino for some gaming and a bite to eat. He'd been handed a free ticket to the Palomera fellow's check presentation, and not having ever seen so large a sum—or so physically large a check—he'd elected to attend. Okay, yes, he admitted sheepishly, perhaps the possibility of winning something for himself at the balloon drop had been part of the event's appeal, but he was loath to admit it, since it seemed an unflatteringly selfish notion. "And anyway," he said—gesturing to his swollen, bandaged face; his mangled, splinted knee—"you can see how well such greed served me."

He'd been nursing a drink—gin and tonic, and a damn fine one at that; it's rare on his librarian's salary he treats himself to Bombay Sapphire—and waiting for the presentation to begin, when he spotted something amiss. An angry-looking man, angling determinedly through the crowd toward the stage, knife in hand. At first, he tried to signal to security, but their attentions were elsewhere, so—foolishly, he realizes now—he attempted to accost the man himself. He cut through the crowd as quickly as he could manage, coming up behind the man and grabbing him by the shoulder. It was clear he startled his attacker, though his startlement sadly did not last long. To this very moment, Engelmann said, he hasn't the faintest notion of what he intended to do once he reached him, but the man rendered any decision moot by attacking him. The man kicked his leg out from beneath him—"breaking something in the process, I fear"—and smashed a glass into his face.

"And I think he would have killed me, too," Engelmann concluded, "had that other fellow not started shooting. Then the balloons fell, and he fled. Shortly after, I lost consciousness. When I came to, he was gone."

"Do you think you could describe this man to a sketch artist, Alan?"

"I think so," he said, "although I may be able to do you one better."

"How's that?" Garfield asked.

"When I came to, I spotted these." He removed a handkerchief from his pocket and handed it to Garfield. It rattled as Garfield took it.

"Careful," Engelmann said.

Garfield unwrapped the kerchief. In it were three curved triangles of glass. "I don't understand," he said. "What exactly am I looking at?"

Engelmann smiled and puffed his chest out with pride. "Those are pieces of the glass he hit me with," he said. "I collected them off the floor before the paramedics brought me out here, because I thought there might be prints or DNA on them, like in the movies, and I worried they might be trampled. I hope it's all right that I moved them—I didn't handle them directly."

He more than thought there might be prints on them; he'd inspected the shards carefully, and—given that the prints were made in blood—he knew damn well they were his quarry's. He didn't worry about them pulling his own prints or DNA from the glass—they wouldn't find either in any database. But his intel on his quarry—and his first-hand assessment of his fighting style—indicated the man was former military, which meant he likely *was* on file. He hoped he was right in that regard, because that assumption represented his last chance to take down his quarry before the Council elected to do the same to him.

"Huh," Garfield said. "Gimme a minute, would you?"

Garfield stepped away from Engelmann's cot, but not so far away that Engelmann could not hear. Into his radio, Garfield barked, "I got a line on ID'ing our guy. Some evidence in need of processing. This could be the break that we've been waiting for—I need a crime scene tech here on the double."

That done, Garfield talked to the pretty young paramedic, and to two uniformed police officers as well. Then he returned to Engelmann's bedside.

"Listen, Alan, you've been a big help. If you don't mind, I'd like to send you along to the hospital now to get you patched up. Ms. Alvarez and these two officers are going to ride with you."

"Of course," Engelmann said. "I'm not in any danger, am I?"

"No, no, no," said Garfield, not entirely convincingly. "Nothing like that. But you've had one heck of a day, and your testimony may prove just the break we need—I'd like to repay you by ensuring you're well taken care of."

"That's very kind of you, Special Agent Garfield. Honestly, I'm not sure what I've stumbled into here, but I'm not ashamed to say I think it's more excitement than I care for."

Though Garfield knew the man had simply read off his ID, which was at present on a lanyard around his neck, he smiled at the use of his proper title. Engelmann smiled as well. He knew the seed he'd sown had taken root. All that was left to do was give it time to grow, and then he'd reap his reward.

As they hoisted him onto a rolling stretcher and wheeled him toward the waiting vehicle, he unfastened the buttons on his filthy periwinkle-checked shirt and reached his right hand inside, as though massaging a knot, or checking his ribs for bruises.

"Are you all right, sir?" asked the pretty paramedic, Alvarez. "Something you'd like me to look at?"

"I'm fine, dear," he replied, fingering the Ruger LC9 hidden in his concealment holster. "In fact," he said, as she and the two officers loaded him into the ambulance beneath lights flashing red, slamming shut the doors as they climbed inside behind him, "I believe my day is finally looking up."

30.

THE ERSATZ Mr. Gunderson and his security escort—whose name, Hendricks learned, was DeShaun—rode in silence down the elevator toward the gaming floor, the day's events rendering small talk impossible and leaving grim glances and awkward shuffling in its place.

Hendricks watched the floors tick by, hope and fear playing tug-of-war with his guts. When the count reached one, the floor rose to meet him—and made Norm's boat shoes pinch. Then the doors slid open with a ding so cheery it seemed sarcastic, and Hendricks's worries, aches, and pains evaporated—or, more accurately, were rendered so unimportant as to go unnoticed.

The gaming floor had been transformed into a war zone.

The comparison wasn't an idle one: Hendricks was a man familiar with combat. In his time in Afghanistan, he'd seen his share of bombed houses and burned-out cars, men once warriors wailing at their wives and children being reduced to so much charred meat. Collateral damage, the reporters back home called it, as though it were a side effect, or some minor and acceptable transgression. A sanitary term for a modern war. But war wasn't sanitary, and war wasn't modern. It was bloody and it was savage. And looking into the tear-filled eyes of those left with nothing but their grief to cling to, Hendricks had learned the lesson so few back home could grasp: *no* damage was collateral. Every limb lost, every hovel burned, every wife left husbandless, and every child orphaned created ripples of anger and resentment. Create enough of them, and we'll one day wind up with a wave that will wash us off the map.

Leonwood had created his share this day.

And by not stopping Leonwood in time, Hendricks had, too.

The gaming floor was nearly empty, but far from quiet. Though no one was there to play them, banks of slot machines clanged and whirred and called out to nonexistent passersby like the soulless, faceless carnival barkers they were. Balloons, some speckled red, drifted past on AC currents, a morbid parody of good cheer. Broken glasses, cocktail napkins, and upturned buckets spilling chips were everywhere, though those shell-shocked few who zombie-walked among them were too dazed and horrified for opportunism to kick in. A few bodies lay akimbo on the ground, ashen and unattended to, the living taking priority over the dead. Armed men were stationed throughout the massive room—some stock-still beneath their flak helmets, hands resting on their gunstocks, while others ushered the crying wounded toward the massive lobby doors.

Hendricks watched awhile from inside the elevator,

stunned into immobility. He didn't understand at first how so many could be hurt—the shooting had taken place in an enclosed banquet hall, not on the gaming floor—but then a woman with a sticky purpled bruise on her upper arm staggered past, and he recognized the imprint of a sneaker tread.

These people had trampled one another.

Leonwood had opened fire and started a stampede.

When the elevator doors began to close, Hendricks realized DeShaun no longer stood beside him. He'd stepped out when the doors first opened and was now looking back at Hendricks expectantly, a hand extended to prevent the door from shutting all the way.

"I'm sorry," he said. "I forgot you hadn't seen this yet. I should have warned you. You okay?"

"I'm fine," Hendricks said weakly, not sure if his tone was an affectation for his cover's sake or not. He cleared his throat and tried again: "I'm fine."

"C'mon, then. Let's go find your wife."

Together, he and DeShaun traversed the gaming floor— oddly brothers now, it seemed, bonded by the horrors that surrounded them. They stopped to help a man with a bleeding gash through his eyebrow—DeShaun blotting at the injury with the sleeve of his Pendleton's sport coat, Hendricks linking elbows with the man to lead him back to daylight. When they stepped outside into the covered drop-off circle, the man was taken by an EMT to God-knows-where.

After a moment's consultation with a uniformed cop, DeShaun indicated a makeshift pen to one side of the parking lot—two ambulances and a couple hundred people contained inside. "They've set up a sort of nerve center over there, where evacuees not badly injured can check in and find each other. I'm sure your wife will be there."

"Thank you," said Hendricks—and he meant it, too. Never mind that he was lying to this kid, or that he was painfully aware of the two dozen news cameras aimed his way as they ambled over to the barricade. The cameras were still some distance off—kept at bay by police tape patrolled by what must have been half of Kansas City's uniformed PD—but Hendricks wasn't fooled. They were close enough to pick him up just fine. A pretty picture for his growing file, perhaps, provided the Feds elected to confiscate the footage. He did his best to look away.

When they reached the penned-in area, they were greeted by an FBI agent in an agency windbreaker and aviator sunglasses, her dirty-blond hair pulled through the back of her matching agency baseball cap. She and DeShaun exchanged a solemn nod, after which DeShaun placed his hand briefly on Hendricks's shoulder—a simple if heartbreakingly kind gesture of goodwill and reassurance.

Hendricks's eyes met the agent's, or tried. Proper eye contact is key to selling any con—too little and the mark reads the swindler as shifty, too much and he comes off overeager and creepily intense. But with the woman's eyes hidden behind two reflective slabs of glass, her stare was cold and alien and gave up nothing of her receptiveness or her intentions. Hendricks felt exposed, uncertain—a feeling only bolstered by the three dozen sets of eyes amid the milling, haggard crowd that turned hopefully toward him, only to drop away, disappointed, as they realized the new arrival was not the one they waited for.

"Name?" the agent asked, her pen hovering above the

clipboard in her hand. Hendricks glanced down at it and saw two lists: one printed and dotted with check marks—no doubt the hotel registry; one scrawled on a scrap of loose leaf—the day-trippers for whose visit there was no record, Hendricks supposed. He wished his cover allowed him to claim membership in the latter camp, whose identities were harder to confirm—but DeShaun still lingered within earshot.

"Gunderson," Hendricks said quietly—hoping neither Patty nor Norman was close enough to hear.

The woman scanned her list. Her earpiece crackled loudly. Then she looked at him as if for the first time, her glasses bouncing his own image back at him in duplicate. "I'm sorry," she said, frowning—distracted or suspicious, he wasn't sure. "What was the name again?"

Hendricks's heart pounded in his chest. His mouth went dry. A ripple of unease spread through the crowd. He wondered if its source was Patty Gunderson. If she'd just told the folks around her the man at the gate was an impostor.

"Gunderson," he repeated. He felt his fight-or-flight response kick in and readied himself to make a run for it if it proved necessary.

Then he realized the guard's distraction and the crowd's unease had nothing to do with him. All the nearby emergency responders' radios had crackled to life at the same time—the gate agent's included. Seconds later, half the cop cars on the security perimeter lit up and took off at once.

The agent in front of him stood with the index finger of her writing hand held to the earpiece in her ear as though straining to hear what was being said—or perhaps simply not believing it. As Hendricks watched, she dropped her clipboard and her pen. Her left hand went to her neck and worried at the gold cross she wore around it.

"What happened?" Hendricks asked.

"There's been some kind of accident," she said. "One of the ambulances leaving the scene. They were escorting a patient, when…" She trailed off, her sentence lost somewhere in the middle distance with her gaze.

"An accident," Hendricks echoed. It was clear to him from her reaction that whatever happened had been anything but.

"They…they didn't make it to the hospital. Two officers, the driver, and an EMT."

"And the patient?" Hendricks prompted, afraid he already knew the answer. "What happened to the patient?"

"He's gone," she said, anger strengthening her tone. "But he won't stay that way. Not for long."

About that, Hendricks thought, she was right—but not in the way that she meant.

He was sure the man in question was the one who'd tried to kill him. That Hendricks had failed to finish him as he'd so foolishly hoped. That he'd somehow bluffed his way onto that ambulance and then murdered his way out of it.

And that now that this man had Hendricks's scent, he wouldn't stay gone for long.

31.

J ESUS CHRIST," breathed Garfield. "This was no fucking accident."

The intersection of Campbell and East 22nd was a mess of pebbled glass and sundered metal, with splashes of crimson all around. Local PD had set up a wide perimeter around the scene—a small act of kindness to any pedestrians who might happen by. Not many did. Campbell and East 22nd crossed in the short stretch between the highway overpass to the east, and the gentle rise of Hospital Hill to the west—a squat, unattractive no-man's-land of overgrown, chain-linked vacant lots, low-slung yellow-brick commercial buildings, and satellite parking for the rambling medical complex that sprawled across ten city blocks.

The ambulance lay on its side in the center of the intersection, resting at a diagonal to the right angles of the streets. The driver was facedown in a pool of his own blood some twenty yards from where it sat—thrown by the force of the crash, Garfield thought at first. But the windshield, though fractured, was intact, and when he examined the man, he found his back riddled with bullet holes, as if he'd run and been gunned down.

Garfield circled the ambulance, its undercarriage still warm enough to raise a sweat on his brow as he passed. As he reached the back, he saw the left-hand—now bottommost—rear door was open, gravity keeping its right-hand mate closed. Across it lay the remains of the pretty young EMT Garfield had tried to flirt with—Sofia, he recalled. "You'd do well to remember it," she'd told him, though looking at her now—arms extended, fingernails split against the sun-bleached blacktop as though she'd tried desperately to escape, her head a pulpy mess thanks to a couple close-range gunshots—he failed to see how the knowledge did him any good.

Garfield crouched beside her. One glassy eye devoid of life stared vaguely in his direction. He resisted the urge to close it. Doing so would only serve to contaminate the crime scene. A glance past her into the ambulance showed a mess of upturned medical equipment amid which lay two crumpled uniformed officers. One's face was gone—shot clean through, a hollow concave like a gore-filled watermelon left behind. The other took two to the chest, but must have kept on ticking, because he'd also been choked with what looked to be some kind of handmade garrote— his face gray-blue, his lolling tongue purple, his eyes bulging and splotched red from burst vessels.

There was no sign of the patient they'd been transporting. Of Garfield's witness.

Garfield cursed again. Looked away.

A black-and-white stopped alongside him. The back door opened. A haggard-looking Charlie Thompson stepped out. "What've we got?" she asked, her voice suggesting exhaustion so profound, she was beyond the capacity of registering any further surprise.

"A fucking mess is what we've got. Both cops and EMTs are dead, and our witness is missing. Guess your ghost just jumped a couple spots on our Most Wanted list."

"How do you figure?" she asked.

"Ain't it obvious? We had a witness who'd laid eyes on the guy—tangled with him, even—and he knew it. So he somehow gave our boys the slip at the casino and came here to take our witness out."

Thompson shook her head. "Doesn't track," she said. "Witness or not, we had eyes on my ghost already—*my* eyes. He could have killed me in the banquet hall and didn't. And I can't have been the only other soul to see him—once our questioning of the casino patrons is complete, there'll be a few more folks who did. Not to mention, the whole damn building's wired for video, which means some camera somewhere must've captured him. So going to all this effort just to kill one witness of many doesn't make a load of sense. Besides, even if he wanted to, how'd he beat them here to make his play? They were in an emergency vehicle traveling at speed with the benefit of lights and sirens. No way he could have gotten here ahead of them."

"Okay, then, Matlock—what do *you* think happened here?"

"Matlock was a lawyer, dumbass—if you wanna play all snide, at least get your reference right." Her comeback was a reflex, and she regretted it as soon as she said it. Garfield's prick-mode was a defense mechanism, nothing more, and she should know better than to rise to the bait. Particularly when she was about to make his day a whole lot worse.

"I think your so-called witness did this," she said. Garfield made to object, but Thompson overrode him. "We know he tangled with my ghost and lived. And we know my ghost's job didn't go as planned. He meant to get to Leonwood before Leonwood got to Palomera—that much he made clear in the banquet hall. So my guess is, your witness was, in fact, here to get my ghost—to kill him, I mean. Only my ghost got away."

Garfield paled. "No—it had to be your guy. It *had* to."

"I'm sorry," she said, not unkindly, "but it wasn't."

"You can't know that for sure," he said. He looked away from her, toward the lights of the medical complex.

"I can, Hank," she said. "I do. And you would, too, if you weren't so blinded by what you'd prefer to see."

"The hell're you talking about?"

"The shots," said Thompson, nodding toward the up-turned vehicle. "They came from inside the ambulance."

As her words sunk in, Garfield sat down hard on the pavement. He felt dizzy. Sick. Worthless. He was complicit in these deaths—an accessory, an accomplice. He'd given the bastard an escape route. Practically marched him past the barricades. He knew he'd never forgive himself for what he'd done.

The bass-drum thud of an approaching helicopter roused him slightly. A news chopper, likely peeling off from the swarm that hovered over Pendleton's like blowflies over carrion when they caught wind on their scanner of yet another juicy morsel for their never-ending misery buffet just down the road.

"Hey!" Garfield called to one of the uniforms manning

the cordon. "Get them out of here, would you? This is a crime scene."

"Actually, sir, dispatch just patched them through—they said there's something the agent in charge should see!"

Thompson and Garfield exchanged a glance, and then both took off at a run for the officer. Garfield's legs were longer, his soul more desperate in that moment for a win, and he beat his partner there. When he grabbed the radio, he didn't bother to identify himself, instead saying: "Tell me you people have eyes on the guy who did this."

"Wish we did!" came the shouted, radio-garbled reply.

"Then why're you calling?"

But their answer didn't make any damned sense. Garfield asked them to repeat it, assuming he'd simply misheard, but he hadn't. They'd said, "There's something written on the ambulance."

Garfield and Thompson trotted back over to the up-turned wreck. After a moment's hesitation while she considered scaling it herself, Thompson laced her hands together and offered them to Garfield. He placed a foot inside, and Thompson hoisted him up. He clambered awkwardly onto the skyward-facing side panel of the ambulance and was faced with letters, upside down and three feet high—letters scrawled in blood.

He tilted his head. The message resolved. Garfield read it along with several hundred thousand viewers at home—to say nothing of the millions who'd see it that night when the story of the day's events went national:

BE SEEING YOU, COWBOY.

32.

MICHAEL HENDRICKS crouched in darkness beside a red-brick foursquare on a quiet suburban street, hidden between its porch and an azalea bush. The night sky was full of stars. The air had taken on the sort of chill that always struck Hendricks as summer's death knell. His breath plumed. His muscles ached. His shoulder throbbed dully in time with his heartbeat.

The metal cover on the outdoor electrical outlet clacked loudly when he opened it. He winced and glanced toward the window to his left. But no one inside noticed. The children suggested by the swing set out back had long since gone to bed. The couple who owned the place were glued to CNN, which was broadcasting helicopter footage of the message left for him in blood. But although it held their interest, it was nothing for them to worry about. It had happened almost four hundred miles away.

Once the call about the ambulance came in, the Feds were forced to reallocate their resources to search both the hotel and the neighborhood surrounding the crash site, which left local PD and Pendleton's security in charge of wrangling the frightened casino patrons. It was easy enough to slip past the barricades.

Hendricks knew he'd be likelier to escape suspicion if he weren't traveling alone, so he'd cozied up to an octogenarian gambler who'd been separated from the rest of her senior-center tour group. He bummed a Windbreaker from a kind stranger on her behalf, which, once zipped, hid her neon-yellow GAMBLIN' GRANNIES T-shirt. She was grateful for it, because the temperature was dropping, but when he offered to help her find her friends, she balked.

"Son," she said, "I'm old, not stupid—and you don't want no such thing." Her tone was sharp enough to chastise, but she was smiling when she said it, and her suspicion was of a benign sort. It was clear she wasn't afraid of him—why would she be, when he'd already been cleared by the agent at the gate?

Hendricks smiled, too. "You got me," he said. "I'm just tired of standing around. Plus, my girlfriend must've seen the news by now, and I've got no way to tell her I'm okay. You wanna help me get outta here so I can let her know I'm not dead?"

"Sure," she said, "but it'll cost you."

"Excuse me?"

"You heard me, young man. I left eighty bucks in chips on the table when they made me leave, and Lord knows these yahoos ain't gonna give it back. So if you can make it right, I'll help you get back to your little lady-friend."

"You want me to *pay* you?"

"Damn right I do. You're lucky I didn't ask you for double. I expect I-ain't-dead whoopee's great. And if you want some, you're gonna hafta pay the piper."

Hendricks laughed and took his bankroll from his pocket. The old lady's eyes went wide. He peeled off two hundred even and handed it over.

"Shit," she said—though it came out more *SHEE-it*—"I shoulda gone higher. You must be one lucky sumbitch."

"You don't know the half of it," Hendricks said.

But as sarcastically as he'd intended that, he *was* lucky in one respect: Lorraine—this was the woman's name—went from mark to coconspirator in the time it took her to pocket Hendricks's payoff.

She's the one who hatched the plan. She'd toddle, addled, up to the greenest officer they could find. Hendricks—the doting grandson—would follow close behind, apologizing for her sorry state; she gets confused when she hasn't had her medicine. It's at home, and hours past due. No, they wouldn't need a ride: Hendricks's car was in the garage at the edge of the lot. That part was true, not that it mattered—Hendricks had no intention of returning to his rental car, for fear it had been burned.

Lorraine played it to the hilt, and the kid bit so hard he might've cracked a tooth. Hendricks had to suppress a laugh when the officer slid aside a panel of steel barricade just wide enough to let them pass, and Lorraine shuffled through, arms out like a blind man's, headed back toward Pendleton's.

Hendricks trotted after and, with affection not entirely faked, gently turned her around so that they faced the outer lots and the parking garage beyond. Then they strolled arm-in-arm into the distance.

They entered the parking garage just for show and exited the other side, out of sight of the casino. It was there they parted ways. "You sure you'll be all right?" Hendricks asked her. He was reluctant to strand her so far from her group, in the vast commercial stretch that surrounded the Pendleton's grounds.

"I ain't an *invalid*," she replied. "I've got a cell phone, and thanks to you some spending money, too. I'm gonna call a cab, and I'm gonna have him take me to Winstead's for a bacon cheeseburger and a chocolate malt. I'm convinced that low-fat crap they feed us at the home don't actually make you live longer—all those years of not being able to taste your food just makes it *feel* that way. I'll cab it back when I'm good and ready."

Hendricks smiled and peeled another hundred off his roll for her. "In case you ever feel the need to break out for a decent meal again."

"You're a dear. You care to split that cab?"

"That's all right," he said.

She looked appraisingly at him a moment. "Take care of yourself, would you?"

"I will try."

Lorraine pecked him on the cheek, and Hendricks set out walking, heading south until he hit the Missouri River, then following its lazy eastward arc until he disappeared from Lorraine's sight.

Hendricks walked for miles in Norm Gunderson's godawful, pinching boat shoes before he came across a set of railroad tracks. He knew the Feds would be covering all passenger rails out of town, as well as airports and rental-car companies, but that was fine by him, since he didn't plan on availing himself of any of those. He followed the tracks until they crossed a roadway, then waited for a freight train to roll by. It wouldn't take long, he reasoned—Kansas City was a major shipping hub, servicing freight carriers both local and national—and he knew that trains crossing streets were required to slow. He waited just beyond the intersection in a shallow ditch, shielded from view of the street by a stand of trees. An hour later, his waiting paid off, and he climbed onto an empty cargo car headed for Peoria—not that Hendricks knew that until he'd arrived.

The last thing he wanted was to tangle with a railroad cop, so when the squeal of brakes indicated they were approaching their destination, he hopped off the train, rolling as he landed to cushion the blow. Then he walked—filthy, stiff, exhausted—into town.

Hendricks's first priority was to call Lester. He hadn't dared from Kansas City, because he assumed the Feds were monitoring traffic through all the local cell towers—and by the time the train had taken him far enough away to chance it, his burner phone was dead.

His charger was in the rental car he'd left behind. That was okay—cell-phone chargers were easy to obtain; the lost-and-found bins in every coffee shop in the country were full of them. He made three stops before he found one that fit his burner. The girl behind the counter eyed his filthy clothes suspiciously and seemed dubious when he said he'd been in earlier, so he decided not to stay to charge his phone. Instead, he wandered around the adjacent neighborhood until he found a spot with an outlet private enough to suit his needs.

Hendricks plugged in the phone. It booted up. Lester answered on the first ring.

"Jesus, Mikey, are you all right? I've been going outta my head!"

"I'm all right," Hendricks said, his voice just above a whisper. "Barely."

"What the hell happened out there? The news says Leonwood went on a rampage."

"I fucked up, Les. I didn't get to him in time. I was jumped before I got the chance."

"By who?"

Hendricks sighed. "I wish I knew."

"This the guy who left the message on the ambulance?"

"Yeah," Hendricks replied.

"I thought that mighta been directed at you," Les said. "Gave me hope you were still kicking."

"What's the press saying about the guy?"

"Nada. Official story is, he's an accomplice of Leonwood's."

"I don't think Leonwood knew any more about him being there than I did."

"You want me to do some digging? Maybe poke around the Feds' system? I could see how much they've got on you, while I'm at it."

"No," Hendricks said. "It's not worth the risk. As good as you are, Les, you can't make me disappear from Pendleton's security-cam footage, and it's too late for that anyway. By now, my picture's probably been circulated to every airport, train station, bus terminal, and rental car agency from Colorado to Kentucky. But there's no way they've got my name, since as far as Uncle Sam knows, I'm dead and buried. Which means right now, there's nothing that connects this fucking mess to you; the last thing you should do is stick your neck out and change that."

"Let me hook you up with a new ID, at least."

"What's the point? My face will still be the same. Don't worry about me—I can make my own way home. I've been through worse than this."

"But this dude's still out there, hunting you."

"All the more reason for you to keep clear. Whoever this guy is, Les, he's bad news—I don't want you on his radar. Promise me you'll lie low until I get back."

"Aw, listen to you, all cute and worried-like. We're gonna hug it out when you get home."

"Sure," Hendricks said. "Then, when we're done, we're gonna find this guy and end him."

Hendricks disconnected the call and left the phone in the bushes to recharge. Then he looked around for somewhere to lie low and get some sleep. He found a boat out back, behind the house—a twenty-footer that looked like it hadn't seen the water for a couple years. He undid a couple snaps on its canvas cover and crawled inside. It was musty but dry, and the tiny cabin had cushioned benches.

Tired as Hendricks was, he dropped off almost immediately. As he slept, he dreamt of dying. Of rebirth.

And as the sun crested the horizon to the east, Hendricks awoke and braced himself for the long journey home.

33.

T HE BLONDE AT the bar wasn't Garfield's type.

Big, fake basketball tits. Dime-store acrylic nails. Brown roots showed beneath her peroxide locks, and a quarter acre of spray-tanned skin bracketed either side of her tube-top-and-miniskirt combo. At first, he couldn't tell if she was even winking at him, or if the gobs of mascara that made her lashes look like gothic Venus flytraps had gummed up, hindering her ability to reliably open both eyes. But Garfield had struck out with the first two women he'd approached, and this DC dive bar didn't boast a lot of prospects at one thirty in the afternoon. Turned out this chick had a fondness for whiskey and men with badges, so he figured she was as good as he was gonna do.

Garfield and Thompson had been summoned back to DC late last night. They spent all morning in the director's office. A debrief, he called it. It felt more like a dressing-down.

The director called the Pendleton's disaster—his phrase—their biggest clusterfuck since Waco. Said the balloon drop—which had popped up in shaky cell-phone footage on YouTube and gone viral—made a mockery of the Bureau. Said Congress would likely have his head for his agents letting a suspect escape.

Thompson did her best to deflect the director's ire, pointing out Pendleton's was her op, but it was clear Garfield was largely to blame for what had happened—and anyway, she was ahead of the rest of the Bureau on her ghost, which made her valuable. By the time they broke for lunch, Garfield was pretty sure he was on his way to being scapegoated, and he couldn't stomach the thought of spending the next four hours playing party to his own professional demise. So he told Charlie he needed to step out for some air and set out walking until he found a place that looked as shitty as he felt to drink his lunch. He eventually found a romantic prospect bleak enough to match.

"Lemme see your gun," she slurred, her breath whiskey-sweet and tinged with a bitter menthol bite.

"Maybe later," he replied. His cell phone buzzed in his pocket. It was his partner texting him for what must have been the tenth time this afternoon. He ignored it and returned his attention to his drunken companion.

She leaned in close. Large pores caked with makeup loomed before his drunken gaze. "Aw, c'mon," she said. Her hand ran up the inside of his thigh.

Garfield tossed back his drink and closed his eyes. It was a gesture of self-loathing more than anything, but she mistook it for pleasure and slid her hand up farther. "That ain't my gun," he said.

"Coulda fooled me," she said. "How 'bout we head back to your place, and you can at least show me your cuffs?"

Garfield looked at this woman—whose name, he realized, he'd never caught—and then around the bar, wondering idly at his chances of scoring something less likely to leave a rash. If she noticed, she didn't let on that she cared.

Garfield snapped and wagged his fingers at his empty glass, and hers as well. The barkeep poured Beam straight for each of them without a word. "Fuck it," said Garfield, a glass in his hand and a strained grin on his face. She clinked with him, they tossed back their drinks, and then they staggered out of the bar together, Garfield grimly resigned to do just that.

Charlie Thompson stood in the bustling hall of the Hoover Building, thumbing another desperate message into her phone. They were supposed to be back in the director's office forty minutes ago, but Garfield was nowhere to be found. Thompson had begged the director for a brief delay, claiming aspects of the investigation needed tending to. He agreed—reluctantly—to extend the lunch break another half an hour. As it stood, she was officially ten minutes late.

"Charlie!" came a voice from down the hall. Thompson looked up to see her supervisor, Assistant Director Kathryn O'Brien, walking briskly toward her. She wore a crisp gray suit, a white silk blouse, and heels. Her hair was swept into a bun that suggested authority without tipping to severity. "I was hoping I'd catch you."

"You barely did. I'm supposed to be back in with the director now."

"How's it going in there?" she asked, her hand lightly touching Thompson's elbow, a subtle kindness.

"The only way it could, I guess—which is to say, not well. There are twenty-three people dead. One of them doesn't seem to've existed before two years ago, which suggests he was in Witness Protection. Another was his shooter. And four of them were first responders, escorting what they thought was a witness to the hospital. There are seven people in intensive care who're touch-and-go—nearly one hundred injured in total. My ghost is in the wind. Ditto the guy who tangled with him. I can't blame the director for being pissed."

"Pissed, yes, but not at you. You were ahead of the curve on this new hitter, Charlie, and Kansas City would have been even worse had you not been there. No one blames you for what happened."

"Thanks," Thompson replied. "I just wish the same could be said of Garfield."

"I'm surprised to hear you come to his defense."

"He's my partner. And for all his bluster, he's not a bad guy. He was trying to do good out there, the same as me."

"Where is he, by the way?"

Thompson shrugged. "I wish I knew. He disappeared over an hour ago, and he's not answering my texts. I'm worried about him; he's been a wreck ever since the op went sideways."

"Yeah," said O'Brien, "he's not the only one."

Thompson felt a stab of guilt when she saw tears brimming in O'Brien's eyes. The air between them was charged with the buried tension of words unspoken, like power lines beneath the earth. Thompson opened her mouth to reply—but just then, a crowd of suits jostled past. When they disappeared around the corner, it was O'Brien who broke the silence—her voice quiet, fragile, tremulous.

"You scared me half to death, you know. Reports from the scene were sketchy. I knew you were inside. I didn't know until hours later you made it out again. For a while, I thought I'd lost you."

A tear spilled over, cutting a trail through O'Brien's makeup. Almost without volition, Thompson raised a hand to brush it away. "I'm sorry," she said. "Things were crazy. I didn't think."

"Goddamn *right* you didn't think," O'Brien said. "You couldn't have called in?"

"You're right," Thompson said, her voice breaking. "I should have."

They'd been together for six months now—the happiest six months Thompson could remember. She hoped that Kate felt the same. Times like this, she thought Kate might.

It was Charlie who'd insisted on keeping their romance a secret. Kate wanted to tell the world. But Charlie had always kept her romantic life separate from her career— not that it stopped the whispers and the dyke jokes from Garfield and his ilk. Chatting about relationships is so common among coworkers that the absence of such talk creates a void quickly recognized.

It's not that she was ashamed of who she was—far from it. If the woman she loved were anyone but her direct superior, she wouldn't give two shits what a few loudmouthed misogynists thought. But she'd worked hard to excel in the male-dominated Bureau, and she didn't want a soul to think she'd done so on anything but her merits.

"Does your family know that you're all right?" O'Brien asked.

Thompson nodded. "I talked to Jess a couple hours ago. Asked her to call Mom and Dad for me. You know what they think about me being in the field—I didn't have the energy to get into it with them."

"Have you eaten?"

It was sweet of her to ask, Thompson thought. After twenty-four years of looking after Jess, it was nice to have someone look after her for a change. "Not really. I had a candy bar from the machine a few hours ago."

"In that case, when you're done here, we'll do dinner at my place. I'll cook." Charlie raised an eyebrow skeptically. "Okay, I'll order."

"I'd love to, but the fingerprints we pulled from the glass Garfield's witness supplied are due back sometime today—I want to be around when they come in on the off chance they prove legit."

"Oh," O'Brien said, her disappointment obvious. "Okay. A rain check, then."

"Any chance I could convince you to bring that order to my office?" Thompson asked.

O'Brien flashed a dazzling smile. "It's a date," she said.

34.

THE WOMAN FUCKED like a Viking, thought Garfield—violently and with abandon. The way she yelped and hollered, it's a wonder she didn't have half the building banging on his door. Then again, Garfield mused, it was the middle of the afternoon—there might be no one in the building to hear her.

They'd gone at it once already, but she showed no signs of letting up. When he finished a second time—sweating, exhausted—and rolled her sideways off him in a not-so-subtle hint that fun-time was over, she looked back at him wild-eyed and smiled. Her hands reached toward him beneath the sheets. "Hell, lawman, I was just getting warmed up."

"Pretty sure that's a goddamned Indian burn you're feeling," he replied, rolling free of her grasp, his overworked bedsprings squeaking in gentle protest underneath him. "I'm gonna need to ice my junk, you keep this up."

"I know something that might just change your mind."

"Yeah?" he asked, curious despite himself. "What's that?"

"Same something that got my motor running," she said. "But first, you gotta promise you'll be cool."

Garfield raised two fingers in the air. "Scout's honor."

"Your Boy Scout bullshit's what I'm worried about."

He rolled his eyes. She frowned briefly, as if trying to decide what to do. Then she grabbed her purse from off the floor and riffled through it. When she found what she was looking for, she held it out to him, her expression triumphant. It was a small hunk of emerald plastic, ovoid like a too-large Advil Liqui-Gel.

A bullet snorter. He'd seen the kind. They held two grams inside. The head shops that sold them would tell you they were used for snuff—just like they'd say those bongs inside the glass display case were tobacco water pipes. Maybe the old-fashioned pewter bullets you'd find in nicer shops were once used that way, but Garfield would put good money on the fact that no one had ever snorted snuff out of a plastic one.

No, these ones were just for coke.

"You want some?" she asked, twisting the lid and inhaling the dispensed dose.

"Uh," Garfield said, voice hoarse. He was just shy of six months clean. Six months, and four dead bodies. More, if you counted the human wreckage Leonwood had left behind at Pendleton's. By the sober light of day, Garfield knew he'd done his best to minimize the damage there. He knew those deaths, at least, weren't on his head.

But half-drunk, twice fucked, and staring down a little bump that could make it all just go away, Garfield was inclined to count them anyway.

If he was headed toward chemical absolution, might as well clear the decks of as many ills as he could claim.

He took the bullet snorter from her and loaded up a dose. One nostril held closed. A short, sharp snort. Then numbness. Then regret. Then bliss.

The euphoria of coke's a tricky balance. Too little and you come down quick: edgy, anxious, hungry for more. Too much and your heart races, your palms sweat, you wind up jittery as shit and paranoid as all hell—and good luck getting it up for the likes of ol' What's-Her-Name here. But if you ride that razor's edge just right, you'll feel good enough to flush your whole life down the toilet and laugh doing it.

He didn't even notice she was riding him again until she was almost there: face flushed, eyes fluttering, muscles contracting involuntarily around him. This time, though, he wasn't finished. Wasn't out of steam. This time, he rose into her with everything he had until she wasn't moving atop him anymore, and then he threw her down and kept on going—a God in his own mind, a stallion in hers, a grim, determined metronome making vulgar, parodic love to a lonely barfly in the middle of the afternoon to anyone else who might have seen.

Thompson finished with the director around four thirty. At five, O'Brien came by her office with Chinese. The fingerprint results came in a little before six. It took another hour for Thompson to obtain clearance to view the file they pointed toward—and even then, the file was heavily redacted.

She'd been worried the prints would prove a dead end. That the glass shards Garfield's fake witness pointed them toward were no more than a red herring tossed their way so Garfield would provide the guy an exit. But as soon as she saw the grainy file photo looking back at her from her computer screen, she realized they'd hit pay dirt. God knew what the sadistic bastard who'd pointed them this way was playing at, but he'd been right about the prints, at least.

The photo was of a lean, fresh-faced kid—cheery, she could tell, but trying his best to look stern for the camera—whose features would soon sharpen into the man she'd seen kill Leonwood at Pendleton's. His name was Michael Evan Hendricks, according to the file. A foster kid—no family listed—who found his way to Special Forces. The fields for group and battalion featured black bars where text should be—and the file was so slight, it was clear it couldn't contain two tours' worth of mission information.

That, to Thompson, suggested the government didn't want those missions known.

That, to Thompson, suggested black ops.

And that wasn't even the most interesting aspect of Hendricks's file. The most interesting aspect was the fact that—according to the government, at least—Hendricks was dead, the victim of a roadside bomb outside Kandahar. Wiped out his whole damn unit, save one. She'd done some digging and discovered—in a document so whitewashed it was clear the bulk of it was bogus, a casualty report sanitized to feed to the press—that the sole living member of his unit was a man named Lester Meyers.

The document contained only names, so she had no social security number, nor any idea where this Meyers was from—and DOD was stonewalling her at every turn.

A quick search indicated there were a few dozen Lester Meyerses the country over. She had agents sifting through the information now, trying to determine which was theirs. Maybe this Meyers was still in contact with his undead brother-in-arms. Maybe he wasn't. But either way, he might be able to provide them with some kind of lead on where Hendricks might be.

She was dying to share all of this with her partner, but Garfield hadn't ever returned, and he wasn't answering her texts. Her concern for him had blossomed into something more immediate, unignorable. Finally, she broke down and called him. After six rings, his voice mail kicked in.

"Garfield," she said, "where the hell are you? Call me as soon as you get this. Those prints came back. We've got an ID on my ghost."

Garfield woke slowly to darkness. The only light in the apartment was that of the streetlights through the blinds. His head was pounding. His skin crawled. His mouth felt like it was packed with cotton.

For a moment, he just lay there, taking stock. He knew that he'd fucked up big-time today. That he'd fallen off the wagon hard. That he might've just torpedoed his career. He knew he needed to clean up, fly right, and take his lumps if he wanted to come out the other end okay, but he couldn't quiet the voice in his head that told him another bump of coke would make everything all better.

He glanced at the woman who lay beside him, facedown and tangled in the sheets. On the small of her back, she had a tattoo of a cross—once black, but now faded to fuzzy blue.

Judge not that ye be judged, Garfield thought.

She'd set the bullet snorter on his nightstand. He

reached over her toward it—trying not to wake her—but it was just beyond his grasp. As he strained to reach it, he slipped, and put his hand down on the edge of the mattress in front of her to catch himself. The whole bed rocked, but she didn't stir.

And when he lifted his hand back off the bed, it was bloody.

Garfield rolled the woman over. Her throat was slit. Her eyes were open and glazed over. Blood soaked her side of the bed and dripped onto the floor beneath.

He leapt out of bed and scanned the floor for his holster, his gun. That's when he saw the man pointing a Ruger at him from the armchair in the corner.

The man's face was swollen and bruised. His right eye was rimmed with lacerations. Beside the chair were Garfield's shoulder holster and cell phone, as well as one of Garfield's kitchen knives—the latter streaked with gore.

"Hello, Special Agent Garfield," the man said, smiling. "It's a pleasure to see you again."

35.

H EADLIGHTS DRIFTED toward the shoulder in the darkness. The car's front-left tire hit the rumble strip, and Hendricks jerked awake—fishtailing as he swerved back into his lane. Once he got the car back on the road, he rolled the window down, hoping the air would keep him alert.

He'd tossed and turned all night in the musty boat cabin. His injuries had nagged at him. The cuts on his hand and neck itched maddeningly. His bruises were hot and tender to the touch. His shoulder clicked when he moved it wrong, and felt like it was full of rusty nails. At dawn, Hendricks found the boat's first aid kit and chewed four aspirin as he cleaned his wounds.

Hendricks had waited until he heard both cars in the driveway leave before he climbed out of his hiding place and retrieved his phone. Then he walked barefoot toward Peoria proper, his too-small stolen loafers in one hand.

In a Goodwill parking lot, Hendricks had jimmied open a donation box and started dumping bags at random. After a little digging, he'd grabbed a plain black T-shirt, a pair of Levi's, a hooded sweatshirt, and a pair of paint-spattered black Chuck Taylors. He felt a little guilty stealing from a charity, but as bedraggled as he looked, walking into a store would've drawn too much unwanted attention—and anyway, he was a little short on cash. The way Hendricks saw it, a fugitive from justice twelve hundred miles from home with less than seven hundred dollars to his name was entitled to a little charity.

He'd cleaned up in a nearby Hardee's restroom and put on his new clothes, burying his old ones beneath a layer of paper towels in the trash bin.

Not far from the Hardee's was a Best Western. Hendricks strode into the lobby like he belonged there. The bored young woman playing a game on her cell phone behind the front desk didn't even look his way. He helped himself to their continental breakfast, and then he pulled up Craigslist on the computer in their business center.

Three hours and a bunch of phone calls later, he was the proud owner of a '93 Civic. The tires were bald, the backseat was all chewed up, and the cabin smelled like dog, but at three hundred bucks, the price was right—and deals for two other cars had fallen through already, so he couldn't afford to be too picky. Hendricks offered the owner another hundred to bring the car to his hotel. Once he dropped the guy back at his house, Hendricks was on his way.

Stolen wheels are fine for short-term transportation, but when you've got twenty hours of driving ahead of you, it's nice to know the cops aren't looking for your ride.

Now, the lights of Cleveland beckoned to him in the distance. Hendricks figured he could find some food there, some Advil, and maybe even a shower and a proper bed—provided he could find a motel shady enough to accept cash no-questions-asked. He knew Cleveland well enough to assume that wouldn't be a problem.

Hendricks turned on the radio, scanned the dial until he found a classic rock station playing the Stones. Cranked the volume and drummed along on the steering wheel.

For the first time since Purkhiser double-crossed him, things were looking up.

When Thompson's phone played Garfield's ringtone, she nearly jumped out of her chair trying to answer it. "Garfield, where the hell have you been? Are you okay?"

Thompson heard shuffling on his end of the line. She wondered for a moment if he'd dropped the phone. "Huh?" he said. "I mean, uh, yeah...I'm fine."

"You sure?" she asked. "You sound distracted."

Garfield barked with laughter. It sounded more desperate than amused. "Distracted? Nah. Rough night, is all."

"Listen, your lead panned out—we got a hit on those prints. Some badass Special Forces type by the name of Michael Hendricks. And get this: he's been presumed dead for years. We're tracking down a known associate of his now—a soldier from his old unit."

"That's great," Garfield replied flatly. "E-mail me the file, and I'll take a look at it on the way in."

"Sure," she said. "It's on its way. You picked a hell of a time to disappear, you know. The director is furious. I tried to cover for you—I told him you were sick—but he's not an idiot. He knows damn well I was lying."

"Thanks, Charlie. You didn't have to do that. Not after...the way I've been to you."

Thompson was taken aback. "Hey," she said, "what are partners for?"

"Still," Garfield said, his voice tinged with regret, "for what it's worth, Charlie, I'm sorry."

36.

THE BELL ABOVE the Bait Shop's door jingled as the sandy-haired man let himself inside, sunlight streaming in around him on all sides. It was a little after four p.m. on Saturday. The bar had been open for all of five minutes, and save for Lester, it was unoccupied.

When Lester heard the bell, he peeked over the bar toward the door. He could just make out his would-be patron's head and shoulders from where his wheelchair sat. Black sport coat. Black turtleneck. Black kid gloves, evidenced when he raised a hand in hello. And the palest of blue eyes. The man limped slightly, and his face was bruised, but his expression conveyed no discomfort—the slightest of smiles graced his lips, as if he'd just remembered the punch line of a joke long since forgotten.

"Afternoon," Lester called to him. "Kitchen's closed,

so if you're hungry, keep walking—but if a drink is what you're after, I'm happy to oblige. What's your poison?"

"What, indeed?" asked the man—his smile coming out in full now. His English was flawless, but its edges were sharpened by an accent that clearly marked him foreign. Austrian, Lester thought, or maybe Swiss.

The man looked around the bar's small dining room. Empty booths, empty barstools, empty chairs. There was something sinister about him, Lester realized. Something predatory. Fear uncoiling in the pit of his stomach, he said, "Yeah, it's been a little quiet around these parts today. But no worries: this place'll be hopping in no time." He hoped it sounded less a bluff to this man than it did to his own ears.

"Yes, Lester," said the man, sliding the bolt on the door behind him and flipping the sign on its inset pane to CLOSED. "I suspect it will be."

The threat was hard to miss. Lester didn't hesitate. He tripped the panic button hidden beneath the lip of the bar—signaling Hendricks—and went for the Beretta M9 Velcroed to the underside of his chair. Maybe if he'd gone for the gun straightaway, he might have had a fighting chance. The man, mongoose-quick, grabbed a wooden chair from the nearest table and hurled it at him. Gun hand and chair legs connected. Lester's Beretta slipped from his grasp and shattered the mirror behind the bar. In seconds, the man was on him—vaulting over the bar, his knee connecting hard with Lester's groin. The pain was excruciating. Lester's world went a little wobbly around the edges.

"That was hardly the most hospitable of welcomes, Mr. Meyers," the sandy-haired man hissed as he back-handed Lester across the face. Lester's head rocked sideways at the force of the blow.

Black-gloved hands zip-tied Lester's arms to his wheelchair's armrests with practiced grace. A whole lemon from the garnish station was stuffed as far as it would go into his mouth. Juice bled from it where Lester's teeth pierced its skin, invading the cuts those same teeth had left in his own lips—twin bee-stings, top and bottom.

As quickly as the man was on him, he was gone. A terrifying, animal grace. He strode calmly but with purpose around the perimeter of the bar—closing blinds, checking the restroom for occupants. Briefly, he disappeared into the kitchen—checking the storeroom and service entrance, Lester supposed.

Whatever's about to happen, Lester thought, it ain't gonna be pretty.

Once Special Agent Garfield had supplied Engelmann with Hendricks's file, finding Meyers was a simple matter of placing a phone call. His Council contact let it ring so long, though, it was clear that he—and by extension, his organization—wished to register his displeasure at Engelmann's lack of progress.

"What?" his contact answered, eight rings in.

"I need a favor."

"So far, you've needed plenty of favors, and we haven't seen much in return. What makes you think you deserve another?"

"I'm close," said Engelmann. "Closer than anybody else has come."

"You'd best be. What, exactly, do you need?"

"I assume you have sources within the military, yes?"

His contact hesitated. "Maybe."

"I need to find a certain Lester Meyers. All I know for sure is that he's a military veteran. Late twenties, I'm guessing—maybe early thirties."

A long, calculating pause. "He our guy?"

"No," said Engelmann, "he's not. But I believe him to have information I require."

"This Meyers…is he underground?"

"I have no reason to assume so, but his military record is under lock and key."

"Seems to me the bucks we're paying you, you oughta be able to do your own goddamn legwork."

"I understand—but time is of the essence," said Engelmann.

"Law's onto this guy, too?"

"Yes. And if they locate him before I do…"

"I get the picture," his contact said. "Gimme five minutes to do my thing, then call me back. And Alexander?" He said Engelmann's first name with exaggerated care, as if mocking his hired killer's mannered grace.

"Yes?"

"That call better be the last I get from you until your target's dead."

The sandy-haired man returned from the bar's back room and fetched from his inside coat pocket a black leather kit the approximate size and shape of a woman's clutch, zippered on three sides. It looked to Lester like a particularly extensive lock-pick kit.

And after a fashion, it was.

The man unzipped the kit and set it on the bar. He made a show of unfolding it—three panels, all told. Its contents, held in place by a series of leather loops, snapped at one end, were the stuff of nightmares.

A set of scalpels. Awls and chisels in assorted shapes and sizes. Something that looked like a cross between a ball-peen hammer and a hatchet. A small bow saw. A hand drill with an assortment of bits. And sundry forceps, clamps, and scissors.

They were old, no doubt—antiques, perhaps, dull-looking and rust-flecked—but there was no mistaking their purpose. They were surgical instruments. But in this man's hands, they were meant to undo rather than repair.

Lester's chair rocked from side to side as he struggled against his restraints. The sandy-haired man cooed over him as though he were a crying child, but made no move to stop him. Lester struggled until his limbs and chest burned from exertion, and sweat plastered his hair and clothes to his body. The zip ties dug into his flesh, drawing blood. It dripped onto the hardwood in quiet, rhythmic taps. Even-tually, Lester's struggles ceased, and he eyed the man be-fore him in unadulterated fear.

"Are you quite finished?" asked the man. Lester was silent. "Good. Allow me to introduce myself. My name is Alexander Engelmann. Now," he said, one hand hovering over the open surgical kit a moment before selecting from it a small, wooden-handled awl, "you're going to tell me everything there is to know about one Michael Evan Hen-dricks."

37.

SATURDAY AFTERNOON, and the New York Thruway was slow going. It seemed to Hendricks as though the entire stretch from Syracuse to Albany was being paved. The roadway was reduced to one grooved lane for miles on end. Hendricks rolled along at twenty miles an hour, cursing the traffic. At this rate, it would be midnight before he got home.

He planned to spend the night at his cabin and head to Portland in the morning. He figured hunting this guy could wait a day, at least—and the way his last forty-eight hours had gone, Hendricks thought he'd earned a little peace and quiet.

Traffic moved at a crawl. Hendricks played chicken with the Civic's gas gauge, watching the needle tip toward E and hoping he'd make it to a gas station. The thruway was bumper-to-bumper as far as he could see in both directions.

He coasted into the Guilderland Plaza five minutes after the indicator light came on. The electronic road sign in the median told him he had five more miles of construction to look forward to.

Hendricks was gassing up the Civic when his burner phone vibrated in his pocket—one short burst, signaling a text. He fished it out of his pocket with his free hand.

The phone's screen read 911.

It was the message triggered by the panic button behind Lester's bar.

A helpless dread gripped Hendricks. Lester was in trouble, and here he was five fucking hours away.

He climbed back into the Civic and eyed the backup on the thruway. Saw cars trying to leave the plaza's parking lot idling as they waited for the chance to merge. Knew he'd go out of his mind sitting in traffic like that for the next five miles.

At the far end of the parking lot, there was a metal gate separating the plaza's lot from the one its employees used, there to keep people on the toll road from leaving without paying. It was a risk. He could be seen. Reported. Chased. Arrested. And if that happened, Lester would be on his own.

With gritted teeth, he jerked the wheel toward the gate and hit the gas.

The gate slammed open, and he drove through—leaving the traffic jam behind and disappearing down the narrow access road.

Engelmann worked on Lester quietly and without urgency. His expression was one of both care and ecstasy—a master composer conducting his opus before a rapt audience of one. He'd told Lester at the outset that Lester was going to tell Engelmann everything there was to know about Hendricks. It wasn't a question, Lester noted at the time, but in the agonizing hours that followed, it was as close as Engelmann ever came to asking one.

Lester, unlike Engelmann, was far from quiet. He screamed. He cried. He begged. He pleaded. Most were muffled by his makeshift gag—the lemon, at first, though he bit through it within the hour, at which point Engelmann replaced it with his own belt.

Not that Lester's protestations mattered much. The Bait Shop was a sturdy old brick building, made to withstand Maine's hard winters. The bar next door played host to a reggae band most Saturdays, today included. And once the dinner hour hit, the Old Port came alive, its streets full of tourists, buskers, and barhoppers. Anyone who heard Lester's cries over the din failed to take notice.

Lester told himself all he had to do was stay strong. That Engelmann didn't know about the panic button, or hadn't realized Lester'd triggered it. If he could hold out long enough, Michael would come for him—even though Lester always told him if he ever got that message, he should run.

Mikey was still a soldier at heart—he'd never leave a man behind.

That thought carried him through the first excruciating hour. Taunted him for half the second. But eventually, Lester realized Michael would not come soon enough, so he began to root for Engelmann to get carried away and kill him inadvertently.

For a time, that grim strand of hope sustained him. But Engelmann was talented. Exacting. Creative. And Lester, for all his resolve, was no match for him. There was no shame in it. No betrayal. There's not a man alive who wouldn't sell out his own mother after two hours of Engelmann's ministrations. Most wouldn't last five minutes.

As the sun glinted orange off the western faces of the low-slung Portland skyline, Lester Meyers began to talk.

38.

M Y GOD," said Thompson. "What happened here?"

Thompson stood on the threshold of Henry Garfield's bedroom, her hands sweating inside her disposable nitrile gloves, a pair of paper booties on her feet. Crime scene techs were everywhere, gowned and masked and solemn as they laid down numbered evidence markers and dusted surfaces for prints. The room flashed white as the crime scene photographer took photo after photo of the bodies.

The woman was unfamiliar to her. She lay on the bed, her throat slit, her naked flesh mottled. It looked like she'd been rolled over—there was relatively little blood beneath her, but the left side of the bed was soaked with it, and the floor beside as well.

Garfield was naked, too, and slumped at the foot of the bed, a gunshot to the center of his forehead. It looked like he'd been kneeling when he was shot.

Her question was more involuntary response than legitimate inquiry, but the DC homicide detective who'd greeted her at the door answered anyway. "We're still piecing that together," he said. "We just got here ourselves. No one seems to've heard the shot. Downstairs neighbor called it in when her ceiling started bleeding. When we found out he was one of yours, we figured we oughta loop you in."

The detective had introduced himself when Thompson arrived, but she'd been in a fog. Now she struggled to remember his name. Newman? Newsome? Neubauer.

"Time of death?" she asked.

"Hard to say. Lividity's fixed. Rigor mortis has set in. The bodies are room temp. I'm guessing it's been twenty-four hours at least. The ME will probably be able to get us closer."

Thompson's heart sank. Twenty-four hours ago, Garfield had called her and asked for Hendricks's file. She'd e-mailed it without a second thought. "That's close enough," she said.

"If it's any consolation, your buddy didn't suffer," Neubauer said. "There's no other trauma to the body. No defensive wounds to indicate a struggle. Just the gunshot. Stippling indicates it was close-range. He would've died immediately."

Thompson shook her head. Garfield didn't even put up a fight—he just gave the bastard what he wanted.

"Could be this was drug related," Neubauer mused aloud. "We found some coke and paraphernalia on the nightstand."

Thompson shook her head. "This wasn't drug related."

Neubauer scowled. "Look, I called you out of courtesy. If you know something you're not telling me—"

But Thompson wasn't listening. She was ringing up HQ. Three transfers later, she got someone on the line worth talking to. "We've got a problem," she said. "Henry Garfield is dead. Our ghost's ID has been burned." A pause. "I'm guessing it was the perp who flipped the ambulance." Another pause. "Yeah. It's bad. We've gotta get eyes on every Lester Meyers on our list ASAP."

Michael Hendricks fought through the crush of drunken revelers that crowded the lamp-lit streets of Portland's Old Port, his impatience tipping toward panic. Every glance his way felt hostile. Every idle bump was a potential threat. The live music blasting from open bar doors set his teeth on edge. The bass thump from the dance clubs knocked the breath from his chest.

A twenty-something meathead—popped collar and backward ball cap, tequila breath and cheap cologne—shouldered Hendricks hard as he staggered by.

"Watch it, dipshit!" he said.

Hendricks sized him up. Eyes glazed from drink. Veins bulging. Fists the size of country hams. He was clearly spoiling for a fight. Hendricks wasn't keen to give him one, so he kept walking.

"Hey!" He wrapped a hand around Hendricks's upper arm and yanked. "I was *talking* to you, asshole."

As Hendricks turned, his right hand lashed out and grabbed Meathead's trachea in a pinch grip. The guy let out a pained cry, which dwindled to a gurgle as Hendricks applied pressure. Hendricks knew he could crush the asshole's windpipe easily. Leave him to choke to death in the street, where he'd be mistaken for another weekend drunk until it was too late. And for a moment, he was tempted.

But Lester was in trouble, so Hendricks couldn't afford any complications. By force of will, he released the man, who backed—bug-eyed and gasping—into the throng.

When Hendricks finally reached the Bait Shop, it was shuttered and dark, and its sign read CLOSED—unheard-of on a Saturday night. Ten agonizing minutes spent surveilling the place indicated no discernible activity inside. Once he'd satisfied himself that no one lay in wait for him, he ducked into the alley that ran alongside the bar and used his key to slip in via the service entrance.

The first thing he noticed was the scent. Sweat and pennies, and beneath them, something even less pleasant, like garbage left too long. Though the gloom of the bar was impenetrable, Hendricks knew precisely what that olfactory cocktail signified. He'd smelled it more times than he wished to recall: sometimes on the field of battle, though more often in cold, gray, stone-walled basements—long shadows cast across the floor and walls by naked bulbs and naked zealots, strapped to chairs and taken apart piece by piece until they gave up either their secrets or their ghost. It was the scent of death drawn out—of a body letting go of blood and bile and bladder and bowels long before it's granted the reprieve of death.

As Hendricks's eyes adjusted to the darkness, the lifeless form of his only friend swam slowly into focus. He was in the center of the restaurant's small dining room, slumped forward in his wheelchair. A bar rag dangled from between his swollen, bloodied lips. The only thing that held him upright were the zip ties that bound his forearms to the wheelchair's armrests, looped through the spokes of his wheels to keep him from rolling off, and cinched so tight his pained struggles had stripped skin from sinew like insulation from a wire. Hendricks felt sick as he took in the grisly scene: a blasphemous Rodin's *Thinker*, an ode to suffering rendered in bound and bloodied flesh.

Hendricks ran to his friend's side, tears welling as proximity revealed fresh horrors. Lester's shirt lay in tatters on the floor around him, cut from his body by his assailant so that he could better access his living canvas. Lester's chest was marked with plier-bites as if snacked on at leisure by some kind of carrion feeder, plucking flesh from bone here and there at random. A series of inch-long slices—fine, as if made by razor blade or surgical scalpel—etched his muscled shoulder like a woodcut. What should have been blood-caked was instead glazed and sticky, with a residue whose scent suggested whiskey—poured onto these cuts to inflict maximum pain. One ear dangled loose. Three fingers on his left hand were missing; a length of rubber hose was tied tight around his left elbow to prevent him from bleeding out as they'd been taken one by one. The floor before him was littered with teeth, pinkish-white amid the puddling scarlet. His skin was gray. His chest was still. His eyes, mercifully, were closed.

Hendricks crouched before Lester and touched his forehead to the dead man's. "I'm sorry, Les," he said, tears falling as he clenched shut his eyes—a vain attempt to keep his grief at bay. "I'm so sorry."

So this is what this life he'd chosen had come to. What his bullshit quest for atonement—for absolution—had wrought. He'd once believed that God and country were worth killing for. After, when that moral certainty abandoned him, he thought that balancing the scales might make things right again. But now—too late, perhaps—he knew, as he wept over his departed friend, that his new crusade was as delusive as his last. There was only one thing in this world worth killing for—worth *dying* for. The lives of those you love.

He wished that he were dead instead. That the man who did this to Lester had bested him at Pendleton's—or that he'd died alongside the rest of his unit in the high desert of Afghanistan. Then the horrors of the past three days would have never happened.

Could he die? he wondered. Or was he too good at this? Too tough? Too stubborn?

Apparently, Lester was.

Because at that moment, the broken man opened his eyes, spit the filthy, blood-caked rag out of his mouth, and began to scream.

It was a noise unlike any Hendricks had ever heard. Every one of Lester's muscles clenched as he expelled breath from his lungs, and he thrashed violently against his restraints, loosing fresh gouts of blood from his many wounds and rocking his wheelchair so hard it nearly toppled.

Hendricks had no idea how Lester had survived this long. Had no idea how *anybody* could have. But by the look of him, and the severity of his wounds, his vise-grip on life wouldn't hold for much longer.

"Jesus, Lester—I thought you were a goner!" Hendricks exclaimed. "Just hang on, buddy," he said, plucking his phone from his pocket. "We're gonna get you to a hospital."

But Lester grabbed his wrist and held him fast. Through gritted teeth—what few he had left, at least—he barked *"NO!"* his voice hoarse and weak, his neck bulging from the exertion required to speak. Blood trickled from the corners of his swollen, ruined mouth.

Hendricks mistook Lester's gesture as protective of Hendricks. "Don't worry about me. All I care about is getting you—"

"*NO*," Lester once more insisted. He closed his eyes and focused. Then, calmer than he'd sounded prior, though thick and wrong from the trauma to his mouth, his face, he added, "Evie."

Hendricks froze. Fear crawled up his spine like living ice.

"I'm sorry," said Lester, tears streaking his blood-caked cheeks. "I tried to wait. I didn't want to tell him..."

Hendricks touched his friend's shoulder—gingerly, for he was loath to cause him further pain, and there was little undamaged flesh left on him—and said, "It's all right. I understand." And he meant it. He didn't blame Lester for having told his assailant of Evie—he *couldn't*. After all, it was Lester himself who insisted on safeguarding against knowing anything that, if disclosed, could compromise Hendricks's safety. No one could hold out forever while tortured. All they could hope for was to bide their time until shock, unconsciousness, or death took over. It would seem Hendricks's adversary was clever enough to stave off all three. And one look at Lester told Hendricks he'd resisted, valiantly, regardless.

"Tell me what happened," said Hendricks.

Lester nodded, wincing at the effort. Both he and Hendricks knew that whenever help came, it would be too late. Lester was too far gone to save. Five minutes wouldn't make any difference. The only thing that had kept him here this long was sheer force of will—he was determined to redeem himself for having given up Evie.

Lester told Hendricks everything he could—beginning with the fact that Engelmann had left no more than an hour prior, armed not only with the knowledge of Evie's existence, but with her address as well. He spoke haltingly, struggling for every breath, growling his words out as fast as he could force them. Hendricks held his hand and listened, rapt, until finally one of Lester's pauses stretched on forever, and Hendricks looked up to find two dull eyes staring back at him.

Lester was gone. But in holding on—in delivering his message—he'd bested his tormentor, who'd left him to die rather than killing him quickly in a cruel attempt to prolong his suffering. In holding on, he'd given Hendricks what he needed most in that moment: the chance to end this. To save someone who mattered.

39.

A S HENDRICKS raised a hand to close his dead friend's
eyes, there was a banging on the door.

He rose from his crouch beside Lester's wheelchair and
headed for the window. Parting the blinds slightly, he saw
a pair of unmarked black sedans parked just outside—one
blocking the alley through which he'd entered. Two men
in dark suits were at the door. Two more hung back a
little—weapons drawn, eyes darting all around. FBI, he
guessed.

He ran into the bathroom and shut the door. It was
dark but for the streetlight through the window. The window frame was painted shut, so he wrapped his sweatshirt
around his hand and knocked out the lower pane. He
climbed out as the men out front kicked in the door and
stormed the place. Then he strolled as nonchalantly as he
could around the corner—his mind reeling, his stomach in

knots—and plucked his cell phone from his pocket, punching in a number from memory.

"Hello?" The word was high and thin and tinged with fear.

"Hello, Edgar."

"*You*," Edgar Morales spat. "Do you have any idea what my involvement with you has put me through? Some psychotic motherfucker damn near killed me in my own bed because of you! I've barely slept since, and when I do, it's with a gun under my pillow. I'm goddamn terrified he might come back."

You wouldn't have been alive long enough for Engelmann to visit you if it weren't for me, Hendricks thought but didn't say. Instead, he said, "Actually, Edgar, that man's precisely why I'm calling. See, I've got a bead on where he's headed, and I aim to deal with him—permanently. But he's got a head start on me, which means I'm gonna need a favor."

"Yeah?" asked Morales. "The fuck is that?"

"You own a fleet of charter jets, don't you?"

There was a pause on Morales's end, as if he were weighing a decision. Then he sighed and said, "I've got planes on ready at every airport in the country. Just tell me where you need to go."

It took eleven minutes from the moment Thompson put out the order to get eyes on all their Lester Meyerses for the Portland, Maine, office to call her back. Turns out, Portland's Lester Meyers was the Lester Meyers they were looking for. Emphasis on *was*.

Seems he ran a bar in some touristy section by the water. The first agents on the scene found the place empty, save for Lester Meyers's mangled corpse. They would have assumed him dead for hours but for the fact that he was still warm. Only a coroner could say for sure, but it seemed they'd missed saving him by minutes at most—assuming he could have been saved at all. Given the pictures of his injuries they'd forwarded to Thompson's cell, that was one hell of an assumption.

How he'd managed to survive the trauma he'd endured for as long as he had, Thompson hadn't a clue. But one thing she *did* know was Meyers wasn't L'Engle's big play. If he'd meant to use Meyers as bait to draw Hendricks out, he wouldn't have tortured him and left him for dead—he would have taken Meyers and left behind a grisly message like the one on the ambulance for Hendricks to follow. No, the evidence suggested the killer had extracted information from Meyers, which meant he had bigger bait in mind—and that Meyers himself was the message.

Thompson had no idea whether Hendricks had received that message, but still, she thrilled at the prospect of catching the two of them at once. First, though, there was the matter of discovering what it was L'Engle was onto.

Whatever it was, it must be somewhere in Hendricks's file, hidden beneath the black redaction bars.

Thompson scrolled through her cell-phone contacts, dialed up an old friend in the DOD.

"Charlie Thompson. I never would have guessed I'd hear from you today. How are you?"

"I'm fine," Thompson said. "Did I wake you?"

"Nah, I was up," she said. "What can I do for you?"

"Actually, Diane, I need a favor. Got a file on one of your guys by the name of Michael Hendricks. Real cool customer, from what little I'm allowed to see. File says he's dead, only it turns out, not so much."

"What do you need, Charlie?"

"Someone's hunting this guy. Someone bad. I think he's got a bead on some major bait to draw him out. Guy's an orphan—no siblings, either—so I'm thinking it's a partner. He wasn't married, so this partner could be male or female."

"And you need my help in finding said partner?"

"Yeah. Anything you can give me. His death benefits. Where his checks were sent. Whatever you can think of."

"Files like these are sealed for a reason, Charlie. I do this, I could lose my job."

"You don't do this, that partner of his might just lose their life."

Diane sighed. "Hell," she said. "I never could say no to you. Keep your phone handy. I'll call you back in twenty minutes. And Charlie?"

"Yeah?"

"It's good to hear from you. We should grab a drink sometime. Catch up."

"Yeah," Charlie agreed. But she knew they never would.

40.

TWO A.M., and Dulles's long-term parking was deserted. Hendricks's footsteps echoed through the concrete parking structure while he eyed license plates.

The flight from Portland to Dulles had taken less than two hours. The next commercial flight wasn't for another six. Hendricks assumed Engelmann would be on it. He hoped to God Engelmann didn't have a Morales of his own.

On the fourth floor, he found a car that met his needs: an early-nineties Porsche convertible with doctor's plates. The ragtop made breaking in a breeze. The engine was fast enough to get him to Evie's quickly. And the car was old enough to be susceptible to hot-wiring.

Hendricks had raided the charter plane's tool kit on the way down. Took a utility knife, a hammer, a couple screwdrivers, some electrical tape. He used the knife to cut a slit in the car's roof, right behind the driver's-side window.

Then he reached inside and unlocked the door. It took some wrestling to pop the cover off the steering column, and in the dark of the garage, the multicolored wires were hard to tell apart, but eventually, he teased out the ones he wanted. He connected the ignition on-off wire to the battery, and the dashboard came to life. Then, taking care because it was live, he stripped the starter wire and touched it to the join between the other two.

Two hundred forty-seven horses' worth of power roared.

Hendricks left the parking lot and kept the needle pinned at eighty-five all the way to Evie's. Even with the doctor's plates, there was a chance they'd try to pull him over. He didn't care. They could chase his ass the whole damn drive, he thought—all that mattered now was Evie. All that mattered was keeping her safe. Leading a parade of cops to her front door seemed as good a way as any to do it.

But no one tried to pull him over. On those dark back-country roads, beneath the low ceiling of clouds that blotted out the stars and threatened rain, no one noticed him at all. And so Hendricks wound up standing on Evie's front porch, alone.

He knew at once Engelmann hadn't beaten him here. If he had, he would have made a show of it—trashing the place, causing a scene, maybe leaving a grisly souvenir to lather Hendricks up into an ill-advised rage. But all looked normal, and quiet, and dark.

Still, Engelmann would be here soon enough. And Hendricks aimed to be ready for him when he showed.

He wished he'd had time to procure weapons. But his whole way here, all Hendricks could think was that the hours he spent tracking down the gear he needed might make the difference between beating Engelmann to Evie or allowing the only woman he'd ever loved to fall into a madman's hands. And besides, he had no idea how compromised he was. There was a good chance every law enforcement agency in the country had eyes out for him. And with Lester dead, he had no backup, no tech, no way to reach his usual suppliers in time, and no access to the money he'd need to pay them if he did. That meant he'd have to either reach out to untested contacts or steal what he needed, either of which might well alert the authorities to his location. He couldn't run the risk of getting caught before removing Engelmann from play—the cost of doing so was far too steep.

Hendricks's pulse raced. He was horrified at the prospect of confronting Evie—of confessing everything to her. Of allowing her to see the monster he'd become.

And still, he pounded on that door.

"Evie!" he shouted, his voice oddly tinny and distant to his own ears. "Goddamn it, Evie—open up!"

It was almost three a.m.—plenty late for most decent folks to be asleep.

If I were Evie, Hendricks thought, and some nutjob was banging on my door shouting my name, I might be reluctant to answer, too. Which is to say, he should've figured on what happened next.

The inside light came on, spilling yellow through the decorative glass panel in the door. Then the door flew open. As Hendricks squinted against the sudden light, a hand grabbed a fistful of his shirt. Next thing he knew, he was up against the doorjamb, the business end of a baseball bat in his face.

Fucking Stuart.

It was all Hendricks could do not to end his ass right then and there.

Instead, Hendricks tried to talk to Stuart—to calm him down. It didn't take.

Stuart was riled up—anger masking fear. A king defending his castle. Lots of "Who the fuck are you?" and "The fuck you think you're doing, pounding on our goddamn door in the dead of fucking night?" The whole time, Hendricks was a little bummed Stuart didn't recognize him. Guess Evie doesn't keep too many pictures of me around, he thought.

Then again, even if she did, you couldn't blame the guy for not putting two and two together. No one expects his wife's dead fiancé to come knocking in the middle of the night. But Stuart kept getting angrier and angrier—spit flying, veins pulsing, nose almost touching Hendricks's—and the whole time, all Hendricks could think was This is the guy who gets to lie down next to Evie.

So Hendricks took the bat. Pushed Stuart back into the house—harder than was strictly necessary—and closed the door. Stuart toppled backward into the hallway, crashing ass-over-teakettle through the console table along the wall and coming to rest amid a hail of keys and cell phones and spare change.

Of course, that's when Evie showed up.

When Stuart took the table out, Evie half-ran, half-stumbled down the stairs calling his name, as though she'd been listening from just out of sight the whole time. Then she spotted Hendricks standing over Stuart with the bat, and the air around Hendricks seemed to gel. He couldn't move, couldn't speak, couldn't breathe—he just stood there staring as Evie's fear turned to confusion, as recognition turned to shock.

"Michael?" she said, her voice tremulous.

Hearing her say his name tore at Hendricks's insides worse than any bullet could. It hurt like love. Like dying.

Her hand to her mouth, she sank to her knees. Slowly, as if through water. Seeing her like that—mouth open, chest hitching beneath her husband's borrowed undershirt, no noise coming out—reduced Hendricks. Broke him. All he could think was: I did this. I made her feel this way.

The bat clattered to the floor, forgotten. The distance between her and Hendricks melted away. And for a few blissful moments, he held her—her swollen belly warm against his own, her face buried in the crook of his neck as she cried.

"So let me get this straight," she said, gripping her coffee mug in both hands, her bare legs curled under her on the couch. "This man is coming. Coming for you. And you don't know when he'll get here. But you mean to kill him when he does."

"Coming for *you*," Hendricks corrected. Abigail, a smooshy little bulldog puppy when Hendricks had seen her last, was now full-grown, and shaking her tiny butt in sheer delight at his return. Stuart looked less pleased.

"But to get to *you*."

"Yes," he said. "But that distinction doesn't make you any safer."

"No, I imagine it doesn't."

"But I can protect you both. Protect all of you," he amended, scratching Abigail behind her ear while his eyes settled on Evie's swollen belly. "You just have to trust me and do exactly as I say."

"Oh, for fuck's sake!" This from Stuart. "I don't know why we're even listening to this bullshit! You let her think you fucking *died*—why in God's name should we trust you *now?*"

"Because I have no reason to lie about this. I let Evie think I was dead to protect her. From this life. From this job. Why would I show up and ruin that now, if it wasn't to keep her safe?"

Stuart snorted, rolled his eyes. "You're a psychopath who kills for a living—who lives his life to kill. And now you've brought another killer to our door. Give me one good reason to do anything you say."

So Hendricks told Stuart the bit that he'd left out. The bit he didn't want to say aloud. The bit that, once he'd heard it, Stuart couldn't dare ignore.

"Look, Stuart, you want the truth? Fine, here it is. Engelmann *needs* Evie. He needs her alive, because he thinks he can use her to get to me. Now that doesn't mean he needs her in good condition—and this guy is not a nice man. In all likelihood, he'll torture her, just for the pleasure of hearing her scream. And you won't be able to do a thing about it, because you'll be dead. See, he needs Evie, but *you?* You he doesn't give a shit about. He doesn't give a shit about you because as far as he's concerned, you're not worth a thing to me."

Stuart made like he was going to object, but Hendricks raised a hand to silence him. "I know, I know, that's not how it really is. Any claim I had on Evie died a long time ago. But you've got to understand just what we're up against."

Evie's face darkened in thought. "Say you kill this man," she said. "His employers will only send more, won't they? And they'll keep sending more until they finish the job. We'll never be safe."

"Maybe. Maybe not. This guy's got all the earmarks of a freelancer. That means he only gets paid if he's the one to kill me. Guys like him, they tend to keep their information close to the vest, because they don't want anybody scooping their hit and making off with their fee. I know this better than just about anyone. That means there's a good chance we can end all this tonight." It was, Hendricks knew, an oversimplification—if not an outright lie—but it was one he needed her to believe to get her through this.

"And then what?" This from Evie. "Say you save the day. Kill the bad guy. What happens afterward?"

Hendricks shrugged, his nonchalance forced. He struggled to keep his tone even, uninflected by the tumult within. "I disappear. Leave the two of you in peace. There's nothing for me here—no reason for me to stay."

"You're goddamn *right* there isn't," said Stuart, once more the king in his castle, bristling at this pretender to his throne. But Evie said nothing—her face twisted in the pain inflicted by Hendricks's words, tears brimming in her eyes.

That was good. That was what he wanted. He needed her to hate him every bit as much as he hated himself for the plan coalescing in his mind to work.

He needed her to hate him so he could find the strength to walk away.

When she finally did speak, her tone was calm, her face impassive.

"Once you're gone, what do we tell the police?"

"Tell them the truth," Hendricks said. "Tell them whatever you like."

"You wanna tell me why we're doing all this?" Stuart's voice strained from exertion as he and Hendricks wrestled the queen-sized mattress from the master bedroom down the stairs.

The breaking dawn was rendered barely perceptible by the dark of the coming storm. The house shook with the bass rumble of rolling thunder, and the first fat drops of what looked to be a deluge smacked like finger-taps against the windowpanes. The sound brought Hendricks back to his childhood—to a Richmond group home he lived in when he was ten. A converted church—thirty kids to a bunk room— with a roof that leaked like a faucet every time it rained and stained-glass windows that projected distorted tableaux of suffering against the walls with every lightning strike.

"No," Hendricks replied. He had no interest in talking strategy with fucking Stuart, of all people; the only man he ever shared such thoughts with was by now on a coroner's slab in Maine. "Do you two own a grill?"

Stuart nodded. That was something, at least: Hendricks had already discovered Stuart had never owned a firearm of any kind—not even a childhood BB gun.

"Gas or charcoal?"

"Why, you gonna criticize my goddamn grilling?"

"No. I'm going to try and save your life, and the life of the woman you love."

"It's gas," said Stuart. "That help or hurt?"

"Too soon to tell if it does either," Hendricks replied, though secretly he was pleased.

Evie, too pregnant to haul anything larger than a gallon of milk, came back wet-haired and breathless from the garage, a box of supplies propped up on the crest of her belly. Two boxes of nails. Three cans of spray paint. Some bug spray. A jug of spent motor oil. "I got some of the sup- plies you asked for. Looks like there's some plywood and two-by-fours and ten gallons of gas out there besides. You want me to bring them in?"

"No!" said Stu and Hendricks in unison, neither wanting her to tax herself. "I'll go get it," Stuart added, abandoning his end of the mattress and disappearing out the French doors off the dining room—Abigail waddling along behind, whining with every distant rumble of thunder that announced the coming storm—leaving Hendricks to drag the mattress into position atop the other two he'd gathered alone.

"This place got a basement?" Hendricks asked Evie. "A root cellar?"

"Both," she replied.

"Show me."

They checked out the root cellar first. Some yards away from the house proper, it was dank and damp, and in no small measure of disrepair. Then they headed to the basement. There, Hendricks spied Evie's old boom box on a shelf crowded with homeownerly supplies: Christmas lights; an old coffeemaker, sans pot; two pairs of Rollerblades; a box labeled STEMWARE. That boom box—a squat gray rectangle, too old to play CDs, with a tape deck in the center and round, black owl-eye speakers—and the box of tapes that sat beside it on the shelf were once all they had for music at the cabin. Her father had left it there years before, along with a four-cassette boxed set of Mahler symphonies; the rest of the tapes, Evie'd cultivated one by one from shoe boxes at garage sales, people selling cassettes cheap because their stereos were too new to play them. The result was a collection at once dated and timeless, tiny and all-inclusive: Bowie, the Stones, Blondie, Booker T, the Clash, Aretha, Zeppelin, Benny Goodman, Joan Jett,

Prince, Elvis Costello. To this day, Hendricks couldn't hear a one of them without thinking of her.

"That thing still work?" he asked, a smile tugging at the corners of his mouth.

"Far as I know," Evie replied.

He brought it—and the box of tapes—upstairs and plugged it in. Popped in a tape and hit play. "Raspberry Beret" blared briefly from the speakers, incongruous in its cheer. Hendricks shut it off.

"You got any blank tapes?" Evie shot him a look like he'd asked where she kept her horse-drawn carriage. "Right. How about some Scotch tape, then?"

She fetched him some, while in the kitchen, Stuart dropped an armload of two-by-fours, swearing as they cracked a floor tile. If he only knew what Hendricks had in mind, he'd be swearing a whole lot more than that.

Evie returned with the Scotch tape. Hendricks ejected the Prince and put it back into its case. Then he popped one of the Mahlers from the boxed set and taped over the tabs.

Evie, watching him, asked, "Why that one?"

"No reason," he replied—but in reality, he couldn't stand the thought of taping over the ones she'd collected.

Hendricks called Stuart into the room. Told them both what he needed them to do. Then he left them to it and set about readying the house. He fetched the box of stemware from the basement and broke the glasses one by one, wrapping them with a tea towel and whacking them with a hammer. Then he scattered the shards inside each window in the house, save one.

He filled a mop bucket with cold water from the tub. Nailed shut all the upstairs doors. Closed blinds and shut off lights. Hung a midnight-blue sheet from the linen closet over the French doors that faced the backyard to prevent prying eyes from peering in. Dragged their china hutch in front of the bay window that faced the front.

That done, Hendricks retired to the kitchen, where he loaded up the microwave with the cans of bug spray and spray paint. Then he threw the contents of their silverware drawer in for good measure and set the timer. A button-push and ten seconds from a very big boom. Might come in handy if this didn't shake out quite how Hendricks envisioned, provided he had a chance to trigger it. It'd kill him too for sure, but if he wound up needing it, then so be it. Dying didn't seem so scary provided he took that bastard Engelmann with him.

Hendricks, without a word of explanation, collected bottles from Stuart and Evie's liquor cabinet and walked the house, dumping their contents. Stuart and Evie watched in domestic horror as he ruined rugs and furniture at every turn. It was a little trick he'd picked up stalking a hitter for the Genovese crime family a few months back. Hendricks didn't let the guy live long enough to find out if it actually worked, but in theory, it was sound—and if the fight the dude put up before Hendricks finally killed him was any indication, the guy knew what he was doing.

Booze gone, Hendricks raided their fridge and cupboards, enlisting their help in dumping mustard and eggs and peperoncinis and vinegar—even a tin of pickled herring—into every corner of the house now that his prior circuit with their booze rendered any objection moot. He emptied the contents of their bathroom's spray air freshener into the air and dumped their trash onto the kitchen floor. Stuart looked as though he thought this was perhaps some kind of spiteful joke, but to his credit, he said nothing.

Then, the house marinating in rot and filth, it was time to hide the lovebirds. He told them where to go, and what to do. He watched them stroll arm-in-arm away from him, Abigail toddling between them, until they vanished from sight.

His preparations done, Hendricks wandered Evie's house to ensure there wasn't anything he'd missed. His plan didn't allow for any error—not with an adversary as formidable as Engelmann. He had precisely one shot at pulling this off, and it was a long one at that.

When he finished his patrol, he made a quick trip to the kitchen to fetch a chef's knife and one of Stuart's longneck PBRs. Hendricks tested the heft and balance of the knife in his hand and decided it'd do. Then he cracked the beer and retired to the couch, to sit and listen in the darkness.

He wondered if Engelmann was minutes away, or hours, or perhaps already here—watching, waiting for the opportunity to strike.

It didn't matter. Eventually, Hendricks knew, he'd come. All Hendricks had to do was wait.

And he was very good at waiting.

41.

THE TORRENTIAL RAIN against the leaves reminded Engelmann of the hiss of white noise through a listening device. The tree trunks he braced himself against were spongy from the damp. Fallen leaves and pine needles were slippery beneath his feet. His injured knee protested with every step as he limped through the thick Virginia forest toward Evelyn Walker's house, and his sodden clothes stuck to his frame.

But he did not falter. He did not slow.

At thirty thousand feet, the sun was shining—the sky a clear, fine blue. Engelmann had watched the clouds flicker like paper lanterns beneath the morning's United Airlines shuttle—tiny, distant, insubstantial. His fellow passengers had seemed insubstantial to him, too, so heady was the afterglow of his time with Lester Meyers. Though Engelmann had washed up since, he'd been certain he could still detect the faint whiff of violence—of death—upon his clothes and skin. When he discovered it, he'd breathed deep, savoring the taste. It restored him. Invigorated him. It marked him as superhuman, as a killer of men. And as he grudgingly released it from his lungs—a profound sense of purpose settling over him—he'd wondered if the others on his flight could sense it, too.

When the plane descended toward Dulles, the foul weather had enveloped it. A dark portent of things to come, he'd thought. Perhaps his arrival had been foretold.

The notion fueled Engelmann as he pressed onward through the forest.

Occasionally, as he cut a rough diagonal from the turn-around at which he'd parked his rental car to Evie's house, he spied other homes through the trees. He saw TVs tuned to the weather, to cartoons, to morning news programs; couples reading the paper over cups of coffee; families eating pancakes in their pajamas. In every house he passed, lights blazed to dispel the rainy Sunday morning gloom. But when he finally spied the Walker house, he saw no movement, no light, no sign of life—and not a sound could be heard over the constant roar of the rain against the leaves.

He broke from the tree line, rain soaking him to the bone, and slinked along the perimeter of the house, staying low so as not to be seen—clinging to the foundation, the bushes, the latticework that framed the base of the deck, only popping up long enough to peek into the occasional window. But the curtains on the windows were all drawn, and those low enough to climb into were boarded shut.

His quarry, he realized, had beaten him here.

The realization angered Engelmann. He didn't understand how Hendricks had outflanked him. He thought he'd been so careful—so clever. Perhaps he should not have left that cripple to die slowly, but Engelmann had enjoyed the notion of prolonging his suffering too much to kill him outright. Still, his miscalculation mattered not a whit. He wanted his quarry to come, and come his quarry had.

Now the killing time was near.

Engelmann drew his weapon, a knockoff Ruger purchased not twenty minutes before from a less-than-reputable pawnshop a few miles from the airport. He'd bought a knife as well—this one designed for gutting deer—which he wore inside his boot. He knew it would perform admirably on human game should the need arise.

Though the storm clouds blotted out the sun, and sheets of rain blurred everything around him, intermittent lightning blazed—brief snapshots clear enough to navigate by. On his second circuit around the farmhouse, he noticed the front door. Open, but only a crack, the darkness showing at its right-hand edge an invitation.

Engelmann grinned. Bold, he thought. Too bold. Hendricks must think him a fool, an amateur. He bypassed the open door in favor of the bay window farther down—not nailed shut like the others on account of its shape, but instead barricaded with a large piece of furniture.

He broke three panes with the butt of his gun and climbed onto the cushioned built-in bench inside. Then he placed both feet onto the heavy wooden piece—a hutch, or entertainment center perhaps—that barred his entrance to the room and kicked it over. His knee flared with pain. The hutch toppled inward with a crash of breaking plates.

Engelmann stepped low and light across the room, taking up a position behind one couch arm. The house reeked like a landfill—alcohol and vinegar and a thousand other smells combining to turn Engelmann's stomach and set his head reeling. He wondered if disorientation was Hendricks's intent when he unleashed this olfactory horror upon the world. If so, it was hardly enough to dull the diamond edge of his focus.

He held his breath and listened. From somewhere deep in the house, he heard a woman's cry and the low growl of a dog, both quickly silenced—the former by a short, harsh "*Shhh*," and the latter, it seemed, by a muffling hand. The dog whined quietly, mouth held closed. The woman and the man who shushed her said nothing.

Engelmann smiled luxuriously. "I confess, Michael, I'm impressed," he said, hoping to draw Hendricks into the darkened room. "I didn't expect to find you here when I arrived. Very kind of you to extend an invitation, by the way," he said, referring to the open door. "You'll forgive the impertinence of my declining your proffered method of ingress. And if I might be so bold, you could have *cleaned*."

"There's no need to bring Evie into this," called Hendricks from somewhere deeper in the house. "How about you let her leave so we can settle this just you and me."

Engelmann, realizing his quarry was not nearby, scampered low across the room, ducking into the next one down the farmhouse's main hall just long enough to call, "My pleasure! The front door's still open, if you'd like to send her out that way. I only hope something unpleasant doesn't befall her—the forest is quite dangerous." Then he ducked into the room across the hall and waited to see if his misdirection would bear fruit in the form of Hendricks chasing after.

It didn't. But Engelmann's words did have an effect on Evelyn, at least, as he heard her wail in fright. Her terror gave him a quiver of satisfaction—not least because he realized it wasn't coming from the same location as Hendricks's calls. That meant he'd stashed her somewhere—along, he assumed, with both her husband and her dog, if the photos on the walls revealed by the lightning strikes were any indication. And unless he was much mistaken, that somewhere was not far from the spot where he'd taken refuge—closer, it seemed, than Hendricks himself.

Thunder shook the house like battle drums, in perfect synch with the many lightning strikes. The storm was precisely overhead. Engelmann's face tingled with excitement.

As the storm outside raged, Engelmann rose and headed down the hallway, drawn like the hungry predator he was to the quiet, muffled sounds of Abigail's frightened whining.

Charlie Thompson pushed the needle of her Ford Escape past ninety, her wipers sluicing back and forth at top speed but making little headway against the driving rain. Dim yellow spots jittered in her rearview as she struggled to stay on the winding country drive. Her backup's headlights, she hoped. She couldn't stomach the thought of facing two stone-cold killers by herself.

Diane had told her she'd call back in twenty minutes. It took her over seven hours—but she'd come through with the intel Thompson had asked for. Turned out Hendricks sent letters every week for most of his deployment to a woman named Evelyn Jacobs. Girlfriend or fiancée, Diane wasn't sure. She'd married since—her last name was

Walker now—and settled down in rural Virginia, about an hour from DC.

Thompson was certain that's where Garfield's perp was heading—and that her ghost would follow. Which meant she had to follow, too. For the bodies carted out of Pendleton's. For her dead partner. For herself, no matter the cost.

Her GPS piped up with a flat, monotone command, instructing her to turn, and informing her that her destination was four-tenths of a mile away. She took the turn at speed, nearly one-eightying in her haste. She thanked God when the headlights in her rearview did the same.

Whenever she allowed her attention to wander from the task at hand, no matter how briefly, the crime-scene photos of Lester Meyers's ruined flesh haunted her. Shook her resolve. Whispered at her to turn around before it was too late.

And every time that happened, she reacted the same way: by putting the pedal to the floor and moving forward—ever forward—her headlights slicing through the storm.

In the kitchen, Engelmann rose to his full height and cocked his head in puzzlement. Sitting in the middle of the floor was a portable radio, probably thirty years old, of the type associated with break-dancers and the like. Ghetto blasters, he thought they called them. He hadn't seen one like it in ages. It was practically an antique. And as he looked at it, a strange sound emanated from its speakers: a dog's whine, accompanied by a woman, quietly crying.

"Disappointed?" Hendricks asked. Engelmann looked up to find him framed by the arch that separated kitchen from dining room, some fifteen feet away, backlit by the lightning flickering through the sheet that covered the French doors. He was dripping wet and panting—the former perhaps from time spent in the torrential rain, the latter no doubt from playing the same game of call-out-and-double-back that Engelmann had. "She's not here," he said, his right foot inching forward to distribute his weight evenly between the balls of his feet. "I got them out hours ago. You want to get the drop on me, you're not going to do it flying commercial."

"Disappointed?" echoed Engelmann as he shifted his own stance, too. "Quite the contrary—I'm *impressed*. Our encounter in Kansas City left me wondering if perhaps I'd overestimated your abilities. Had we not been interrupted, I think I might have gotten the best of you." Hendricks shrugged as if to say *We'll never know*. "But now, it seems, you've rallied nicely. I cannot tell you how much I am looking forward to this."

Lightning showed blinding white through the gaps in the drawn curtains, a clap of thunder on its heels. Evie's house trembled at the sound of it.

"Is this the part of the movie where you say 'We're not so different, you and I'?"

Engelmann laughed. "Oh, no, Michael. You and I are little alike. You require a reason to kill, a motivation, one sufficient to allow you to soothe your conscience—to overcome your hesitation. And you're prone to forming attachments, to people such as Evelyn, or dear Lester. For me, the killing is in itself enough. How *is* Lester, by the way? Dead, by now, I should think. If you like, I'll arrange to have you buried alongside him, so your guilt for the pain you've caused him may sustain you for all eternity."

"Sometime, you'll have to tell me how you tracked him

down," said Hendricks, jaw clenched. He said it more to keep Engelmann talking long enough for him to regain his composure than because he expected any answer.

"Oh, it's hardly a secret—I asked a lovely Federal employee named Garfield for your file, and he was more than happy to oblige. I'd say it's funny your tax dollars pay that turncoat's salary, but then, he'll no longer be drawing one— and you don't pay taxes anyway, do you?"

"I've paid my share," Hendricks said.

"While we're chatting," said Engelmann, "what is the story behind this wretched stench? It's as if you left a grocery store to rot in every room."

"Place was like that when I got here," Hendricks deadpanned.

"You're a fool to've come, you know—a slave to your own sentiment."

"I would have been a coward not to."

"Perhaps. Tell me, how did your dear, sweet Evelyn and her husband react to your return? I understand that she's with child."

Hendricks said nothing.

"A shame, that—but if it's any consolation, you won't be around to wallow in regret much longer."

Hendricks held the kitchen knife in his right hand at the ready. It glinted in the storm's flickering light. "Maybe," he said. "Either way, I say let's get on with this."

Engelmann raised his pistol. "Oh," he said, his grin seeming in the near dark to take up half of his rain-slick face, "I think we've tested one another's knife skills to my satisfaction. And my knee, unfortunately, still troubles me; I'm afraid close-quarters combat would place me at a disadvantage. So please forgive the anticlimax, but…"

Engelmann's knockoff Ruger spat.

In the millisecond before it did, Hendricks cracked the faintest smile.

And prayed.

Thompson spied the Walkers' mailbox, and beside it, a dirt drive disappeared into the trees. She yanked the wheel, spraying twin tails of mud behind her as her tires sunk in and finally bit. She only made it fifty yards up the winding driveway through the rain-driven muck before the night was torn asunder by a fireball four stories high, which spread warm across her face and buffeted her car with debris.

In an instant, she realized what it would take her backup team an hour to confirm.

The Walker house was gone.

Hendricks lay singed, bloody, and wincing atop the stack of mattresses on the deck. His chest hurt like hell from Engelmann's gunshot, but Evie's cast-iron griddle stopped the bullet and dispersed the blow enough to only bruise— not break—his ribs. Chunks of wood and bits of shingle rained down from overhead, pelting him occasionally, but he didn't mind. He was just happy to be alive. Truth be told, he never thought his plan would work.

He laid his head back on the mattress in exhaustion, but lifted it again in pain as soon as it connected. When he probed at the injured area, his fingers came back red. A piece of glass was wedged into his scalp, thanks to his trip through the French doors. Not for the first time, he wished he could've knocked the panes of glass out ahead of time, but then the gas would have escaped, and all his preparation would've been for naught.

He had to hand it to that Genovese hitter—his trick had worked. Between the gas oven leaking steadily once he'd blown out its pilot light two hours ago, and the propane tanks Hendricks had scavenged from the grill, the house was so full of noxious fumes, moving around inside it was difficult—he wound up dizzy, disoriented, euphoric. But as it turns out, the odorants they add to gas so folks can tell they've got a leak only work if people realize what they're smelling. Saturate the air with potent scents—like whiskey, or pickles, or rotting garbage—and the warning scent of rotten egg is masked. Handy if you're a hitman trying to make someone go boom.

Also helpful were the cans of gasoline Hendricks had stashed in the cupboard beneath the kitchen sink, and the microwave full of aerosol cans beside it. He'd turned Evie's kitchen into an IED. Engelmann's gunshot served as the detonator, and the force of the explosion—guided as best as Hendricks could manage by the doorway to the dining room and the bits of plywood he'd rigged up on either side to channel it, a large-scale version of the countless shaped charges he'd employed while in Afghanistan—had thrown Hendricks clear as if he were the bullet and the house were the gun. He'd staved off the worst of the burns he might've sustained by dousing himself with a bucket of cold water just prior to his little showdown. Heat boils off moisture before flesh—the explosion left him red and tender, but unblistered and intact. Engelmann, at the center of the explosion, was not so lucky. Investigators would no doubt be picking charred bits of him from trees a mile around.

Stuart, Evelyn, and Abigail were holed up in the root cellar, protected from the blast by a layer of stone and earth. He'd told them not to come out for any reason until an hour after they heard the sirens. That way, even if he'd failed and Engelmann had bested him, they would have still been safe—and if his plan worked, he'd have time to get away. To disappear. To leave Evie to pick up the pieces of this life she'd built for herself—a better life than he ever could have provided her.

Stuart's ATV was all gassed up and stashed behind the garage. Even sitting atop it, Hendricks could scarcely hear it start—partly the aftereffects of the explosion, partly the twin roars of the storm and the fire that consumed what little of the farmhouse still stood.

Hendricks sat there for a moment, tears threatening, while debris from the ruined house rained down upon the root cellar. His last moments with Evie—as he loaded her inside—played through his mind.

Stuart had entered first, carrying Abby. Evie'd followed close behind. She was filthy and exhausted after their frenzied preparation of the house, and her expression was clouded with frustration because Hendricks had refused to tell her what he had planned. Still, he thought she'd never looked more beautiful.

He'd guided her across the threshold—his hand gripping hers, Stuart glaring from the darkness all the while. When she was inside, she'd turned to him and said, "This is it?"

The words were tossed off for her husband's benefit, but in that moment Hendricks caught the pain, the hurt, the implicit plea written across her face: *How can this be it?*

"I'm sorry," he'd told her.

"Me, too," she'd replied. And before she released his hand, she squeezed it tight.

Hendricks thought about it now and felt something suspiciously like hope.

He thumbed the throttle, and the four-wheeler lurched forward. He rode alone into the rain-swept countryside, once more leaving Evie behind.

42.

IT WAS A BEAUTIFUL October day in Washington, DC—the air cool and crisp, the sky cloudless, the leaves all brilliant reds and yellows against the blue. The National Mall was flush with tourists and locals alike, the former snapping photos of the foliage with the monuments as their back-drop, the latter simply enjoying a moment of peace amid the city's endless bustle. Charlie Thompson and Kate O'Brien strolled arm-in-arm down the crowded promenade, admiring the view.

Times like these, Thompson thought, I can almost imagine the events of last month happened to someone else.

She and O'Brien had been shacking up for weeks. It happened almost by accident—after Pendleton's and losing Garfield, Thompson couldn't stand to sleep alone. Her apartment was too quiet, and after seeing what had befallen

Garfield in his, she felt too vulnerable. By daylight, she was okay, but every time her head hit the pillow, Leonwood and Engelmann came knocking. She woke up screaming most nights, scrambling for her gun.

O'Brien's stately white brick Federal proved a respite from her dreams, and Kate's gentle breathing beside her every night as she drifted off to sleep felt like home. The first night there, Kate gave her a toothbrush and a drawer. Two weeks later, they decided to let Charlie's lease lapse and go public, the assholes at the Bureau be damned.

As they walked, O'Brien pointed out a food truck she'd been meaning to try—donuts, made to order. "You want? I hear their cider donut is to die for."

"Sure," Thompson said. "Get two. I'll grab a bench."

O'Brien got in line. Thompson cut through the crowd toward the nearest set of benches, looking for a free one.

She was stopped by a hand grabbing her wrist—not forceful, but insistent.

Thompson wheeled.

It was Hendricks.

He was dressed to blend in with the autumn crowd: barn coat, work boots, jeans. A Georgetown baseball cap sat low atop his head, shading his eyes. His face was grim, drawn, tight.

"I know it was your partner who led Engelmann to Evie," he said. "It's because of him that my best friend is dead."

Thompson looked around, her heart galloping in her chest. But though the promenade was crowded, no one was paying any attention to them. They were surrounded by people, but alone.

"And he paid for it with his life. You've got a lot of nerve coming here," she said, defiantly. "Half the Bureau's looking for you as we speak."

"Let them look," he said. "I came because I need a favor."

Thompson let out a nervous laugh. "You need a favor," she said, incredulous. "From me." Her right hand crept toward her purse. Toward the gun inside it.

"That's right."

"Okay," she said, as much to keep him talking as to find out what he wanted. "Let's hear it."

"I need you to get Evie and her family into WITSEC, I need you to keep her safe."

"And how do you propose I do that?" she asked.

"Convince her to testify against me," he replied. "After what I put her through, it shouldn't be hard. Then, once she's agreed, you need to sell your bosses on the notion that she's in danger. From folks like Engelmann. From me."

"Wait—is *that* why you blew up her house? To get her to hate you so she'd agree to testify?"

"Evie's stubborn," Hendricks said. "Given the choice, she'd dig in her heels and defend the life she's built for herself. So I took away that choice. I did what I had to do to ensure her safety."

"What makes you think I'd help you?"

"Because you understand how important Evie is to me. Much like I understand how important your sister Jessica is to you. Or your girlfriend, Kathryn. I'm glad to see you've been sleeping better since you moved in with her, by the way."

Thompson flushed with fear and anger. Her stomach felt like it was full of crawly things. "You're bluffing," she said, praying Hendricks wouldn't notice her slowly unzipping her purse. "You wouldn't dare hurt them."

"Maybe I'm bluffing. Maybe I'm not. But the hand you're holding's not strong enough to call and find out."

"If you touch them, I swear—"

"Save your breath," Hendricks said. "There's nothing you can do to me that's worse than what I've already been through. As for your loved ones, I've told you what you need to do to keep them safe. You've seen what I'm capable of, so I know you respect what's at risk."

Thompson fell silent for a long moment. As surreptitiously as she could manage, she slid her hand into her purse. "But what if I fail?"

"Don't fail."

Thompson heard O'Brien calling her name from somewhere in the crowd. First puzzled. Then worried.

"Kate!" she shouted, eyes darting toward the sound—toward the promise of backup. As Kate came trotting over, Thompson drew her gun.

Kate saw the gun. Dropped the donuts she was carrying. Went for the piece she wore on her left ankle. "Charlie, what's wrong?"

Thompson scanned the busy promenade, her eyes wild, but it was no use.

Michael Hendricks was gone.

ABOUT THE AUTHOR

Chris Holm is an award-winning short story writer whose work has appeared in a number of magazines and anthologies, including *Ellery Queen's Mystery Magazine*, *Needle: A Magazine of Noir*, and *The Best American Mystery Stories*. His critically acclaimed trilogy of Collector novels, which blend fantasy with old-fashioned crime pulp, appeared on over forty Year's Best lists. He lives in Portland, Maine.